Sudden Desire - Lauren Dane

Tess Marshall has finally had it with her boss, spoiled but handsome actor Trevor Ryan. She quits and heads off for some much-needed vacation. But Trevor shows up on the doorstep of her cabin, demanding another chance. It's then that he realizes just how beautiful and sexy the woman he's had under his nose for two years is.

Their mutual attraction is incendiary and the next four days are filled with lovemaking and a deepening of emotion for both. Tess knows she loves Trevor and can't settle for being his bit on the side but Trevor isn't ready for forever.

Tess knows what she wants and it's not to be a back door secret lover or second-best to Trevor's career or any other women. What remains to be seen is whether Trevor can get his priorities straight before it's too late and he ends up losing her forever.

Dominant Boys of Summer - Katherine Kingston

Julie is in love with Dave. But if he really is the man for her, why is her sexual response to him so tepid?

Dave's best friend Nick joins them for an explosive and erotic beach weekend. Julie had no idea about her secret yearning to be mastered and dominated. Accepting that need and using it to build a relationship on that basis challenges her. Accepting that Nick is a part of the relationship with Dave adds another layer of complexity to an already complicated situation.

Knockout - Hannah Murray

Having the man of your dreams sweep you off your feet— that's what every girl dreams of, right? Except when it happened to Nina, it was because she knocked herself unconscious. By literally running into the man of her dreams.

The man she's loved from afar for five years, the man she's finally gotten up the nerve to approach. The man she's going to finally have, or get over once and for all.

She's off to a great start…isn't she?

Wild Oats - Nikki Soarde

Samantha has only ever slept with one man, but she feels no need to look further. Until Trent rips the rug out from under her. He makes a proposition that threatens everything she's ever believed about commitment and fidelity. She refuses, but Trent is adamant. Their future marriage is at stake. He won't go through with the marriage unless she agrees.

Furious, but unwilling to turn her back on the kind of love she sees in Trent's eyes, Sam consents. She never guesses how far he'll go to assure their future together. And she never guesses the heights of pleasure she'll experience along the way.

Undying Magic - Ravyn Wilde

Vampire hunter Jane Nichols is mourning the death of her best friend, Marissa. When she meets Rissa's brother Ricardo, one very hot Druid-mage, her thoughts turn to life. And sex. Unfortunately for Jane, Ricardo vowed never to love another mortal. They die after only a handful of years and he's been down that path before. He's determined to enjoy this woman for the short term, but nothing else.

In a race against time, the couple searches for potion ingredients needed to resurrect Marissa. You know, things like mermaid scales, zombie toenails, Druid lust-sweat—the usual. As they scour the Florida Keys, the only thing steamier than the tropical locale is the heat between Jane and her Druid lover.

LAUREN DANE
KATHERINE KINGSTON
HANNAH MURRAY
NIKKI SOARDE
RAVYN WILDE

ELLORA'S CAVE
ROMANTICA PUBLISHING

An Ellora's Cave Romantica Publication

www.ellorascave.com

Sexy Summer Fun

ISBN 9781419950520

Edited by Ann Leveille, Briana St. James, Mary Moran, Sue-Ellen Gower and Kelli Kwiatkowski
Cover art by Syneca.

Trade paperback Publication May 2007

Content Advisory:

S – ENSUOUS
E – ROTIC
X – TREME

Ellora's Cave Publishing offers three levels of Romantica® reading entertainment: S (S-ensuous), E (E-rotic), and X (X-treme).

The following material contains graphic sexual content meant for mature readers. This story has been rated E–rotic.

S-*ensuous* love scenes are explicit and leave nothing to the imagination.

E-*rotic* love scenes are explicit, leave nothing to the imagination, and are high in volume per the overall word count. E-rated titles might contain material that some readers find objectionable — in other words, almost anything goes, sexually. E-rated titles are the most graphic titles we carry in terms of both sexual language and descriptiveness in these works of literature.

X-*treme* titles differ from E-rated titles only in plot premise and storyline execution. Stories designated with the letter X tend to contain difficult or controversial subject matter not for the faint of heart.

SEXY SUMMER FUN

ℰℴ

SUDDEN DESIRE

Lauren Dane

Trademarks Acknowledgement

જી

The author acknowledges the trademarked status and trademark owners of the following wordmarks mentioned in this work of fiction:

Armani: GA Modefine S.A.

Kodak: Eastman Kodak Company

Lakers: The Los Angeles Lakers, Inc.

Lexus: Toyota Jidosha Kabushiki Kaisha, TA Toyota Motor Corporation

Porsche: Dr. Ing. h.c. F. Porsche AG

Prada: Prefel S.A.

Chapter One

ဆ

In a fit of annoyance, Tess Marshall looked up from the stack of papers she'd been putting together in order of importance and sighed, blowing a curl out of her face. "What the hell am I doing here?"

She'd started as Trevor Ryan's personal assistant two years ago. Two years she'd had a crush on him. Wanted him. Watched him with other women — and he never gave her more than a look destined for the help. Okay, so he did get that she made his life easier and he seemed to understand that she was really good at her job. But aside from the occasional moments when he let go of his position and really saw her as a person, most of the time she felt like a machine.

Worse, he was selfish and often ungrateful. *Thank you* rarely came from his lips. He was fond of picking at things he knew little about and she had no power to change. And while she certainly had no complaints about how well she was paid, she was fed up with feeling unappreciated.

Just that afternoon he'd had two tickets to the Lakers game, and he'd given them to his gardener. His gardener! She worked her ass off for him all day, every day and many times in the middle of the night. Hell, she bought him condoms and boxer shorts and he'd never given her tickets to anything. He was richer than god, everyone loved him and watched his stupid movies, and he sent his agent to Hawaii and gave her a gift certificate to a day spa. Very nice and all, she appreciated it and certainly couldn't have afforded it herself, but she had as yet to use it because she worked for him all of the time.

And frankly, she just didn't think she could watch him lure yet another brainless actress into his bed. He never cared

11

about them and they never cared about him. Oh he was nice to them and all. Bought them pretty things while they had his favor, but in the end, he walked away, on the prowl for a new conquest.

"Tess." His voice jarred her out of her thoughts as he walked into the room. "I said I wanted a Cobb salad and they didn't put enough eggs on it. Take it back and get more eggs." He tossed the container on the stack of papers she'd been trying to organize for him.

Her vision went red for a moment but then everything shifted and she had a moment of clarity. She'd officially had enough.

Standing up, she grabbed her bag and shoved her picture frames in it. "Take it back yourself. Better yet, let me shove those eggs up your ass! You ungrateful bastard."

"Whoa! What's your problem today?" The man had the gall to look handsome and cocky as he said it. He even looked amused.

"You! You're my problem every day, Trevor. You know, it wouldn't hurt you to actually utter *thank you* every once in a while. It took me seven months to track down that copy of your first script for you and you grunted at me when I handed it to you. Like uttering two words would have killed you? But oh no! Instead of thanking me, you actually complained because the cover had a fold on it. I've worked for you for two years and you've never once remembered my birthday. You remember the cook's birthday—the cook who I found and hired for you, by the way! You even remember the housekeeper's birthday—someone else I found and hired for you. You call me at two in the morning and ask me where your extra condoms are! My god, do you even understand how messed up that is? You called me when I was on vacation. Every day! I had to change hotels because you had me paged at the pool. I'm sick of it. I'm done. I'm too smart to be running your fucking salad back for more eggs." She rounded the desk and headed for the door.

She paused after she'd opened it. "Fuck you very much. I quit." Freedom claimed her as she slammed the door behind her, stalked out to her car and peeled out down the drive.

Trevor Ryan looked at the door, blinking in confusion and surprise. Who the hell was that? Hot damn, had Tess always had such a fiery temper? Had he always been an ungrateful bastard? Had she always been so beautiful? She'd been under his nose for two years and he hadn't noticed the way her breasts jiggled when she moved? He chided himself for that serious breach of attention and vowed to make it right.

* * * * *

He drove his Boxster down the road, looking for her address. He'd meant to go to her house sooner but he didn't know where she lived and she was always the person who found out such things for him. Hell, she'd even go to the trouble of printing out directions for him in easy-to-read big fonts and colors.

Yes, he'd come to realize her worth to him over the past three days. He'd rampaged around the house when confronted with the knowledge that no one knew where his stuff was. None of his staff could be counted on to know which tie he liked best with the Armani suit and which shirt with the Prada trousers. He had no idea where his dry cleaning was and he was running out of his special shampoo and no one seemed to know where Tess had gotten it. Thank god her notes were so meticulous, he at least knew his own schedule moment to moment for the next year.

More than that, when he really thought about it, he missed Tess the woman. Why he didn't notice her beauty while it was in his reach he didn't know. But as he lay in bed at night, it seemed like all he could think of was her. Her sense of humor, the way she sounded on the phone, her laugh. She made him laugh all the time and he took it for granted. Thoughts of her had taken over his day and crept into his dreams.

In desperation, he'd finally called his accountant, who looked up her information from her W2 form. He meant to get her back as his PA and to set about getting to know Tess the woman better. A lot better.

Triumphant when he sighted her house, Trevor pulled into the driveway and got out of the car. Jogging up her front steps, he set his alarm and gave a look around. The house was nice, in Westwood, not too very far from his own. Confident, he tapped on her door and a stranger opened it a few moments later.

He sent the woman his sexy boyish smile. "Hello, I'm Trevor Ryan. Tess' boss? I'm looking for her. Is she around?"

"Hello, I'm Tess' mother and you're not her boss anymore. So I'm thinking that you don't need to know her whereabouts."

His smile turned down but only slightly. "Ah. She told you about me, did she? Can I talk to you, please?"

Looking him suspiciously up and down, she nodded shortly and waved him inside.

And an hour later he was back at his house packing a bag. Or doing his best at it. Damn, it had been a very long time since he'd had to do this kind of thing on his own. Tess was right, he was spoiled.

But the difference now was that he knew it. He knew all the things she did for him and he was set on making her understand he planned to rectify his bad behavior.

He wanted to get her back because she was one of the few people in his life he could count on to really care about him and tell him the truth even when it sucked to hear.

So he shoved the casual clothes he could find into a small case and picked up his toiletry bag—pre-packed by Tess and always ready for travel—and headed for the door.

His agent had sent over a temp to help while Tess was out

and he'd already charmed the woman into utter incompetence. He told her to cancel all of his appointments for the next day and left her gaping at him.

Chapter Two

ℬ

Holy crap, was Crescent Lake in the middle of nowhere! Annoyed, Trevor wondered yet again why the hell Tess would come all the way up to Washington to a lake a million miles from the airport when she could summer anywhere.

But once he stopped to really look he began to understand. It was perfect there. While L.A. was hotter than hell in the middle of July, along the road to the lake, lush green trees filled the landscape and the air smelled sweet and clean.

The resort Tess' mother gave him directions to was gorgeous, he had to admit. A big rustic main lodge and smaller cabins dotted the area around the lake. It was nearly ten at night but it was still the pinkish light of late sunset.

After parking the rental in front of her cabin he got out, relishing the crunch of pine needles beneath his shoes. He could smell the warm earth, the sap from the trees. How long had it been since he'd done that?

Leaving his bags in the car for the moment, he marched up to the door and knocked.

She answered after a few moments and stood there, utterly surprised. Then she scowled, crossing her arms over her chest. Which alternately annoyed and confused him more because he realized he'd never noticed what world-class breasts she had until that day she quit. And there she was— there they were—mouthwateringly creamy mounds heaving out of the top of the camisole she wore. And her legs were exposed to the top of her thighs by a very short denim skirt, and he saw a woman he'd never imagined worked for him for two years.

"What do you want, Trevor? I sent your house keys back and wrote out instructions on how to reset your alarm codes in case you're worried I'll break in. How in the hell did you find me? I can't believe you hunted me down for that."

"I got the keys but I haven't changed the codes. I threw myself on your mother's mercy. Can I come in?"

Warily, she stepped back and opened the screen door and waved him inside. He looked around. The cabin was one large room with a loft space he guessed housed the bed. The front was all glass and looked out over the lake. The rising moon glimmered overhead, reflecting off the water. The interior had what he believed was a coastal Indian décor. Beautiful and simple.

"This is a really great place." He looked at her and motioned toward the couch. "Tess, uh, can I sit down?"

Rolling her eyes at him, she waved in the general direction of the couch and tossed herself into a chair. Swinging her legs up onto the ottoman made her skirt ride up, briefly exposing a scrap of red fabric covering her mound. He blinked a few times and sat down.

"Well, what is it, Trevor? You came two states and several hours on two-lane roads to get here. You'd better not be here about buying you condoms."

"I want you back," he blurted out.

She snorted. "I'm sure you do. You've discovered how hard it is to run your own damned life, haven't you?"

"Yes." He wasn't happy about the admission but there it was.

Watching her to gauge her reaction, he couldn't stop himself from looking at the body he'd totally ignored for two years. Good god, her nipples were hard. Mouth beginning to water, he wondered what color they were, strawberry pink or deeper raspberry, maybe even coral pink.

"Are you even listening to me?" Her voice broke into his

naughty, naked ruminations. While in nipple fantasyland, he hadn't heard a word she'd said. That couldn't be good.

"No, damn it. Have you always been so sexy? How am I supposed to think when your nipples are hard and you have on red panties?" he said grumpily. She raised her eyebrows. Standing up, he began to pace. "And what's with the short skirt anyway? Have your legs always been so long?"

"Yes and when you're around my nipples are always hard." She looked up at him with a sardonic smile.

Shocked into stillness by her admission, he looked at her closely. "Really? How come I never noticed?"

She sighed. "A question for the ages, Trevor, I'm sure. As I was saying—I'm not interested in coming back to work and having you treat me like shit. No matter how well I'm paid."

"What color are your nipples?"

"What? Trevor! God, never mind, go home." She stood but he grabbed her arm and pulled her closer.

All finesse was gone. He was on fire for her. Every cell in his body wanted to claim this woman he'd had under his nose all this time. "Suddenly, Tess, I'm finding myself obsessed with what you look like while you're coming. What you'd feel like as I slid inside of you. What your pussy tastes like," he growled, running his hands up and down her arms.

Holy crap! No wonder those starlets jumped into the sack with him. No rational woman with a clit could withstand the assault of the sex appeal of this man. Her heart pounded. She gripped his shirt to keep her hands from shaking. Nervously, she licked her lips as she looked up at him.

"Shall we see, Tess?" His voice was soft and velvet, his hand trailing up her thigh.

"I already know what color my nipples are." Her voice was faint and breathy, and he rewarded her with a wicked smile that flooded her pussy with honey.

Those questing fingers reached her inner thigh and then

higher, brushing the fabric of her panties. A moan escaped her as he flicked his index finger across her clit through the lace. "Are you wet for me, Tess?"

"This is a bad idea." *Yeah, really convincing if you thrust your cunt into his hand when you say it.* She should have been ashamed of her response but she wasn't. She'd crushed on him for so long. Watched him with other women for two years. Even though she knew he'd walk away in a bit, she wanted him.

"No it isn't. Take your skirt off." His voice was quiet but it wasn't a request.

Reaching behind her body, she quickly unfastened the skirt and it fell to her feet, leaving her in red thong panties and a tank top.

"Very sexy." Circling her like a shark, he ran a finger underneath the waistband of her underwear. "A thong. Nice choice for someone whose ass is as juicy as yours. Tell me, Tess, why is it that I never noticed your body before?"

"I don't know. You barely noticed me at all for two years. Enough to know I kept your life moving but not as a woman. Not even as a human being really." That still hurt.

"I'm sorry, Tess. I really am. For lots of things. I've obviously been missing quite a bit." Stopping behind her, he leaned to speak in her ear. "Take your panties off."

She hesitated for a moment.

"Tess."

Quickly, she slid the panties over her hips and down to join the skirt at her feet.

"Will wonders never cease? Tess, you're bare. I like that very much." Running his fingers over her mound, he stopped to dip one into her pussy. The fleshy pad pressed over her clit, sliding side to side. Hips bucking forward, she moaned as he slid a finger inside her and then back out.

"Your clit is pierced. Tess, you look so innocent on the

outside but you are such a naughty girl just beneath the surface. I find I like that very much."

Putting the finger slicked with her honey to his lips, he locked eyes with her as he licked it with relish. "Juicy. So sweet and hot and wet. Is that for me?"

"You know it is." Anger began to edge into her system. Duh! Who else would she be wet for? Arrogant ass!

"But I didn't." He tipped her chin so that she was looking into his face. "I didn't know." And why didn't he? Trevor kicked himself for his lack of attention. He leaned down and licked over her mouth. Tongue tracing a hot, wet line across her pouty, full lower lip before catching it between his teeth.

Her taste burned through him, intoxicated his brain and teased his senses. She tasted heady and sweet but real. There was nothing artificial about this woman and that may have been the biggest turn-on of all.

She was fire in his arms. Fluid, hot sex and damn it if she wasn't the most beautiful sight he'd ever seen.

His cock strained against the fly of his jeans, aching to be inside her body. The muscles of his abdomen trembled with restraint. This woman knew him. She knew his history and he didn't want that to bar the way. He had to show her pleasure first. Bring her off, take her higher and higher until she shattered around him. Then he'd fuck her.

Lips skating down the arch of her neck, he feasted on the place just below her ear. The wild fluttering of her pulse fed his desire. The knowledge that he affected her so deeply seduced him.

"I think it's time I see those breasts, Tess." He pulled her tank off with a flourish and couldn't hold back a sigh of happiness when he sighted her bare breasts. "Ah, coral. A lovely color. I would have guessed more pink. Surprises are a wonderful thing." They were high and full, nipples drawn tight and calling for his mouth.

"Only a movie star would call it coral," she breathed out.

"Fucking metrosexual."

He laughed. He'd missed her humor. Something else he'd failed to appreciate until it was gone. "There's my smart-assed girl. I may know my color palette but I know a few other things, too." Drawing his hands up her stomach, he brought them to her breasts. As he palmed them, the nipples begged for attention and he complied. He kissed down the upper curve until he found her nipple. Her skin smelled like summer. Warm and sunkissed. As he swirled his tongue around that hard bead, her cry of pleasure shot straight to his cock. Unable to resist, he took the entire nipple into his mouth, grazing his teeth over it before sucking hard. She arched into him, her hands sliding up his shoulders to cradle his head to her.

Hazy with the shock of the utter unreality of the moment, Tess slid deeper into his spell. Yes, she'd wanted this but the fantasy had nothing on the reality. She had no idea what inspired this move from disinterest to thrusting his erection against her thigh so quickly.

"What brought this on? What are you doing?" she managed to gasp out as he bit her nipple.

"I'm going to fuck you, Tess. But first, I want to be sure you're good and wet. I want to taste you on my tongue as I lick you into orgasm. And then I'll back you over this couch and slide into you from behind and fuck you just hard enough to make those luscious breasts bounce."

"What makes you think I want that?" *Yeah, right.*

He chuckled wickedly. "Your cream is running down your thigh, Tess. Your pussy is hot and wet and soft for me." He dropped to his knees before her, leaning in to part her pussy. Exposed, her clit throbbed in the cool air.

"Damn it, this ring is so sexy. Just looking at it makes me so hard I can barely move." Moving his mouth to her, he flicked his tongue over her clit rapidly until she had to lean on the couch for support. He gently pulled on the ring with his teeth, bringing a mewl from her lips. "Do you like that, Tess? I do. Oh I enjoy you so much." Pushing her back on the couch, he brought her thighs up to his shoulders. Pausing to spread her open and look at her again, he flicked his gaze up to hers before bringing his mouth to her pussy.

So soft and creamy. Trevor speared his tongue into her, swirling it around her gate. He lapped at her, bringing the flat of his tongue through her folds and over her clit and the silver ring there. Pulling her clit into his mouth, he slowly sucked it in and out while he stroked two fingers inside her. She was so good, so luscious that he wanted to eat her for days.

"Oh yes, more like that, please," she whispered softly and he complied. "Don't stop, god, what you're doing, don't stop." His mouth on her was heaven. Wet against wet, his tongue sliding over her and into her, pushing her into a place where her muscles trembled with the rush of endorphins through her body. It wasn't impersonal at all. Not a quick, nameless blowjob. He made love to her with his mouth. The intensity of that frightened her but did not halt the freight train of her climax from slamming into her cells at full speed. Arching, a cry on her lips, she clamped her thighs over his ears as wave after wave of pleasure rolled through her.

After she'd stopped fluttering a bit he pulled back, kissing the sensitive spot where thigh met body. He moved up, capturing her lips in a hard kiss.

Responding to her taste, her residual warmth on his mouth, she licked at his lips, nipped on his chin and sucked on his tongue. He felt good there against her lips. And she wanted more.

"Please tell me you have condoms. Because I really, really need you inside me. Fuck me now, Trevor."

Reaching back, he pulled a foil packet out of his wallet and grinned.

She put her hand on his to stop him from ripping it open. "Not just yet." Standing, she reached out and grabbed his belt. She loosened it, a shiver working through her at the hiss of leather and the soft jingle of the buckle. More quickly, she undid his jeans, shoving the pants and his boxers down until his cock was free. Hot and hard in her hands. A bounty. She didn't know where to begin.

But first, she dropped to her knees. "Mmm," she hummed her pleasure, looking at the thick length of him. The meaty head of his cock glistened, beckoning her to lean in and lick him from sac to crown. Loose fingers dropped the condom and she retrieved it, putting it on the edge of the couch.

His balls were smooth and drawn tight against his body and he groaned when she drew one and then the other into her mouth gently. Hands replaced her mouth as she kissed her way back up the length of him, finally taking him into her mouth. Mary Poppins was so wrong when she said enough was as good as a feast. His cock was more than enough and Tess still wanted more. The salt of him, the tang of his body, tantalized her tongue. The heat of him bathed her face. He held her head gently but firmly.

"My, another surprise. You really like cock, don't you, Tess?"

Looking up at him, seeing him watch her, she pulled off him with a smile. "I love cock." Her voice was a whisper.

"Okay, well. That does it." Grabbing the packet, he ripped it open with his teeth and rolled the condom on in mere seconds. Before she could finish admiring his speed and handiwork he'd bent to pick her up and move her over the side of the couch. He nudged her feet apart and reached to spread her open before thrusting into her in one hard push.

He'd never in his life had a hotter experience. She was real, alive under his hands. Her breasts swayed with each press into her body. Sweat glistened down her spine. And she was wet. Oh god, so wet and inferno hot. That sweet pussy clenched him, milked him with agile muscles as he slammed into her. The noises she made—she was on fire and he'd caught the blaze, too.

Reaching around, he found her clit and flicked it and the ring. And what a surprise that was! A shaved pussy with a piercing? On his personal assistant? Yeah, he'd seen dozens of shaved cunts, but thinking that this sex bomb was sitting on his estate, within reach for two years while he flitted around with shallow bimbos drove him crazy.

Stuttered half words came from her mouth as he felt her pussy flutter and grip his cock. Triumph roared through him, *fuck, she was coming again!* Shuddering, she pushed back against his cock, taking him in even deeper. The clutch of her cunt drove him past madness, pulling him down with her. Letting his head fall back as he drove into her body in feral digs, he came.

Slowly, he pulled out and walked into her bathroom, shutting the door behind him. He splashed his face with water and looked at himself in the mirror. False modesty was not one of his traits, he knew he was handsome. But he was also a bit scared. What he'd just experienced was unlike anything he'd ever done before. He was emotionally off balance and not sure why. One thing he was sure of—he wanted more of Tess. A lot more. Perhaps he'd figure it out after he'd had her three dozen more times.

Bolstering himself with a deep breath, he opened the door and went back out to the main room. He didn't see her. Panic rose that she'd run again but he saw her on the deck just outside, facing the water.

He joined her out there, looking long and slow at the way she was lying across the lounge chair, a beer in her hand. He wasn't happy to see she was clothed once again.

"You're wearing clothes, Tess." His voice was serious but amused. He'd work to get them off her very soon.

She held up an extra beer and he took it and sat down on the chair next to hers. "Yes, very observant of you, Trevor."

"We can't do that again if you put your panties back on."

She raised an eyebrow at him. "Trev, why are you here?"

"I told you, I want you back."

"You know, if you think a blowjob and a mind-blowing fuck over the couch will erase what a bastard you are to work for, you're sorely mistaken."

"We can work it out, I can change. Especially if we can do that every day."

"Oh, so you think I'll buy you condoms at two in the morning and you can fuck me when you don't get enough eggs on your salad?" Her jaw was set, eyes narrowed.

He shouldn't be turned on by how pissed she appeared to be but desire coursed through him. "Who are you! Damn it, Tess, you are not the woman who worked for me for two years."

"Of course I am. You only just noticed me now. Yet again it's about you, Trevor. I haven't changed. I'm the same person I've always been. The only difference is that I finally had enough and walked out. And I'm not going to be your whore at the office."

"Whoa! I don't want you to be a whore, I never suggested that. Don't put words in my mouth, Tess."

"Trevor, you said you wanted me back, especially if you could fuck me every day at the office. That makes me what? Your PA with benefits? It sure doesn't make me your girlfriend."

He stilled. "Is that what you want? To be my girlfriend?"

She exhaled in disgust. "Jesus, Trev, don't have a stroke. I'm not trying to claim you after one sexual encounter. I'm merely using your own words and then pointing out the obvious differences between what you're suggesting and what I am not."

After several moments of silence, she shrugged. "I'm looking for another job, Trevor. I can't afford to wait around. In fact, I've got four offers on my plate right now." And now that he'd touched her, been inside her, there was no way she could be his PA and watch him with anyone else. She couldn't be his bit on the side. She'd hate him and herself, too.

"Look, I came all the way up here to talk to you. Can you just give me a few days, please?"

"A few days for what? Trevor, tomorrow you have a fundraiser to attend, you're taking Marie Jansen."

"This is why I need you back!"

"No, this is why you need a PDA, as I've been advising you for two years to get. Anyone can tell you when your appointments are."

"When is my next free night?"

"No, I'm not going to do this, Trevor. You're going to have to do some of the work on your own. You want to woo me back to work for you, do it. I won't do it for you. But I'm staying up here for the rest of the week. My mother had her vacation booked here and gave it to me. I need a vacation in a place with no phone. My days consist of lying in the sun, swimming in the very cold water, drinking too much beer and reading smutty romance novels."

"Then I'm staying, too."

One of her eyebrows rose. "You're going to vacation at a remote lake in Washington State? People drink beer from the bottle here, Trev. The bathrooms don't have heated towel bars and this place does not have room service."

He moved to squeeze in next to her in the chair. "I don't need room service. I'll have all I need in bed next to me."

She watched him warily. Four days with Trevor Ryan? All to herself to frolic with? Naked? And then she'd go back to L.A. and get another job and have a nice memory of a summer fling with the gorgeous actor to tell her grandchildren about someday. Well, maybe when her granddaughter was like thirty or something. In for a penny, in for a pound her mother always said. And there was the fact that her mother was the one who told him where to find Tess. Tess' mother was no pushover. Whatever Trevor told her, it must have been pretty amazing or she'd have told him to fuck right off.

"You plan to stay here? In this cabin with me?"

"I'd like to. Would that be all right?"

"You know you can't be on your cell phone, the reception sucks out here. There's a landline up at the main lodge but no real privacy. I don't have my laptop here so you can't be wheeling and dealing all day. And you can't bring women here to fuck in my bed."

A fingertip on her chin, he turned her head to face him. "Hey, there's only one woman I want to fuck in your bed. Give me some credit, please. I'm not a slut. And I'm certainly not without a heart or just plain manners." He winced. "Okay, I clearly need better manners. I know that now. Four days, Tess. What do you say?"

"Okay. You need to go and call to cancel your appointments for the next few days, though."

"Right. I'll run up to the main lodge then and come right back."

She shrugged. "Okay, I'll be out here a while. I'm going to light some citronella candles and drink my beer. I'll make a late snack in a bit."

"Excellent." Grinning, he leaned in and stole a kiss before jumping out of the chair and heading out.

* * * * *

Trevor couldn't get her out of his mind as he sat and waited for his call to connect. He still had her tang in his mouth, her scent on his skin. He had a shitload of things to do in the next four days but at that moment, he couldn't have cared less. He wanted to be with Tess in that cocoon of a cabin in the middle of nowhere. For the first time in a very long time, he wanted to be a regular guy on vacation with a woman who didn't want him to read a script, didn't want his money or his fame. Just wanted him.

That was dangerously alluring.

Turned out his new assistant was less than thrilled to be called at nearly eleven at night but she didn't complain or try to talk him out of canceling his appointments for the next four days.

Like a coward, he called his agent's work number and left a voicemail that he'd be out of pocket for several days but would try to check his messages here and there. Ben would flip out when he heard but strangely enough, as Trevor walked away from the lodge and headed back to the cabin, he felt freer and lighter than he had in years.

When he brought his bags into the cabin, she looked up in surprise. "You had this all planned out?"

"No. I had no idea this place would be so far in the middle of nowhere. I thought I'd be able to get a room in a hotel if I needed to. I like this solution much better." He nodded his chin in the direction of the loft. "That where the bed is?"

"You planning on actually sleeping with me, Trev? I'd assumed you were a fuck-and-run kind of guy. There's a pullout down here."

"Well, more than sleeping, but I do like waking up to the right woman."

They both froze a moment and he took the bags up to the loft.

He came back down after changing into loose drawstring pants and a T-shirt. The night air was still warm but not oppressively so.

"Hey, just in time. Food's on the table."

Watching her as she bustled around before sitting down, he felt like he'd never truly seen her before. He'd always had the impression that her hair was plain, a sort of nondescript brown-blonde, but it was glossy and up in a high ponytail. Her eyes were a pretty green and almond-shaped, nearly feline. She had one of those pert little noses and a sweet, soft mouth. Tess Marshall was lovely. Not a knockout in the traditional sense like the women he tended to date, but beautiful in her own way.

"What?" Raising a brow at him, she filled her plate with a sandwich and some pasta salad.

"Nothing. Just looking at you. You're really lovely."

"Mmmm-hmm. So do you have a new PA?"

"Temp. Ben sent her over."

"Why are you trying to get me back, then? You have someone and we're all pretty interchangeable."

"Bullshit. She's not you, Tess. She doesn't know all my preferences. She didn't know what I meant when I said I needed the blue suit."

"Well, you were spoiled." She hid a smile. "You know you're going to catch shit for breaking your date with Patrice Thursday."

"Damn it, how can you remember all of this stuff?"

"I made those reservations after you called me when she was sucking your cock in the background. It was one of those Kodak moments." Her voice was dry.

"She's not even very good at it," he said and she snorted. "Really."

"Trevor, next you'll be telling me that you really respect all of the women that you fuck. Don't bullshit me, boy. I know all of your dirty laundry. I was your personal laundress for years."

"I respect you." He colored when she sent him one of those knowing looks. "Okay, so I didn't. I'm sorry. I took you for granted. But I will treasure you from now on. I'll give you a big raise. More time off. Season tickets to the Lakers. Courtside."

Avarice lit her eyes. "Oh ho! The raise was a so-so

enticement but the tickets, ah!" He laughed. "I didn't know you were a fan."

"Well, you would have if you ever asked me if I wanted the tickets you always gave to everyone else." She snorted.

"Okay, okay. So I've been blind. I'm not now."

Chapter Three

ರಾ

After a night of extremely hot sex, Trevor awoke to an empty bed. Groaning, he picked up his watch from the nightstand to see it was already noon.

Getting dressed in shorts and foregoing the shirt, he went downstairs and saw her in the small kitchen.

"I thought you'd run again," he said with a smile, stalking to her and pulling her close. He dipped down to claim her mouth for a kiss and that heat stole over him again. He'd never been roused this way before. He was practically panting for the woman.

"Well," she gasped as he ended the kiss, "good morning to you, too. Up for an excursion?"

"Like back to bed for some enthusiastic sex?"

She laughed. "No. You probably didn't see much last night but we're right in the middle of a rain forest. There are waterfalls and rivers and mountains and ferns taller than you are. I was heading out to see some petroglyphs today. I've packed a lunch for two if you want to come with me."

How could he refuse her? Her face shiny with excitement, she stood there grinning. No makeup, just cute shorts and a T-shirt with her hair up again.

"Okay, sounds interesting. I'll grab a shirt and some shoes." And some condoms.

And in minutes they'd gotten in the car and she was pointing out some of the scenic highlights. And she'd been correct, the Olympic National Park was amazing and lush. The trees were gigantic and everything was so damned green and clean.

She pulled into a small parking lot.

"What? Is this it?"

"We need to rent a canoe. I called ahead when I arrived. It's reserved. Come on and bring the cooler and my backpack, it's got a blanket."

He followed, happy to watch the sway of that luscious ass. She was just as efficient in renting the boat as she was in everything else. She'd charmed the geezer behind the counter so much he threw in ice-cream sandwiches as a bonus.

On the docks, Trevor watched her as she ate. That was another rarity, seeing a woman with a real appetite and a body with curves. She was fit but rounded. Her hips were sexy to hold on to. She seemed to do everything with relish.

"I haven't had an ice-cream sandwich in years," he laughed as they got into the canoe and he pushed off from shore.

"Ice cream is one of life's greatest pleasures, Trev. You shouldn't deny yourself the simple things."

They were both quiet as they paddled. The muscles in her upper arms were tight and he got harder and harder as he watched her move in the sunlight.

"I brought you a hat, it's in my backpack," she called over her shoulder.

She was fucking psychic, there was no other explanation for her always anticipating just exactly what he needed. He slid the baseball cap on and immediately felt better. The sun was shining off the water and the temperature had risen several degrees since they'd left the cabin.

"Ah, here they are." They brought the canoe up to a natural rock wall and looked at the ancient paintings there. "Amazing." She took shots with her digital camera and they slowly paddled past to the shore.

"Come on then. Let's find some shade and eat."

They pulled the canoe onto shore near a shaded spot and laid everything out.

"First, I'm going to take a dip. I'm hotter than hell." She peeled off her clothes to reveal a bikini underneath and his mouth dried up as she waded into the water and swam out a bit.

He wasn't wearing a bathing suit but no one was around anyway so he got naked and followed her.

"FUCK! This water is cold," he called as he swam to her.

Laughing, she turned her face up to the sun overhead. "It's hot enough to be refreshing. You big baby."

"I'll show you," he growled and pulled her to him, both treading water. She was cool and soft against him, eyes shining with amusement and just plain happiness. "C'mere and smooch me."

"Gladly," she murmured, tipping her head so he could access her lips fully.

She tasted of sunshine and fresh water and sex. Damn it, he should not want her so badly but oh how he did.

He towed her to shore, her arms around his neck, upper body resting on his while he swam on his back.

"We don't have towels."

She laughed. "It's ninety degrees, Trev. We'll dry." Looking down, her laughter caught in her throat. "I see you didn't suffer any shrinkage."

Laughter bubbled from him. "Not at all. Now come back to the blanket with me. I want to warm up by putting my cock inside you."

This Trevor was damned attractive and dangerous to her peace of mind. Tess hadn't seen him *carefree* before. She'd seen cocky amusement and jaded humor. Lots of sarcasm and even an edge of smug bitterness. But never carefree. Which was sad given that he provided entertainment for millions with his movies. This Trevor was someone she *liked*.

Tess pushed him back to the blanket and onto his back. She scrambled atop his body, straddling him. "You have such a gorgeous body. I know you know that, but you do." Leaning down, she kissed a bead of water that had collected on the tip of his nose.

Kissing a trail down over his lips, she stopped to savor the dip in his chin before skimming up the line of his jaw and to the sweet hollow just behind it and below his ear.

His hands rested hot and easy against her thighs. Her skin was cool from the water but his was so warm and hard against hers. The contrast was delightful. When he moved to untie her top she stopped him.

"Let me do this. I want to taste you, give you pleasure."

Grip tightening at the unexpected bloom of emotion in his chest, he swallowed past it. She gave him so much.

"Okay, bossy. Give it to me, then," he said, putting his cocky grin in place to cover his emotions.

Scooting down his body, she kissed across his collarbone and stopped to lave the hollow of his throat.

His cock, already hard, nudged against her and she gasped at the contact. That was one place her flesh was hot.

"God, let me fuck you, Tess," Trevor moaned.

"In due time, Trev. Be patient."

She found her way to his nipple and scraped her teeth over it, bringing a jerk of his muscles and a gasp from his lips. The night before had been frenzied and she couldn't remember details. It was more impressions of yearning, straining, arching, sweating, fucking. But this—this would be a memory she'd savor forever. If she couldn't have him, she'd have her memories.

Her clit might be pierced but she was not a casual dating kind of woman. She felt things for Trevor Ryan, things she couldn't afford to be alone in feeling. It was one thing to be protective of him as his PA. To make sure he ate well and took care of himself. But they'd passed that and she felt more than protective of him. Over the years she'd been telling herself it was just a crush but she'd come to realize the first few days at the cabin and especially after the night before that she loved him. So she'd take the next days and wring every last experience she could out of it. A summer romance beyond her previous imagining. But when she got on that plane back home, she had to put it all out of her mind.

Until then though…

Moving down again, she trailed her tongue over each rib and over the muscles of his abdomen. She swirled her tongue around his navel and looked up into his eyes before moving her body down that last bit and settling between his thighs.

His cock practically shoved into her mouth of its own accord, which was fine with her.

"Oh god, yeah. That's the way," Trevor said in a low, desire-rough voice. His hands slid over her shoulders and up into her hair, releasing it from the ponytail. Cool, wet curls fell over his skin.

She loved the way he felt in her mouth, against her tongue. Loved finding the places that made him gasp aloud, made his muscles tremble. The head of his cock was round and meaty and she loved the way it felt deep inside her pussy. In her mouth it was almost like a salty, tangy candy.

His balls lay in her palm and she squeezed softly, making him take his breath in sharply. In passion, not pain.

"Tess, you're so good. Your mouth on me feels so damned hot. But if you don't stop now I'm going to come."

She pulled off him for a moment. "That's the idea."

Gripping her shoulders, he brought her up to his lips. "Later. Right now, I want to be inside you. I want you to ride me, Tess."

"Condom?"

Reaching out, he grabbed his pants and pulled one out and she laughed. "You must have been a Boy Scout when you were young. Always prepared."

Rolling it on, she quickly untied the side of her bikini bottom and shoved it aside. She moved, positioning herself above him. He felt the inferno of her cunt just above the head of his cock. Catching her bottom lip between her teeth bewitched him for a moment until she slammed herself down onto him.

The shock of the intensity of the pleasure he felt at that moment made his vision swim. "Fuck!"

"Yeah." She grinned and began to move.

He arched, seeking to fill her as deeply as he could. The curtain of her flesh parted each time she descended onto him and pulled back at him as she moved up until only the head of his cock remained inside.

She looked glorious there in the dappled sunshine sifting through the trees. He smelled the warm earth, the water from the lake, the moss. The water lap, lap, lapped at the shore and that seemed to echo off the wet sounds of their union. He smelled her skin, warmed by desire and sunshine and her honey. Oh god, the scent of her desire drove him insane with need. No one smelled like Tess. She was one of a kind. Fuck. He'd never have anything else this good. He knew it to the bottom of his soul.

Reaching down, he dragged some of her lube up to her clit and played around it and that damned sexy ring. He wasn't entirely sure why the clit ring did him in to the extent it had. It wasn't the only one he'd seen up close and personal but on her it worked like gasoline on an open fire.

Her cunt gripped at him as her climax settled into her body. He liked that he knew her body so well after such a short time of being intimate. But she was open. So deliriously, wonderfully open that she was a shining thing. Brilliant really. He watched the flush creep up her torso, saw her nipples darken and elongate. Her head lolled back, hands gripped his thighs as she arched.

A long sigh escaped her as orgasm claimed her. Coming with him embedded deep inside her was nearly too much to process. It felt so good as she squirmed, losing her rhythm in the delirium of pleasure. It went on and on. Dimly she knew he'd begun to thrust up into her. She felt his thigh muscles tighten and loosen against the inside of her own. His pelvic bone ground into hers, dragging out her orgasm.

She looked so fucking gorgeous up there above him, coming. Coming hard. Her face was a mask of concentration, muscles tight. Even as his own climax claimed him he watched her, falling.

* * * * *

They paddled back to the rental place quietly as the late afternoon sun played on the water. They'd shared a lunch, naked beneath the shade of the trees, and taken another swim before deciding to head back.

The intensity of what they'd had on that blanket sobered them both. A quiet kind of desperation filled Trevor as they drove back to the cabin.

That evening, after he'd showered, she'd cooked a simple meal and they cleaned up side by side in the very small kitchen. He liked the natural intimacy they'd developed. There was nothing taxing about Tess. She was straightforward and complicated in the right ways. He realized then that maybe he did know her better than he thought he did. He'd just been blind to the full extent of what he'd been taking for granted.

"I have a surprise, Trev."

He turned to catch the infectious smile on her face and mirrored it. "What? We've already done it on the table and here on the counter."

Rolling her eyes, she opened the freezer and pulled out two popsicles. "Fifty Fifty bars! Or they call them creamsicles now, I guess. Anyway, I saw them at the little store and bought them for just such an occasion." She grabbed his hand and tugged him out toward the lake.

They settled, feet dangling in the water, eating popsicles in the pink light of not quite night.

"I haven't had a summer vacation this wonderful since I was a kid."

She turned to him. "Yeah? Tell me."

"Oh, well, we didn't have a lot when I was growing up but my parents saved all year long to take one three-week vacation every summer. We'd go to Flathead Lake— you know I'm from Montana—and camp in my uncle's pop-up camper. My sister and I would swim and run and play all day and if my dad was in a really good mood—or maybe when he just wanted to be alone with my mom—he'd let us sleep out under the stars in sleeping bags. Cindy, my sister, would ride herd on me during the school year to hoard my extra change so we'd have money to buy Big Sticks at the general store at the campground."

"Yeah, I'm sure a popsicle can't hold a candle to the week you took in the Bahamas three months ago," she laughed, cocking her head.

"You know, it's the other way around. This is better. I haven't had an actual vacation that was this relaxing since Flathead Lake."

The yearning in his voice touched her deeply and she scooted closer to him and put her head on his shoulder. The more he opened up, the more he gave her of his life, the deeper she fell.

* * * * *

"Let me take you to dinner tonight at the restaurant at the lodge. Our last date before we go home tomorrow."

Tomorrow she'd leave and be out of his life forever. The knowledge sliced through her and she closed her eyes against it. "Okay, our last gasp before we go back to our real lives."

"That sounds so final."

She got up. "Let's get changed then."

They walked hand in hand down the path that led from the cabin to the main lodge. He loved the normalcy of that intimacy. He'd never experienced such depth of connection with anyone before. Tess never took, she only gave.

At the restaurant, once seated and order taken, he turned back to her and grabbed her hand. "Tess, you didn't answer me. Your comment back there sounded so final."

"Trev, I can't work for you. You have to know that."

"Why not? Why would I know such a dumb thing? Of course you can work for me!"

"Because I can't..." she paused, taking a deep breath. She wasn't one for subterfuge and after the next morning, she'd never see him again anyway. "I can't go back to the way it was. Not after the last days."

"I told you, I'll be better. I see you now, Tess. I appreciate you. I need you. I won't take you for granted, I swear."

"Trevor, is this a relationship or a job you're offering me?"

He let go of her hand and sat back in his chair and the hand in her lap fisted, nails digging into her palm to keep from begging. "I love you, Trevor. I didn't mean to. Hell, I don't even want to. But I do. And you want me to go back to buying you condoms in the middle of the night. I can't."

"There won't be any of that. I'll buy condoms for us."

"You want me to work for you and you can fuck me but you don't want a relationship? So what would that be? I'm confused as to what that makes me to you."

"You're a friend. A good friend. I need you, Tess."

"For what? Are you going to take me to the openings and gala parties instead of Patrice and her ilk?" She really needed to shut up, this conversation would only end in pain. Hers. But out of some perverse impulse, she couldn't stop the words.

"The studios like me to be seen out and about with the actresses I work with. It wouldn't mean anything." And even to him it sounded pathetic.

When their food came she picked at it, looking miserable. "So I'd handle your schedule, buy your presents, order your suits, be available when you're done with your glamorous public life for a solid fucking? That's your definition of good friend?"

"You make it sound dirty! Why are you doing that? You know it wouldn't be that way." His heart pounded in his chest, a cold sweat ran down his spine at the very thought of her not being in his life every day.

"It would make me *feel* dirty, Trev. Does how I feel matter at all to you? I told you I loved you and you offer to be my friend." She snorted. "Look, let's just have this short summer vacation fling, okay? Tomorrow we'll go back to L.A. and you'll go your way and I'll go mine. Your new PA will learn what you mean by your blue suit in a while. And after a time the ache will ease and I'll be able to see your face on the screen again and smile."

"Tess, can't we just try? You're special to me. The way you make me feel is special. What do you want? Marriage? It's been only been a few days."

Flinching, she stood up and put her napkin down. "It's been two years for me. If you'll excuse me, I need to pack." He started to get up but she put her hand on his shoulder. "I need to be alone for a while. Please."

Sighing, he nodded. "I'll have them box your food up and be back in half an hour."

"Okay." Turning, she left the restaurant, head held high. Until she got outside and the first sob tore through her gut. She ran back to the cabin and packed up as quickly as she could. She couldn't stay there another night, sleeping in the curve of his body. She knew that her resolve wouldn't be nearly as strong waking up warm and naked against him. He wasn't hers and he had no intention of being so.

She wrote him a quick note and put one of his shirts to her face for a long moment. Then she left. Tossing her bag into the backseat, she started the car and drove away from the best four days she'd ever spent in her life.

Chapter Four

ଛେ

Trevor got back to L.A., relieved the limo was waiting outside baggage claim to take him home because he hadn't slept and was basically in a daze.

He'd gotten back to the cabin and seen that her car wasn't out front and panic had shot through him. Inside, on the bed, was her note.

Trevor, I wanted another night but I can't face leaving you tomorrow morning. I can't pretend that it's okay that I won't ever see you again. I can't pretend that I don't love you and I can't beg. I can't be what you want and you can't be what I want so let's have Lake Cushman and popsicles be one of those memories that summers are made of.

Please be well and make sure your new PA knows you need healthy lunches.

Love,

Tess

He'd stared at the note, a roaring in his ears. She'd left without saying goodbye? Damn it, how could she?

He'd shown up at SeaTac early, storming to her gate only to wait in vain as her plane left without her on it.

His house felt empty when he walked into it that afternoon. Shaking his head, he looked out over the pool to the small pool house that he'd had converted to an office. The place where Tess would arrive at nine every morning and stay until seven every night.

Not able to face seeing that place without her in it, he called down there to let his new PA know he was back. And he thanked her for sending the limousine for him. He made mistakes before, the least he could do was remember to thank his damned assistant.

*   *   *   *   *

Trevor had already planned to be gone for six weeks to shoot a movie in Toronto right after his return from the lake. Gratefully, it kept him from driving past Tess' house every day.

Damn it, he missed her. Not the way she kept his life in order, but her. The sound of her voice, the way she laughed. He had no one to share things with the way he'd done with her. Those days at the lake became more than a fond memory, they became a touchstone.

While on the shoot, his very attractive costar had sent him all the right signals and he'd even tried to work up an interest but he couldn't. He saw Tess' simple smile instead. Tasted her skin on his lips. She was burned into him like a brand.

He'd always thought he had enough money to have everything. Working damned hard, he got past a childhood of privation to an adulthood where his every fantasy was within reach. But the realization came to him with terribly clarity that Tess Marshall was a very fine thing and someone utterly priceless to him. She was it. The one true thing. A woman who knew him and loved him anyway. Knew his flaws up close and personal and accepted them. He was too old and she was too special for him to miss out on having her as his woman because of stupid expectations of other people.

At the end of the shoot he got on a plane and headed straight for Westwood.

*   *   *   *   *

Tess had returned home from Lake Cushman and waited. She was sure Trevor would show up at her door within a few days but he hadn't. She told herself it was for the best and it was, but it still hurt.

Two months had passed and the summer faded into the fall, although in L.A. there wasn't much difference. Still, Tess felt further and further away from those idyllic days beside the lake.

She didn't take a full-time PA job again. Instead she joined an event planning firm part-time and enrolled in school. She'd meant to finish college but it remained one of those things on her to do list until then.

Thankfully, she had enough connections from working with Trevor that she was able to find a spot at UCLA and began to attend classes. Her house was paid for, her expenses other than school were small and she began to settle into a life totally different than what she'd had before and she discovered she loved economics. Who knew?

So she'd pulled back into her driveway in her traded-down car—no use having a Lexus to go to college in—and saw his Porsche sitting there. Her heart leapt. But she steeled herself. She'd learned that she could live with her new life. Yes, she still loved him but she could live without him if she tried. Didn't mean it was easy, she missed him like crazy. But she couldn't live without her self-respect.

Taking a deep breath, she grabbed her backpack and got out, walking to the porch where he sat.

Damn he looked good. Better than she remembered. He had a bit of a beard and his hair was too long, but he looked warm and handsome and oh god how she loved him.

"Hi."

He stood. "Hi. Can I come in?" He motioned toward the door.

Swallowing hard, she nodded. "Sure." After she unlocked the door, he followed her inside. Kicking off her shoes, she tossed the backpack on the table and turned to find him only inches away.

"You look good," he murmured, stepping closer.

Her heart shot into her throat at his nearness. "You look tired. Handsome, but tired. You just finish a shoot?"

Smiling softly, he reached out to cup her cheek. "You know me so well. I just got back two hours ago. Dropped my stuff at home and came straight here. I've asked around, who are you working for? No one will admit to poaching the best PA ever."

"I went back to school. I think I'm going to get my degree in economics. I may do an MBA. In the meantime, I'm working a few nights a week and weekends for an event planning company. It pays my bills."

"I really have to kiss you, Tess."

She gulped and tried to step back but the table was to her right and the wall directly behind her. "I don't think that's such a good idea, Trev." Yeah, could she be less convincing?

"Why is that? Are you seeing someone else? Have your feelings for me changed?" He stepped forward again so that his body was now flush with hers, his arms braced on the wall to either side of her head.

"I…uh, no. No to both questions. But that doesn't change the situation, Trevor."

"The situation *is* changed, Tess. The life I live without you in it is a shadow. It's pale and watery. And lonely. But the life with you in it? It's vivid and beautiful and living and breathing and damn it, I love you. I want you to be with me."

Hope, a tiny ember of it, sparked within her. Okay, there were other things sparking to life too, but hope was more important than lust.

"Your silence is freaking me out, Tess."

"I love you, too, Trevor. But," she put out a hand to stop him from swooping in for a kiss, "what are you offering? Because I haven't changed my mind about not wanting to be some kind of dirty, back-office secret. I can't watch you on the red carpet with other women. I want to be in your life, openly."

"I want you there, too. I want you to marry me. I've called the Lake Cushman Lodge, they do weddings there, did you know that?"

For the life of her, Tess could not find words so she shook her head.

"No? No you won't marry me?" He looked so crestfallen that she quickly kissed him, holding his face in her hands.

"Are you sure you want to marry me? Because I'm old-fashioned, Trevor. Having a clit piercing does not mean I don't expect you to be faithful."

He threw back his head and laughed. "Of course. And babe, I plan to have you keep me far too busy to stray. Even if I wanted to, which I don't. You're it."

"Then why did you wait so long?"

The hurt in her eyes tore at him. "I'm sorry. I left for the shoot a few days after returning from the lake. I wanted to come get you every day since I found the cabin empty. I was hurt when you left but I understand why you did. I couldn't have offered you forever then. I loved you that last night but I was afraid to say it. Afraid to let myself be known enough to love you. So I needed to work it through, be absolutely sure, because you deserve utter devotion and certainty. Every moment of the last two months has been filled with you. All of my dreams, each breath. All you. Will you let me give you forever, Tess? Can you give it to me in return?"

She took a deep breath. "Yes."

"Thank god!" Grinning, he moved his hands to the waist of her jeans and quickly undid them, shoving them down her legs.

The dam of longing between them broke and suddenly it was all hands and mouths and teeth and writhing as they sought to divest each other of clothing.

Greedily, he took her mouth in a kiss so devastating that she went weak over it. His lips brushed hers and then seduced her mouth open, tongue flowing inside to slide sinuously over hers.

Roving hands found her breasts, rolling and pinching the nipples until she was trembling with need. His cock thrust through her fist, the sticky warmth of his pre-cum spread to her belly.

"Inside me," she gasped. "If you don't fuck me now I'll die."

"Just a little death," he said with a chuckle and spun her body, pushing her stuff on the table to the side and laying her on it, legs dangling off the side. "I've dreamt of that beautiful pussy every day. I'm going to eat you first, then I'll fuck you. We may even make it to your bed. I can't make promises just yet."

"Oh dear," she whispered as he leaned over her and put her hands above her head and had her grasp the far end of the table.

"Hold on, Tess, my love."

She didn't have time to laugh as he spread her legs wide and pulled the lips of her pussy apart. He blew softly over that swollen, wet flesh and she whimpered.

"That's the way, baby. I want you writhing and whimpering. I've waited so long for this." Two fingers slid into her cunt as his tongue slowly circled her clit. He hooked the fingers and found her sweet spot, making her cry out with pleasure and arch into his face.

No more words from him then as he got down to the very serious work of eating her pussy. He loved the way she tasted, loved the way she felt against his lips and tongue. Her response to him—that sweet and genuine reaction—was soothing and sensual at the same time. His Tess was flame against his mouth but real. So fucking sexy.

Her clit hardened and swelled and he could no longer deny the lure of that little silver ring. Taking it between his teeth, he tugged it gently and followed up with a stroke to the underside of her clit with rapid flicks of his tongue.

She was close. The trembling of her thighs told him that. He made her this way. Triumph and possessiveness roared through him as orgasm hit her and he claimed her heart and soul.

"You got some mad skills there," she gasped.

God he'd missed her sense of humor. "Yeah, I'm wicked skilled." He rolled the condom on one-handed as she sat up and moved her ass to the edge of the table. Good thing it was oak and heavy or it may not have been up to the beating it was taking.

"Oh!"

He slid into her completely. God, had anything ever felt this good before? Her pussy was made for him, her body made to fit against his. Her legs wrapped around his waist, opening her fully and pulling him closer.

"And the right height, too. We'll have to move it to the house. I don't think my table is very good for fucking." He grunted as he began to slowly thrust into her.

"Yes, my Grandma Marshall's oak table will look right at home in your dining room that's larger than my entire house."

"Oh hush. It's our house and our dining room and I rather like this table. Now let me fuck you. I've been dreaming of this for two months now."

Putting her palms flat on the table behind her body, she arched her back and received him. Her gaze bore straight into his, right into his heart and soul.

"You'll need one of those hands. I want you to make yourself come. I did so love watching you do that when we were in our cabin."

Sucking her finger to wet it, she slid a hand down to her pussy and stroked over her clit, gasping and moaning as she played with the ring.

"I love the way your cunt grips me when you do that." He moved to take a nipple between his teeth, his tongue stroking it as he bit down gently.

The fat head of his cock stroked inside her, making her nerves sing in time to the mouth on her nipple and the fingers on her clit. His unique smell filled her senses. Leaning down, she kissed the top of his head, his cool, silky hair against her lips.

She couldn't wait, she was a terrible masturbator because she never made herself wait. Her orgasm broke around his cock and she loved the way he groaned. Knowing she affected him that way touched her deeply. Made her feel like a goddess.

"My god, your cunt is like a fucking fist. Hold on, baby."

Putting her hands back where they'd been before, she arched and took him into herself over and over. Tiny ripples of orgasmic pleasure rolled through her with each thrust of his cock.

He thrust so hard and so deep that her breasts began to bounce and her breath caught as she saw the look on his face as he watched. So much desire for her.

"Yes, oh yeah. I love you, Tess." The words left his mouth followed by one last, deep thrust as he came.

Moments later, he pulled out and pressed a kiss to her collarbone. "I'll be right back and then I think we should order pizza to refuel. 'Cause then I'm going to fuck you proper-like in your bed. I've got a wad of condoms and a cock that can't seem to get enough of you. Are you up for the challenge?" He grinned but then got a bit serious. "It will be hard sometimes, you know, being my wife. But I'm dedicated to you, Tess. We'll make it work."

She hopped off the table and tiptoed up to kiss him. "We will. 'Cause I'll have to kill you if we don't." Winking, she sashayed past him to the phone and joy surged through him at his unexpected fortune.

Also by Lauren Dane

ಬ

Enforcer

Reluctant

Sudden Desire

Tri Mates

Witches Knot 1: Triad

Witches Knot 2: A Touch of Fae

Witches Knot 3: Vengeance Due

Witches Knot 4: Thrice United

About the Author

ಬ

Lauren Dane been writing stories since she was able to use a pencil, and before that she used to tell them to people. Of course, she still talks nonstop, but now she's decided to try and make a go of being a writer. And so here she is. She still loves to write, and through wonderful fate and good fortune, she's able to share what she writes with others now. It's a wonderful life!

The basics: Lauren is a mom, a partner, a best friend and a daughter. Living in the rainy but beautiful Pacific Northwest, she spends her late evenings writing like a fiend when she finally wrestles all of her kids to bed.

Lauren welcomes comments from readers. You can find her website and email address on her author bio page at www.ellorascave.com.

DOMINANT BOYS OF SUMMER

Katherine Kingston

Chapter One
Day 1

ജ

Julie shivered as she pulled the car into the driveway leading to the beach house. She tried to convince herself the chill came from the cool air blasting out of the car's air conditioning but she knew it wasn't true. Fear made her stomach clench and sent goose bumps racing across her skin.

The beach house was nothing special. About the same size as its neighbors, it had cedar siding, a parking area on the ground level and a wood deck surrounding the upper-level living quarters. From here she could see the ocean behind it but the bulk of a dune hid the beach.

She had to force herself to turn off the motor and climb out of the car.

Whatever happened over this long weekend would change her life and her world. For better or worse.

After much agonizing, she had decided to roll the dice, to give it a try, even though the plan Dave and Nick had presented to her made her stomach roil with fear.

How much did she have to lose? A bit of pride, more than a bit of control, Dave?

She was going to lose Dave anyway if she did nothing. He'd shown remarkable patience with her, but what man wanted a long-term commitment to a frigid woman?

Drawing a deep breath, she raced up the wooden steps to the deck and knocked at the back door.

Dave opened it for her. The smile that spread across his face worked its way under her skin and all the way down into her heart. Then he kissed her. That long, sweet kiss should have fired her blood and made her tingle all over. At least that's what the novels said would happen. It didn't for her. And yet she loved him. Tall, dark, handsome, good-natured Dave would make most women slaver in eagerness. She wanted to burn for him the way the books and magazines all said she should.

She wanted this to work so badly. No matter how hard it was for her, she was going to do it.

"Hi, Jules." A second man walked up behind Dave.

"Nick," she said, nodding to Dave's best friend.

He offered a smile whose coolness made a marked contrast to Dave's warm greeting.

She gave Nick the standard peck on the cheek and drew back. She had to admit his silky blond hair, warm, masculine smell and broad shoulders would be a temptation to most women. The familiar pang of guilt knifed through her. She loved Dave more than anyone in the world and was dismayed that she could find his best friend appealing too. Julie hadn't decided whether she liked Nick or not but she couldn't deny she found him attractive. Still there was something intimidating about him. Given the plans for the week, she'd better get used to it.

One way or another her life wouldn't be the same after this week.

"Julie." Her attention switched to Dave. "I'm going to help Nick bring in your things. I've left linens in the front bedroom. I want you to make up the bed in there, get us each a beer and meet us in the living room in fifteen minutes. Oh, and change into the red two-piece when I bring in your suitcase."

She met Dave's eyes, startled at the stern look in them. Unusually and excitingly stern. Dave's easy-going good nature and good looks had drawn her to him in the first place, but his sharp wit and intelligence had sealed the deal and made her fall in love with him.

From the corner of her eye, she caught Nick's approving nod. So. The games had begun.

She nodded, went back to the front bedroom and hustled through putting sheets on the bed. By the time she finished, Dave had deposited her cases in a corner of the room. She changed into the bathing suit and slipped her feet into the red sandals with the three-inch heels. Studying her reflection in the dressing table mirror unnerved her. How could she walk out in front of Nick like this? Dave, at least, knew all her curves and all her imperfections. Why did she have to display them for Nick? The suit hid almost nothing. For the bottom, a small red triangle of fabric hung from the elastic at the front, turning into another tiny triangle in back, displaying her too-ample butt and heavy thighs. The top featured a two-inch-wide strip of fabric that ran across her breasts and tied at the back. Her nipples showed clearly against the material. She might as well be naked.

She pushed back a few strands of dark brown hair from her face as she drew a deep breath to muster her nerve. At least her face looked good. Maybe it would hold their attention rather than her body. Right.

Time was running out and she still had to get the beers. The heels on the sandals reminded her to keep her shoulders straight and her tummy tucked as she walked, which helped steady her.

The two men came into the living room from the back bedroom just moments after she'd set the three open bottles on the glass coffee table and sat down in one of the chairs.

"Stand up," Dave said.

After hesitating for a second, Julie stood. Since the two men approaching stared at her, she did the same, turning her attention from one to the other and then back. Both were handsome but in very different ways. Oddly their coloring belied their natures. Dave had the sunny disposition but his hair was almost black and his eyes the color of rich, dark chocolate. Cooler, harder, more introspective Nick had blond hair and green eyes. Dave was six foot two. Nick was a couple of inches shorter, with broader shoulders and a deeper chest. Nonetheless even with his slimmer build, Dave had solid muscles. Both men worked out to stay in shape as well as meeting often for tennis and golf.

Dave's expression remained harder than normal. "Turn around."

Julie did, despite the blush rising to her cheeks as she thought about them studying her oversized rear end.

"You can face us again," Dave said after a couple of uncomfortable moments. His expression softened as he approached her. "Julie, I have to know if you still want to do this. You know what it entails. You've had time to think about it. Are you sure?"

She looked over at Nick, considering how it would change their relationship, then back to Dave. "Are *you* sure?"

He blinked in surprise. "If you are, I am. I've told you I'm willing to live with it."

Humiliation warred with anger at herself. "You shouldn't have to. If you think this will help me learn to respond to you, then I want to do it."

"It's not a case of learning to respond," Nick interjected. "But of learning what you respond to. But we can only do this if you're completely willing."

"I am."

"You know the rules? Remember the safe words?" Nick asked.

Julie nodded. "Yellow light and red light."

"Good."

Nick put the athletic bag he held on the sofa, opened the zipper and pulled out several leather straps. Her heart skipped into a double-time beat.

The men flanked her, Nick on her right and Dave on the left. Each buckled a leather strap around one of her wrists, not tight, but just snug enough to stay in place. Then they each knelt and put them on her ankles as well.

"Whenever we put these on you, you'll know that you're expected to be submissive to us until we remove them," Nick said after he straightened up again. "You understand?"

"Yes." The word came out as a bare breath.

"Yes *what*?"

"Yes, Sir. Forgive me, Sir."

"This time," he answered. "Only *this* time."

The two men each reached for a bottle of beer and took a few pulls. Julie followed suit and didn't recognize the error until Nick gave her a hard look. "Julie, did anyone give you permission to drink that?"

"I didn't—" She stopped and looked at them. She did know. She just didn't remember. "No, Sir." She said it as humbly as she could manage.

Nick nodded. "This is the last time we'll give you a pass. You know the rules. I know it's a struggle for you to remember them, but learning to remember, acquiring the mindset is why we're here. So next time you slip up, no matter what it is, you'll be punished. Understood?"

Her stomach twisted with a combination of fear and…was that excitement? "Yes. Sir." The second word was added a bit belatedly but Nick let it go.

"Of course, that doesn't mean we won't decide to punish you just because we feel like it. You've given us that privilege. Haven't you, Julie?"

Her heart hammered in her chest and a coil of heat snaked down into her cunt. "Yes, Sir."

"And you want it, don't you?" Nick demanded.

She sucked in a breath. "I think so, Sir. Yes. Sir." It was true too. She hoped. Their plans terrified her and fascinated her at the same time. It might be her only chance to find out if she was truly frigid or if her needs were just different, as Dave and Nick suspected.

"Good." Dave picked up the thread of the conversation. "For the next couple of days it's going to be all about you learning to submit, to accept and to feel what we think you want you to feel. I know it's hard for you to give up control."

Julie nodded. Her pulse hammered in her temples as she wondered what they would ask her to do.

"Have a drink," Dave told her.

After she'd taken a long pull of the beer, the men exchanged a look. "Take off your top," Dave said.

Julie sucked in a sharp breath. She stared from Dave to Nick. Did they really expect her to—?

"Julie, do we have to punish you for disobedience right away?"

"No, Sir." She reached behind her and pulled open the fastening on the bathing suit top. The fabric slipped off her breasts. A breeze rushed over her, making her nipples bead up into hard pebbles.

"Look at us," Dave demanded.

Julie lifted her gaze from the spot on the floor where it had rested to meet Dave's eyes. Admiration tempered the sternness of his expression. It took more nerve to turn to Nick. His green eyes sparked with lust and anticipation. She shivered from fear.

"You're beautiful," Nick said. "Voluptuous. Spectacular."

Dave nodded agreement. "And now you're going to take off our shirts."

Julie went to him, undid the bottom two buttons of the polo shirt and lifted it over his head. She knew Dave's chest well enough from their sometimes nearly successful attempts at lovemaking. She admired its strong smooth muscles and thick mat of dark hair. The warmth of his skin and masculine aroma pleased her.

Releasing the buttons of Nick's shirt and sliding it down his arms was a far more dangerous undertaking. Nerves made her hands tremble. His broad chest was uncharted territory. The tanned skin felt rougher than Dave's, though he had only a smattering of blond hairs on the sculpted pectoral muscles.

She wanted to stroke the firm skin, to test it with her fingertips as she sometimes did Dave's. The way Dave flinched and sucked in a sharp breath of pleasure when she touched his taut masculine nipples always gratified her. Would Nick react the same way? She didn't dare try it.

Julie backed up a couple of steps once she'd finished the task, waiting for the next demand.

"Kneel on that." Nick pointed to an oversized round hassock beside the coffee table.

She knelt on it, letting her knees sink into the cushioning.

"Spread your legs apart."

The bottom half of the swimsuit offered some privacy, but even so, to display herself like that seemed somehow obscene.

"Julie…" Nick's tone threatened reprisal.

"Yes, Sir." She moved her knees apart.

"Wider."

"They're— Yes, Sir."

"It rankles, doesn't it?" Nick asked. "You don't like following orders."

"No, Sir," she admitted as she shifted her legs so they rested right on the edges of the hassock.

"Good. It'll be all the sweeter when you discover the joys of giving up control."

Julie shivered. It didn't sound sweet at the moment. It sounded fearsome and dangerous. She wondered if she'd end up hating Nick when the weekend was over.

Nick reached into his bag and pulled out a length of black silk fabric that shimmered as a ray of sunlight struck off it. He came to her and wrapped the narrow band of silk around her head, over her eyes, tying it in back.

"We're doing this because we want you to concentrate on the sensations you're feeling and not who's doing what or is about to do what to you."

Julie nodded, hoping she didn't lose her balance in the sudden blankness. Gentle hands stroked down the side of her face and throat. When a finger brushed delicately along her lips, she jumped, startled by the sudden tingly sensation, and nearly lost her balance.

Moments later a strong masculine body stood behind her and hands settled on her shoulders to steady her. She couldn't tell whether it was Nick or Dave behind her, and that disturbed her.

Until she heard Nick's voice say, "Good grief, you're so tense you're like a board." Strong fingers kneaded the muscles of her back and shoulders.

Moments later another set of hands stroked down along her arms, then across her chest and over her breasts. She tried to jerk back and away, embarrassed to be touched that way by one man in front of another. Nick stopped her by pressing himself forward and clasping her shoulders tighter, keeping her from moving far in any direction.

When she tried to reach out to push the hands away, her arms were drawn back behind her and the clips on the leather wristbands snapped together, holding them in place.

Dave spoke from somewhere close. "It's all right, Julie. You don't have to struggle. Just relax. This is what you're here for. We won't hurt you, and if you really don't want us to do this, use your safe word. Otherwise, we're making the decisions here, remember? You gave us that privilege. If you want to revoke it, you know how. Otherwise, just relax and let this happen."

Easy for Dave to say. Hard for her to do. She nodded.

When Nick began to massage her shoulders and back again, and Dave's fingers circled her breasts, she let go inside and gave herself over to it.

With no distracting sights, the effects of their touches seemed magnified. The massaging pressure of Nick's hands dug into her shoulder muscles, finding the knots and tight places and working them until they loosened. By contrast, Dave's fingers brushed over every sensitive inch of her breasts, rousing a pleasant tingle.

The men were in no hurry. Dave spent a long time exploring her breasts, circling, rubbing and stroking every inch of the flesh. She jumped and squealed when he swirled a finger around her areolas then squeezed the tip of the nipple, pinching lightly.

Heat began to simmer deep inside, pouring along her veins and nerves into every corner of her body.

Dave skimmed down her chest to her stomach, his fingertips sliding along her skin with excruciating deliberateness. Shivers ran up and down her body, growing sharper and harder when Nick's lips touched lightly on the skin of her neck, just below her ear.

She'd never guessed her abdomen could be so sensitive, but it felt like a flock of butterflies danced on her skin as Dave explored there. Small shards of pleasurable heat ripped into her. Her breath grew harsher and louder as muscles clenched in response. Not her shoulder muscles so much this time, but those in her groin and thighs.

When Dave's hands moved lower still, brushing along her thighs, the sensation was so exquisite she moaned aloud. Her bones felt as though they were melting, and she leaned back against Nick, letting him support her.

A burst of elation exploded inside her. Dave had touched her before, had spent a lot of time trying to arouse her, with little response. Finally, finally, her body began to respond to his efforts. She wanted to reach out, pull him to her and hug him. Oddly, she wanted to do that with Nick too, though not with the same urgency.

Then Dave's fingers trailed ever so slowly up the inside of her thigh. Tingles and prickles sliced deep. Heat raced through her, driving all thought from her mind for a while.

Sparkling lights burst in fireworks behind her eyes as he stroked up and down the tender insides of her thighs, never quite reaching the apex. A new sort of tension curled from her stomach and lanced down into her groin.

It got hotter and heavier when Nick's hands brushed down her sides, fingers splayed so that his pinkies just touched the sides of her breasts. Even as Dave made her skin shiver and tingle on her legs, Nick roused tendrils of heat in her chest as well. The twin sparks joined to become rivers of fire that surged through her until it melted any remaining resistance.

Something new and intriguing woke within her. Need. A need for more. A desperate, urgent longing for more.

Whatever they wanted, whatever they demanded, she would do, just to get more of what they gave her.

Instead, they stopped.

She shivered as a cool breeze blew over her heated flesh. Making sure she could hold herself up, Nick let her go and began to fumble with the catch holding her wrists together. His hands trembled. It took him two tries to get the knot on the blindfold undone.

Light assaulted her eyes and she had to blink a couple of times to let them adjust. Dave stood in front of her and his breath was far from steady. The bulge behind the zipper of his shorts had to be uncomfortable. Nick still stood behind her. She heard him breathing hard as well.

"Why?" She looked at Dave first then twisted to address the question to Nick as well. "Why did you stop? I was just starting to get it."

"This isn't a race, and just beginning to get it isn't enough," Dave said. "I don't think you went anywhere you haven't been close to before. There's more, lots more, but we're pretty sure it will work better if we don't take it too fast."

Julie drew in a deep breath, struggling to calm herself. If Dave was wrong, she could end up hating him. Nick too.

Nick offered a hand to help her alight from the hassock and then he and Dave unbuckled the straps.

"You can go change if it makes you feel more comfortable," Dave said. "I'm up for a walk on the beach before supper. Anyone else?" He looked at Julie. "When you're not wearing these, it's back to our normal relationship. Can you handle that?"

She thought about it a moment and nodded.

The three of them took a long walk up to a pier probably half a mile away, and back. The sun beat down on them from high in the sky, but a fresh breeze off the ocean kept them from becoming uncomfortably hot. They joked, laughed, teased, splashed around in the shallows where the waves broke onto the shore and picked up shells or other things that caught their eye. They played silly games of tag and tried to lure each other into deeper water.

Later, they grilled hamburgers on an old charcoal grill. They ate those and drank beer and sat in the rocking chairs watching the ocean until the sun sank below the horizon behind the house.

She should have been shy with both men after what had happened earlier, but in fact she found it oddly liberating. What would tomorrow bring though? Better — or worse?

Bedtime brought another surprise. Dave wasn't sharing a bed with her as she'd expected. When she asked about it, he said, "We're not ready for that yet. Oh, and no touching yourself. That's an order."

Chapter Two
Day 2

ഗ

Dave woke to early morning light straggling in his window, the soothing rhythmic sound of breaking waves and the painful throbbing of a hard-on.

Dreams of Julie and how she'd looked yesterday lingered in his head. So beautiful. She was always beautiful, but to see her begin to be turned on was a double bonus.

It gave him hope.

And a whopper of an erection.

He reached down and grabbed his cock. Sighing as the exquisite sensations ran through him, he slid his hand up and down along it. Lightning bolts of pleasure tore through him. His breath speeded up as he pumped harder.

Images of Julie filled his mind. The way she'd looked yesterday, the way she could look kneeling in front of him, begging him to fuck her. Her mouth hovering over his full cock, dipping to enclose him...

He gasped. His hand moved quicker. Balls swelled and ached and felt ready to—

A quick hard jerk, and cum spurted onto his belly, dripping over his hand. A few more spasms followed until he lay back, gasping hard. For a few minutes, he rested quietly, calming his breath in the afterglow.

Then the doubts set in.

Would this truly be what Julie wanted? Was Nick right, that it would free her and allow her to reach the orgasm she'd been unable to find? Her reactions yesterday left him cautiously hopeful, but they had a long way to go yet, and lots of opportunities for it to go wrong.

When his thoughts refused to let him rest any longer, he got up, showered, dressed and went to make coffee.

Half an hour later, Nick joined him on the deck, a cup of coffee in hand. "You're up early," he commented.

"Too nice out here to waste time in bed—alone."

They'd been friends since college and Nick knew him very well. "Trouble sleeping?" he asked.

Dave shrugged. "Some."

"Doubts?"

"Who wouldn't?"

"Nobody in their right mind gives guarantees." Nick stopped to take a drink of coffee. "Based on what we saw yesterday, though, I'm pretty sure we're on the right track."

Dave heard something behind the words, a concern Nick didn't want to voice, and guessed what it was. "What about you?"

"What about me?"

The defensiveness of the words convinced him. "Where are *you* with it?"

Nick gave him the characteristic off-kilter grin. "Stop it. We've been through this, and if you're okay with it, I'm okay with it. Hell, I'm grateful for it. The trust and all. It's a hell of a gift. And yeah, damn it, I'm part of your future as long as you and Julie want it that way, and…" He stopped and shrugged again.

"You'll meet someone. Hell," Dave said, "as many women as chase after you, sooner or later one of them will be *her*."

"If it happens, it happens. And even if it does…I don't see us going completely separate. Do you?"

Dave considered. "Only if Julie or whoever '*her*' turns out to be has a problem with it. I rather doubt Julie will."

"Julie will what?"

Dave turned toward the door where Julie stood, her hair still mussed from sleep and her face bare of makeup. Even so, she looked gorgeous, with her tank top showing a tantalizing hint of breast and the shorts displaying long, lovely legs.

"Julie will want to go down to the beach with us as soon as we finish our coffee," he answered.

She spared him a raised eyebrow but didn't pursue it. Her intelligence and tact were among the many things he loved about her.

An hour later the three of them were down in the water, bouncing on gently rolling waves under a gorgeous clear blue sky. They dove for sand dollars and body-surfed. They stretched out on the sand, slathered each other with sunscreen and enjoyed the soothing pleasure of doing nothing at all.

After lunch they spent time reading and resting.

When Julie got up to get a soft drink from the refrigerator around mid-afternoon, Dave let her get it and take a few sips, then he stood up and said, "Julie, it's time. Finish that and then strip."

Nick followed his lead and got the leather bands out of his case.

She paused with the drink halfway to her mouth. Her face showed a mingling of dismay, delight and surprise. "Strip? You mean...right here?"

"That's what I meant."

She drew a sharp breath and nodded quickly. Watching her pull the tank top over her head sent blood rushing to his cock. Her breasts weren't large, but they were firm and nicely shaped, a neat fit for a man's hands, with nipples that begged to be touched, circled and pinched.

Nick's breath caught as she dropped the tank on a chair and pushed the shorts down her long, lean legs. Her panties were low, flesh-colored and made of some silky material that hugged the curve of her hips.

"The panties too," he ordered when she hesitated, standing awkwardly while the two men admired her body.

She straightened for a moment and he thought she would argue, but then she stuck her fingers in the elastic band of the panties and pushed them down her legs. Her hips were pleasantly round and full, and a triangle of curly hair, the same dark shade as the hair on her head, pointed to her cunt.

After a moment of staring, he and Nick moved closer to put on the leather bands. A faint womanly aroma teased his nose as he knelt to put the strap around her ankle.

Nick blindfolded her with the strip of black cloth.

Dave felt her start of surprise when he picked her up and carried her into his bedroom, the only one in the place that had a king-sized bed. He laid her down carefully and he and Nick ran cords from the hooks on the wrist and ankle bands to each corner of the bed, tying them off on the posts, leaving her spread-eagled, face up.

Dave watched her muscles tense and heard her breathing get harsher as she realized she couldn't move, couldn't do more than just wiggle her arms and legs a few inches. "Relax," he said. "We won't hurt you. And if you can't stand it, use your safe word. Do you want to use it right now? We'll release you."

She sucked in a harsh breath and let it out, then did it again before she shook her head and said, "No."

"Good. But don't forget you can use it at any time."

She nodded but she didn't relax very much.

Nick climbed onto the other side of the bed, holding a large goose feather.

Dave sat on the bed, watching as Nick ran the feather lightly across her cheek and down her throat.

Julie shivered and her lips parted in surprise.

Nick took his time brushing down her arms and along her sides. Julie wiggled and occasionally let out a small gasp. Her breathing sped up when he teased her breasts with the feather, circling, stroking the sides then circling again, but taking his time, moving in slow inward spirals that stopped short of the areola.

A small sob escaped her when he abandoned her breasts and brushed the quill down her abdomen, just to where her pubic hair started, and veered off to run down the front of her left thigh.

Dave couldn't resist any longer and leaned down to kiss her. Her lips were soft, quivering gently, and tasted of cola and sweet woman. They parted on a sigh to admit his tongue. Soft, hot, sweet…her mouth enveloped him in moist heat. Streaks of fire ran straight to his already engorged cock.

He kissed her cheek, her throat and skimmed down her chest and up the swell of her right breast. She moaned softly, deep in her throat as he brushed his tongue over the nipple then drew it into his mouth. He sucked it gently until she squirmed beneath him, making small, mewing noises.

Nick straightened up and signaled for them to change places.

While Dave began stroking her thighs, Nick skimmed the feather over her breasts and brushed her nipples with it.

Julie continued to squirm and moan occasionally. It gave him hope.

Until his exploration took him to her cunt. He parted her labia with gentle fingers and tested the folds within, only to find her completely dry. It took all his self-control to keep from sighing with disappointment.

He looked up, met Nick's glance and shook his head. Nick nodded and they both stood.

"How does it feel?" Dave asked Julie, brushing a hand down her cheek.

"Good," she said on a sighing breath.

"But not good enough."

Nick was already releasing the wrist and ankle straps. Dave joined him. They untied Julie just long enough to flip her over onto her belly then they secured her again. As much as he loved her breasts, the sight of her graceful back and lovely, rounded bottom turned him on in its own way. The pale, creamy skin begged for something to give it more color.

Nick went to the living room to retrieve the bag.

Julie squirmed a little, probably anticipating what would come next.

"You're withholding the thing we want most from you," Dave said to her.

She drew an almost sobbing breath. "I don't mean to."

"I know. I think you need stronger stimulation. You know what to do if it gets to be too much."

She bit her lip, nodding with a quick jerk. It almost dislodged the blindfold, but he moved it back into place over her eyes.

Nick returned. He pulled a pair of light floggers from the case and handed one to Dave before he dropped the bag on the dresser and went around to the other side of the bed.

They'd practiced with everything they'd brought and even tried them out on each other. They agreed they could see why the sensations could be so exciting and that they might want to include them in their play beyond just using them to arouse Julie.

Still a hard knot of apprehension gathered in Dave's stomach. What if she really didn't like it? What if it turned her off completely and made her hate him? What if he struck too hard and really hurt her?

Nick gave him a questioning look then lifted the flogger and slapped it down, almost gently, on Julie's rear end. She made no sound. After a moment a few faint pink marks showed then faded away just as quickly.

Fighting his cowardice, he raised his arm, shaking out the dozen or so eighteen-inch-long leather tails in the process. He let it smack down on her bottom with just enough force that it should sting.

Again Julie showed no reaction and the few small pink marks faded within seconds. Nick's next lash fell a little harder but didn't draw any more reaction.

Over the next dozen or so times they each struck, their blows grew sharper and harder until Julie finally jumped and squealed at a cut from Nick that printed definite, darker pink streaks across her now blushing bottom.

Dave stopped for a moment and let the ends of the flogger fall softly on her neck then trailed them down her spine, along her crack and into her cunt. She jerked hard and made a sobbing sound when the leather tips brushed over a sensitive area.

He slapped the flogger against the inside of each thigh. Julie jerked and groaned, though more from excitement than pain. His cock, already so full and heavy he could barely move, throbbed when he noticed the faint sheen of moisture showing on her labia.

He gave Nick a thumbs-up sign.

Encouraged, they lashed a few more times, spreading their strikes down over the backs of her thighs and even aiming a couple at that tender skin on the inside.

Dave brushed his fingers over her labia, parted them and tested the tender flesh within. It felt warm and slick, and his finger came away coated with her cream.

Julie wriggled under his touch and moaned. "That feels good. Soooo good."

Nick looked at him. At Dave's nod, the other man dropped the flogger and sat on the bed beside Julie. He leaned over to kiss her cheek and a corner of her mouth.

Dave had to fight a surprising stab of resentment and jealousy. He knew Julie loved him. He wasn't sure how she felt about his best friend. She said she liked him well enough, but she sometimes seemed reserved, even nervous, around him.

She had to know that it couldn't be the same man, kissing both her throat and the insides of her thighs, but she wasn't protesting. Dave looked up along her body to see Nick reach around to touch her breasts. She didn't object to that either.

While he continued to kiss his way up and down the insides of her thighs, he stroked a gentle finger along her cunt, stopping to circle and caress her clit. She jerked repeatedly.

The aroma of her arousal made him almost lightheaded. His cock ached and pleaded for relief.

Ignoring it, he stroked her clit then worked a finger carefully inside. He'd never done that before when they made love. She'd never seemed to want it. Her sobbing cries and muscle-clenching reaction when he pumped in and out, though, told him she was liking it now.

He nipped lightly at her thighs, rubbed her clit harder and drilled his finger farther into her until she screamed in surprise and delight as she jerked with the spasms of release.

He continued stroking her until she calmed down. Nick got up and left the room, following their plan that for the first time after she achieved orgasm only Dave would take her.

Julie still breathed hard when he released her wrists and ankles from her bonds and flipped her over. Because he couldn't bear not to see her expression, he also pulled off the blindfold. Then he moved over her, spreading her legs and positioning himself between them.

She watched his eyes as he entered her, her expression utterly radiant. "That was the most amazing thing that's ever happened to me," she told him, raising a hand to cup his cheek.

The glow of joy and delight and love on her face made him feel like he'd grown a foot taller and his cock several inches longer. Not that it wasn't long enough and hard enough right now. "God, Julie," he said. "You were amazing. Beautiful. Magnificent."

He entered carefully but found he slid in easily without the heavy application of lubricant they'd been using. She was hot and slick and held his cock with a tight grip. It felt like heaven, much more so than any time in the past.

She responded to his invasion with a few more jerks and spasms as he pumped in and out. He wanted to make it last, but he'd already had to hold on so long he couldn't contain it for more than five or six plunges.

He yelled as the orgasm all but exploded from him, using up every bit of air in his lungs. Moments later, he collapsed onto her, into the welcoming cradle of arms that encircled him.

"Lady, you take it all out of me."

"Only because you put it all into me." She grinned at him. Her shining happiness struck him in the heart, a spear point of pride and delight that dug itself into the depths of his soul.

He rolled over and stretched out beside her, pulling her close and holding her with her back to his chest as they each came down from the high of their orgasms. Moments later they dozed off.

By the time they woke, the light outside the window had started to fade into twilight. Nick had a pot of tomato sauce bubbling gently on the stove and another kettle of water ready. When he saw them emerge, he dropped a big handful of spaghetti into the water and slid a loaf of French bread into the oven.

Dinner was delicious, but the atmosphere a bit uncomfortable. They discussed the news of the day, the weather, their jobs and everything else they could think of except what was really on their minds. By the end of dinner, though, the red wine Nick had provided with the meal began to mellow them.

Once they were done and the dishes rinsed and set in the dishwasher, they retreated to the front porch with their wineglasses and the bottle. He and Julie settled in rocking chairs while Nick perched on the deck's wide railing with his back against one of the pillars.

It had gone completely dark while they ate, but a nearly full moon shone. It slashed a sliver trough in the ocean, highlighting the white-capped, rolling waves. A fresh, cool breeze blew in from the ocean, carrying its bracing salty scent.

For a few minutes the only sounds were the squeak of the rocking chairs, the roll and splash of the waves, music and voices from the deck of a nearby house. Dave felt peace sink into his bones. He couldn't imagine anything better than being here right now with the two people he cared most about.

They sipped their wine in silent contemplation until Nick said, "It was good for you, wasn't it, Julie?"

She hesitated for a moment then said, "Yes."

Dave tried to see her face in the darkness, but he could only make out a pale oval of light skin. "It wasn't too much for you?"

She laughed. "Not hardly."

"Good," Nick said. "There's a lot more. We've barely touched the surface of what can be. Does it scare you?"

Again a slight pause. "Yeah. A bit. It's so…different. So…against everything I've been taught. I mean it's so un…PC…to let a man—two men—dominate me that way."

"But it feels right to you, doesn't it? It turns you on."

"It does," she admitted. "But what about you, Nick? Today..."

"Today was your first time, and it belonged to you and Dave. But don't worry. Tomorrow will be different."

Chapter Three
Day Three

ஓ

Nick woke to the roar of the waves outside his bedroom window and the first traces of morning light stealing in around the shade. He got up, switched on the coffee maker and went to take a shower while it brewed.

Memories of yesterday flooded his mind while the warm water ran over his night-sweat-slicked body. His cock filled, hard and fast. Just as quickly, he grabbed it and began to pump. He'd jerked off twice yesterday, after he'd left Dave and Julie and then again later, in bed. His breath came quicker and harsher as his balls swelled and throbbed with tension, his cock getting harder and harder until the cum finally burst out and sprayed onto the shower wall.

He leaned against that same wall for a moment or two afterward while he recovered. It had felt good, but doubts began to assail him as he rinsed soap off his body and cleaned the shower afterward. They mostly centered around his place with Dave and Julie in the future.

Now that it looked like they were on the way to sorting out the sexual issue between them, Julie and Dave would probably get married pretty soon. He'd never met two people more obviously made for each other. He rejoiced for them, even while he fought a small worm of jealousy.

He didn't begrudge Dave his Julie. Initially he'd had some reservations about her, doubts that grew when Dave confessed that she seemed sexually cold. The more they'd talked about the relationship, though, the more he realized Julie wasn't indifferent to Dave, that in fact she loved him. She was just wired a bit different sexually. More like himself, in fact, though he preferred to be on the Dominant side of the D/s relationship.

Now, he liked her and found her attractive, but she wasn't the woman for him. His ex-wife Allison hadn't been the woman for him either. Looking back, he couldn't remember why they'd gotten hitched. It had only lasted eight months, and that long only because he insisted on trying to rescue it with counselors and a second honeymoon way too soon after the first one. Allison had stopped caring about a week and a half after the wedding when she found out he didn't live on or spend his dad's money.

He thought Dave and Julie would grant him a place in their life together, and he was grateful for it. In fact, it was an important place, guiding Dave to be the Dominant Julie needed. But could he accept it, knowing that in many ways he was a third wheel? Would he be smarter to guide Dave from afar and not get involved? Maybe today would help him decide.

He had half an hour to himself to brood before Julie and Dave both wandered out, looking rumpled, sleepy and content. When everyone had imbibed enough coffee to get the wheels turning, Nick proposed an outing to the strip of shops and amusement areas a mile or so up the road. The suggestion got an enthusiastic thumbs-up. Julie looked a bit more thoughtful when he added that upon their return they would put the leather bands on her and she would wear them for the rest of the day and evening.

If that thought bothered her, she managed to put it aside for the morning and first half of the afternoon. They parked and walked up the sandy road that paralleled the beach, window-shopping or ducking into the various souvenir places. Dave bought oversized fluorescent pink sunglasses for Julie and a T-shirt for himself. Nick treated them each to a boogie board, a baseball cap with the town's name on it and a box of salt-water taffy. He added to the pile one of those souvenir wood paddles with directions for use burned into the side.

Dave looked at it all. His eyebrows rose at the sight of the paddle, but he only said, "Been dipping into Daddy's piggy bank again?"

Only Dave could say something like that to him and get away with, because they knew each other so well.

"Nah. Been saving my pennies for this trip for a while."

The clerk didn't bat an eyelash as he registered and bagged Nick's purchases.

They had lunch at a place serving delectable crab cakes and shrimp salad sandwiches, and played a couple of rounds of miniature golf.

"I can't believe you beat us both in both rounds," Nick complained to Julie when they were done.

"Just because I'm submissive doesn't mean I'm a pushover. Should I have let you guys win? I'll make a note of it."

"We need a handicap," Dave said. "No more playing with you until you give us a couple of strokes."

Her tawny eyebrows rose. "I thought it was the other way around."

"Not in this game."

"Besides you already have a handicap. You're men."

"Oh, man, that's going to cost you later," Dave said.

"Promises, promises."

"We're men of our word," Nick agreed.

They strolled out over the ocean on the long pier and stood for a while watching people fish off its side. Far out at sea, a dolphin arched in a flash of gray fin. A line of pelicans soared low over the water in stately formation. The warm breeze, the healing rays of the sun, the laughter and pleasant company of his friends all sank into Nick's soul and eased tensions he didn't even know were there.

They walked on the beach and dabbled in the shallow wash of the breakers for a while before they decided to head back to the house.

Once there, they put away their purchases, got refreshments and closed all the window shades before Nick brought out the wrist and ankle bands.

When they'd fastened them on Julie, they demanded she strip. Slowly. As slowly as she could manage it.

"We're not going to blindfold you right now," Nick added. "You need to learn to accept it."

Julie nodded. She stood in the middle of the room and slowly lifted the hem of her tank top, dragging it by fractions of inches up and over her chest and then over her head. She wore no bra beneath. After stepping out of her sandals, she released the button on her shorts, unzipped them and pushed them down her legs until she could step out. The panties followed after a few deliberate, teasing minutes.

She was thin and graceful, her skin a pale cream color. He generally preferred woman a bit more substantial, but he couldn't deny the appeal of Julie's elegantly shaped breasts. Her hips were more rounded, though, and her padded bottom begged for the attention of the paddle or flogger. He knew she considered herself too heavy in the hips. Women.

"Now undress us," Dave told her.

She took care of Dave first, removing his T-shirt, shorts and briefs more quickly than she'd undressed herself.

Her hands shook as she worked the buttons on Nick's shirt free. Once she looked up and met his gaze. Her gray-blue eyes contained a mix of fear, excitement and a surprising, shy affection. Then her attention turned to the snap and zipper of his shorts. The rasp of metal as she lowered the tab echoed in his ears.

He heard her draw a sharp breath before she worked her fingers under the waistband of his briefs and pushed them down. She had to lift the front away to get them over the bulk of his erect cock. She stared at it for a flattering moment and almost reached out to touch it before she changed her mind.

Dave, meanwhile, had brought two of the chairs from the dining table and positioned them facing each other in the middle of the living room. Nick put a hand on Julie's arm to bring her with him when he went and sat down on one.

"Kneel," he said, pointing to the floor in front of him.

She did as he ordered. Dave took the other chair, facing him, and they each spread their legs, moving forward on the chairs until their knees nearly touched. It formed a diamond, with Julie in the middle.

"Now," he said, "you're going to have to earn your jollies today by pleasuring each of us first. You switch back and forth between us. We each get two minutes of your attention at a time, and we'll keep track for each other. You can use your hands, your mouth, whatever you want, but your aim is to bring us off as quickly as you can, while we'll try to see which of us can last longer. I get the advantage because you start with Dave first. You understand?"

Her eyes were wide and shining as she nodded.

"Good. Get ready." He looked at his watch. "Go."

She turned to Dave, rested a hand on either thigh then slid them up his legs to his crotch. Her left palm went under his balls, cupping, while the fingers of her right hand wrapped around his shaft. Almost immediately she began to slide her hand up and down. From the assured way she fingered the tip of his cock and brushed over it again and again, Nick guessed she'd had some practice with him.

Dave sucked in a harsh breath. His fingers curled around the edge of the chair, knuckles whitening as his nails dug into the wood, trying to hold himself steady, in control.

Nick swung his gaze from Dave to Julie to his watch. Only fifteen seconds left and already Dave struggled. His chest heaved and body lurched when she ran a fingertip along the bottom edge of the head of his cock. He muttered something, so low the words were just a rumble.

Then the second hand hit the mark and he called, "Time."

Dave let out a sighing breath as Julie shifted backward, still on her knees, and turned around.

After a moment Dave found the energy to lift his arm, look at his watch and say, "Go."

Julie crept closer to Nick and put her hands on his thighs. She looked up at him, her eyes questioning. He smiled his reassurance and she rubbed her palms up, up, slowly toward his crotch. Her fingers were warm, soft, hesitant and maddeningly provocative. Streaks of fire heated his blood, radiating from the places where she touched him.

Then she slid her left hand up and under his balls. "God," he gasped as shards of sensation, pleasant but nearly unbearable, tore into him. His cock filled and ached.

Though the idea of a contest had roused his competitive instincts, the feel of Julie's soft fingers drove everything else out of his head. He heard himself gasp and moan. Then she put a hand on his penis.

Fire ran through his veins and all he could see were stars and flames. Heat enveloped him. Pressure built in his groin, balls filling and swelling until they ached beyond bearing.

He wanted to grab her and drag her to him, stretch her out on the floor and bury himself in her. *Stay in control. Stay in control.* It was agony. Torture. He couldn't hold out. He was going to explode…

"Time," Dave said.

"Saved by the bell," Nick managed on a long breath.

He wasn't sure whether to be grateful or disappointed. His cock screamed for release, to have her hands wrapped around him again.

It took him a moment to recover enough to check his watch and signal Julie to start again. At first he still struggled to get control and stared at the second hand of his watch. He didn't look up until he heard a loud groan from Dave. It made him feel slightly better to see his friend having just as much trouble.

It looked like Dave was just about to explode. Julie's hand pumped up and down his cock in rapid rhythm. "Jules," he all but sobbed. "You're killing me. I'm going to die if —"

"Time," Nick said.

"Damn it," Dave said as Julie backed away. "The timing sucked. Big hairy eggs."

"What? You want to lose our contest?"

"What's with losing? I was about to come." He heaved a huge sigh and looked at his watch. "Go."

Julie went straight to his cock and balls this time. With her fingers, she explored every inch, every ridge and crevice of him. Her concentration on the task was oddly endearing. He put a hand on her head and ran his fingers into her hair as she sent bursts of furious pleasure shooting through him with palms and fingers. He struggled to hold on, hold back the explosion building rapidly in his groin. He got so hot, so heavy, so desperate and so close. So close. He couldn't hold —"

"Time."

Nick had to resist the urge to yank Julie back and insist she finish it. He wanted to strangle Dave. He clenched his fists and concentrated on breathing for a moment before he checked his watch and told them to go. He stared at the hands on the watch for almost a minute. It took a yell from Dave to make him look up. His friend's body jerked hard once, twice and cum spurted from his cock. Julie continued pumping him until he finished. Dave let out a long sigh and sagged

"Get over here, right now," Nick growled at Julie. "Finish it for me too."

She shuffled over to him, wrapped a hand around his shaft and began to slide her fingers up and down around it.

The fire roared to life, faster and hotter this time. Her touch was sweetness itself. It didn't take long before the flames burned their way past all barriers and his seed burst loose. He roared and leaned forward to kiss Julie as the last of the spasms shivered through him.

They all remained quiet for a few minutes while Dave and Nick recovered, then they stirred and stood. Each man offered a hand to help Julie to her feet.

"You did well," Dave said. "Even if I didn't win. Now it's your turn. First, though, some refreshments."

They each had a bottle of beer before they continued. Julie looked at Dave for permission when he handed her one, and he granted it with a nod.

Nick got out the blindfold and put it on her before they led her to the archway between the kitchen-dining area and the living room, where they'd set a sturdy clamp over the framing woodwork at the top.

Dave reached up and attached two lengths of bungee cord to the clamp and then fastened the other ends to the cuffs on Julie's wrists. They'd measured the cords to be short enough when stretched to raise her arms up over her head but let her stand without having to go up on her toes.

At her sobbing breath, Nick moved up behind her, steadying her with his body against hers. She was all feminine curves, soft and warm. A pleasant flowery fragrance mingled with her more essential womanly odor. "You remember the safe words?" he asked. When she nodded, he added, "You'll use them if you need to?"

"Yes."

"Good."

"See that you do. That's an order."

He stepped back. "I'm going to try out that paddle we bought this morning."

Dave had retrieved both the paddle, which he handed to Nick, and the nipple clamps.

Nick rubbed the paddle on her bottom, measuring where to place the spanks. It was an inch-thick piece of sanded and varnished wood about fourteen inches long. He didn't know how much it would sting or how she'd react, so he swung carefully. The loud crack of the first stroke still surprised him. Judging by her gasp, and the pink streak it left on her creamy bottom, it packed a pretty strong bite. He made his next couple of slaps lighter, just enough to make a smacking sound as they hit.

He paused to let Dave squeeze one of her breasts, gather up the nipple and put a clamp on it. She yelped as he let it close over the sensitive tip and bounced up and down for a moment.

Nick waited until she'd settled a bit before he used the paddle again. Lightly. She might need heavier stimulation, but they'd have to approach that gradually. He didn't want to scare her off with too much too soon. The worry caught him by surprise as he realized just how much trust both Dave and Julie had invested in him. Their relationship was important to them, so much so, they'd both been willing to take this chance to save it. He didn't want to do anything that might damage it.

But Julie wanted this. Needed it. He understood that at a level deeper than rational thought.

He delivered another series of smacks, turning her bottom from pale cream to pink and then to a more blushing rose. Another pause gave Dave a chance to put on the second nipple clamp. She squealed even more loudly and her breath came in a series of harsh pants.

They waited but she didn't use the safe word.

A few more cracks with the paddle had her moaning softly with each stroke. He put it aside and chose another flogger, a bit heavier than the one he'd used the previous day but nowhere near the cruelest one he had. In fact, he'd bought a couple they wouldn't be using that weekend or probably for some time to come.

Dave circled around to get to the bag, picked up a thin, flexible light switch and went to stand in front of her again.

Nick raised the flogger and brought it down on her pink bottom. She moaned and wriggled. Seconds later, Dave snapped the switch across the fronts of her thighs.

He waited for her reaction, watching the pink lines on her bottom form welts. She gasped a few times but didn't say anything.

For some time, he and Dave alternated strikes, Nick on her buttocks and the backs of her thighs, Dave on the front of her thighs, her abdomen and breasts. They developed a slow, deliberate rhythm, leaving plenty of time between strokes to enjoy the way she squirmed and moaned.

The backs of her thighs developed a nice rosy flush to match her bottom.

Than Dave did an unusual strike with the switch that cut upward, under her breasts. The nipple clamps went flying off, drawing a surprisingly loud scream.

Nick winced and hoped none of the neighbors heard and decided to come investigate. Or worse yet, called the police. They'd have to make up a story about her seeing a mouse or something. He looked at Dave, though, and said, "Nice aim." He meant it.

Dave shrugged. "Yeah, but maybe not my brightest idea."

No one knocked on the door or pushed through.

They each delivered a few more strokes. While Julie didn't say anything or do more than groan again, Nick sensed she was approaching her limit. Dave looked at him just then. Odd, how they could be so in tune with each other on this.

Instead of releasing her, they moved together, closing in on her. Dave got down on his knees and began to finger her cunt. Nick plastered himself against her back and reached around to hold her breasts.

They were soft, incredibly soft, the sweetest little handfuls imaginable. And the position let him fit his engorged cock into the crack dividing her buttocks. Each time she squirmed, her bottom stroked him and sent rippling shards of pleasure tearing along his nerves.

He ran his fingertips over her breasts and across the peaks, rubbing softly, pricking carefully with his nails and pinching.

Then Dave stood, put his hands on her waist and lifted her a few inches so he could slide her down on his cock. Nick steadied her with both hands on her buttocks, supporting most of her weight. It let his cock move down a little closer to her anus. Working together like the old friends they were, he and Dave lifted and lowered Julie up and down on Dave's cock. It had the side benefit of pumping his as well.

The only thing he could imagine ever feeling better would be to bury himself deep inside her hot, slick womanly canal. Or the cunt of his own woman. The woman he hadn't met yet but hoped to someday. The woman who could accept his Dominant demands, give herself completely to him but also be strong enough to be his equal in every other way.

In the meantime, his soul rejoiced and gave thanks that Dave and Julie accepted him so intimately.

The warm, soft bulk of her buttocks held him, enfolded him in her womanly essence. The aroma of her arousal perfumed the air as her muscles grew tenser with an impending orgasm.

They moved faster and faster, lifting and lowering. The three of them breathed almost in unison, loud, harsh, panting breaths that sped up as the climax approached.

Nick tilted his hips so that not only was his cock rubbing along the crack of her ass, his balls slapped against her anus.

He filled and burned and flamed until he couldn't hold it much longer. But he did.

Only as he felt the first spasms of orgasm tighten and release Julie's body and heard her cry of shock and delight did he let himself go. The seed spurted from him. Dave roared at almost the same time.

They continued to lift and lower until Julie's spasms had finally worn themselves out. His arm muscles had begun to ache by then. He let her down gently and leaned into her, plastering his body against hers, his chest to her back, his head resting on her shoulder.

Profound gratitude engulfed him, along with a sublime feeling of belonging, of being part of a family. Not the one he'd been born into, but one that had chosen him, had accepted him as part of them. Had given him this gift of pleasure and connection and love.

They stayed that way for several minutes while they came down from the peak. Eventually Dave stirred and straightened. Nick followed his lead. Dave released Julie from the clamp and Nick caught her when she started to sag.

"Are you all right?" he asked, worried that she might be fainting despite the flush that still stained her cheeks.

She leaned back enough to brush a cheek against his. "If I got any better, the world would come to an end. I couldn't contain it."

He smiled and kissed her, suddenly possessive of this unusual young woman. She belonged to his best friend, but part of her belonged to him as well. He wanted to shout it to the world. He wouldn't, though. The world wouldn't understand it.

Dave took her weight from him, picked her up and carried her into the bedroom. He looked back over his shoulder, though, and said, "Joining us for a nap?"

Nick nodded. His legs just barely carried him to the bed. Dave and Julie already lay together there, spooned, with her back to his chest. Nick plopped down on the other side of Julie from Dave. When Julie's arm came around him, her hand resting on his stomach, a profound peace and joy settled into him. It lasted only moments before he sank into sleep.

He woke before the others and managed to slip out of bed without disturbing them. After showering and dressing, he drove down to the market to get what he needed for dinner.

By the time the other two appeared, he had pots of water boiling, ready for the shrimp and corn.

He noted that although Julie had dressed in shorts and a tank top, she still wore the leather bands and deferred to Dave for permission to eat and drink. She looked flushed and radiant. In fact, she almost glowed with happiness.

They took their time over dinner then retreated to the deck again afterward to talk and watch the light fade over the ocean.

"Tomorrow's our last day here." Nick looked at Julie. "Tomorrow you'll have to make the decision for yourself how far you want to go with this."

"How's that?" she asked.

"You'll see. Just keep in mind that all decisions will be yours, but once made, the only way out will be to use your safe word."

She drew a long breath and let it out slowly. "All right." After a moment, she added, "I hate to leave here. It's been…amazing."

Nick smiled. "What happens here *doesn't* have to stay here. We *can* take it back with us."

"We'd better," she said. "This is too valuable to lose. All of it. But I really meant that I just like it here. It's a pleasant interlude."

"We can come again," Nick said. "Pretty much whenever we want. I just have to coordinate it with the rest of the family."

"You own this place?"

"Dave didn't tell you? My family does."

Dave shrugged. "It didn't come up."

"Must be nice," she said on a sigh.

"It is, but I don't like coming alone, and I don't have all that many friends I care to share it with, so I haven't been here much the last few years. I have a feeling that's going to change."

Silence reigned for a few moments, and then Dave turned the conversation to their jobs and how they could manage to get more time off.

They sat for a long time, discussing families, jobs, sports, politics and everything else that crossed their minds.

Nick looked at his watch and was surprised to realize it was close to midnight. A near full moon reflected in a wide silver swath over the water and made the night brighter than usual. Most of the other houses along the strip of beach had gone dark. Only a distant hint of music reached them over the ever-present sound of the waves. After their nap this afternoon, he didn't feel particularly sleepy.

"Anyone up for a moonlight dip?"

"Is it safe?" Julie asked.

"It's a bright night," he pointed out. "As long as we stay in the shallows, yes. In fact, it's a perfect night for a skinny dip."

Dave nodded. "Let's do it." Julie looked at him and nodded.

They went down to the beach and undressed in the shadow of the dune. The hot day had cooled to a warm night, and a fresh breeze blew in off the ocean. The first curls of water hitting his toes brought a bracing chill.

Julie hung back a moment, looking around as if trying to see if anyone watched them, then she plunged in.

"Whooo," she said as the water got to the tops of her thighs. "It's freezing."

"That's far enough," Dave warned. "Sit down in it. You'll warm up." He led by example, crouching down in the water until only his head stuck up out. He pulled Julie down so that she more or less sat in his lap.

Nick could just see their faces as pale ovals sticking up out of the water, but Julie's giggle sounded both surprised and delighted. Nick approached and ducked down as well. A wash of coolness swept him, growing warmer and more comfortable within minutes.

They played around in the water for an hour or so, until the soothing effects of waves and warmth brought on exhaustion. Nick was both surprised and thrilled when they invited him to sleep with them that night.

Chapter Four
Day Four

ဢ

Julie woke slowly the next morning. As awareness crept in, memories of the previous evening bombarded her. First, sharing the bed with two men before she'd drifted off to sleep. Being the filling in the man-sandwich during sex. Nick. The change in the way she viewed him now astonished her.

For a while after Dave had introduced her to his best friend she'd been intimidated by the man. He seemed so cool, so strong, so forceful…and she felt he didn't like or approve of her. She tolerated him for Dave's sake, but she hadn't wanted any closer acquaintance.

When Dave had told her that Nick had a suggestion to try to cure their sex problems, she'd been appalled and repulsed. Until she'd learned exactly what he'd proposed.

How had he guessed at what she needed, when Julie hadn't realized it herself?

She thought she understood Nick more now. He was a good man. One who hid behind a cool, reserved front to protect feelings more sensitive than most people would ever suspect. He'd been dumped by a greedy, grasping bitch who'd wanted him more for what he had—or she thought he had— than for the fine man he was. It had made him wary. Dave probably compounded Nick's doubts about Julie by admitting they were having difficulties in their sex life.

She loved Nick. Not the way she loved Dave, who was everything to her, but more as an extension or an integral part of the man she wanted for her husband. She loved Nick, but she'd never be in love with him. She couldn't cope with his demands and dark moods all the time.

What *had* he meant about making the choices today, though? Wasn't this whole thing about her allowing them to make the choices for her?

She'd find out.

Julie got up and followed the heavenly aroma of coffee brewing. In the living room she encountered the sublime sight of Dave and Nick, both wearing nothing but swim trunks, sitting with steaming cups and plates of toast and jam. A stab of elation shot through her. How many women could claim to have even one handsome, strong and honorable man for a lover? She had two.

"Hey, lazybones," Dave said. "Sleep well?"

"Like the proverbial log."

"We're heading for a walk on the beach," Nick said. "Come with us?"

"Sure. But I've got to have the caffeine fix first."

"One thing, though," Dave said. "You've got to wear the red bikini."

Julie stopped and felt the heat rise in her cheeks. She'd bought the suit to wear for him, never thinking she'd go out in public in it. It was so…tiny. But Dave wanted her to do it. She looked into his dark eyes and saw the pride and the question and the desire. "All right." For him. Only for him. "You'll have to slather me with sunscreen, though. I don't have the kind of tans you guys have."

"Our pleasure," Dave assured her.

An hour later, they made their way down the boardwalk across the dune to the beach. Because she really wanted to hide, Julie held her head high and walked as though defying anyone to criticize the extra weight on her thighs and bottom, displayed all too clearly by the next-to-nothing she wore.

They didn't go very far before attracting attention. She expected it but was surprised she drew as many admiring glances from men as her male companions did from the females. Both men were good-looking, in different ways, and she also garnered many envious glances from the women they passed.

Dave and Nick ignored it all, or at least pretended to. Both were too savvy to be unaware of the attention. They laughed, joked, dodged incoming water or splashed each other, gathered shells and watched the birds soaring above.

Even with some doubts about what might come later, Julie couldn't remember when she'd felt so peaceful and contented.

They went a long way up the beach and took a slow, meandering course back. By the time they returned to the house, it was an hour past noon.

After sandwiches and chips, the men banished Julie to the front porch for a little while.

She took a magazine out with her and attempted to concentrate on it while wondering what they were doing within. When they finally called her to come back inside, she noticed a series of objects laid out on the couch, and a pad and pen sitting on the coffee table.

"Okay," Dave said, watching her. "Here's the deal. You have to tell us exactly what you want. You see the things here?" He nodded to the couch. "Your job is to pick out at least five of them, lay them on the table and put a piece of paper with each saying how many strokes and whether they should be light, moderate or harsh. Once we start you can use your safe word to stop it, but otherwise, what you choose now is what you get. Any questions?"

"Do they all have to be one thing or can I mix?"

"Mix as much as you want."

"Okay."

Julie had to draw a deep breath to quell the riot of excitement and apprehension pulling her tummy into knots.

She recognized the riding crop, the paddle, the belt and the switch, but she didn't even know what some of the other things were called. She picked up a whip-like thing with a handle and about a dozen leather tails, all a couple of feet long. That was probably what Nick had used on her yesterday. Applied with a light hand, it had just enough bite to be rousing but not really hurt. A really hard crack with it, though…

As she considered the various instruments, she realized Dave and Nick offered her the chance to try out the various things at whatever level she wanted. And they needed her guidance to figure out how far she wanted to take it.

How far *did* she want to take it?

She could ask them to give her only a few light swats with each of the things. Or she could go heavier…as heavy as she wanted. Part of her said she wanted it heavy. Another part of her was terrified by the prospect.

Yesterday she'd felt like she could have taken more. Might even have welcomed it. And yet… At the time, it had hurt. She'd wanted it to stop. Only a strong will and a refusal to beg had kept her from pleading with them to stop. But afterward… Oh, afterward, the glow had been fabulous, those fiery welts becoming starbursts of pleasure. And she'd been so hot and needy and ready for Dave.

She wanted that glow again. Even more of it.

Julie hefted each weapon in turn, fingered and tapped them against her hand. Then she made her choices and filled in slips of paper for them.

"Ready," she called.

Dave and Nick came back in and surveyed her work. Nick's eyebrows rose. "You're sure?"

"Sure I want to try this," Julie answered.

"Okay. Get out of the suit."

Julie kicked off her sandals, unhooked the top and let it fall, then pushed down the bottom piece. She shivered as the air conditioning blew a breeze across her.

Nick approached with the ankle and wrist bands and the length of black silk again. "I'm not going to blindfold you this time, but I think we do need a gag. When you screamed yesterday I was afraid someone would call the cops."

"All right."

It was harder without the blindfold. Harder to accept when Nick wound the cloth around her head, stuffing folds of it into her mouth, much harder to let Dave draw her arms above her head and fasten the clips on the wrist bands to the hooks of the bungee cords, and hardest of all not to look back as she heard the men picking up the things she'd lain on the table.

No, check that. It was hardest of all not to look over her shoulder so she could flinch or try to wiggle away when the first strike fell.

"Ready?" Dave's voice.

"Yes. Sir."

She heard them approach, heard the whiz as wood cut through the air, then the crack of the paddle as it landed on her bottom. The smack shocked her with its force. The bite felt like a hundred bees stinging at the same time. This was "medium" force? How would she stand a dozen of them?

The breath went out of her on a gasp.

The second didn't seem quite as hard, although it still burned. The next several blurred together. Each one brought a crack, a shock and then heat. Heat that started as a burning sting in her bottom but shot through her and ended as a heavier, thrilling pressure in her cunt.

She lost count of the strokes somewhere around seven or eight. The paddle ignited a fire in her rear end that was hard to bear without yelling or moaning. She struggled to hold in her cries.

They must have finished the dozen at medium force, because a stroke followed that was noticeably harder, so hard it was all she could do to keep from yelling at the shock of it, and the initial blaze of fire it raised. Then another fell, and another, and thank heaven she'd only asked for three harder ones because she couldn't have stood any more.

But the heat running through her veins was glorious, fierce and devouring, rousing and furious. Her cunt swelled as the pressure gathered there.

A shuffling noise sounded behind her as one man moved away and another took his place. What was the second thing in the row she'd created? A switch?

It must have been. The whizzing sound of it cutting the air was different from the noise the paddle made, and it impacted on her bottom with a soft, sharp zip rather than the louder crack of wood. A slicing pain rushed across the flesh, not deep or intolerable, more surprising than anything else, but a deep sting followed, a burning that sank in further and further as the seconds passed.

Repeated strikes slashed across her flesh. After a while it felt as though they tore her to shreds, though she couldn't imagine either Dave or Nick striking hard enough to risk actually cutting her. The itchy, fiery burn of them accumulated to make her bottom feel as though it might burst into flames from the heat.

Even so, it streamed into her veins and nerves and landed in her cunt, which swelled and pulsed with need.

She didn't bother to count strokes, just accepted them, tried to bear them without screaming, tried to exult in them.

A pause, movement behind her and a different sound split the air. The crack of the belt on her buttocks was loud, but the impact none too fierce. She'd known she couldn't handle harder strokes of it and asked for light. Even light force produced ribbons of fire across her bottom and more of the deep, burning itch that translated into a raging fire in her veins and pressure in her cunt. She felt the slickness of moisture oozing between her legs as the need built.

The belt flicked at the backs of her thighs, pure fire on that pristine skin, ribbons and flashes of pain-pleasure mixed so thoroughly one couldn't be separated from the other.

She stopped trying to count strokes, to listen, to anticipate. She sank into the moment, into her body, into the raging fire the men's efforts stoked.

The weapons changed, the burning grew, heat in her body, light in her vision, pressure in her gut. A few very hard strokes of something finally brought pain so steep she couldn't bear it without trying to yell. The gag muffled the sound. She felt herself writhing, kicking, trying to get away, but it was almost as if that body didn't belong to her. The one she lived in now was turning to pure energy, pure fire, pure need. Need growing so high, so demanding it was pain itself.

Her breath came in gasps and bursts.

A cut of something hot, heavy and beyond bearing had her struggling frantically, moaning, tears leaving hot streaks on her cheeks. The moans turned into a chorus of begging. "Please, please, please..." The demanding need of her body a fire of rage. "Please, please..."

Then they were there. Nick behind, Dave in front, his cock huge, erect, dripping beads of cream. Nick lifted her onto it. No hesitation, no waiting, nothing more needed to prepare her. Dave pushed all the way into her, in one hard, smooth stroke.

Heat behind her too. Something cool and slick rubbed along the crack and into her anus. A cock in her butt as well. Fingers finding the sensitive bud of her clit and stroking, stroking, even as a set of hands on her hips lifted and lowered.

Sensations sublime beyond description tore through her, even while the driving pressure pushed her onward, faster and faster. She wanted to make it last, to keep it going, but she was growing, expanding, pulsing, mad, like someone else…a Julie wilder, more animal, more greedy than anyone she knew.

And then it burst, a volcanic eruption that jerked her around until she was dizzy, screamed past her control, jetted her upward into a zone of pleasure and completion she'd never guessed possible.

Dimly, she heard shouts of joy and release from each of the men.

She wrapped her arms around Dave, leaning on his chest, spasms of aftershocks continuing to tear through her. It took a long time before they wore out. As peace fluttered in to replace the heady rush of the orgasm, she felt completed, stunned, sucked dry and yet astonished at the heights she'd reached.

Nick's breath tickled against the skin of her back when he said, "I think we can say with complete and utter confidence that you are *not* frigid."

"It just takes a different kind of stimulation to excite you," Dave added.

Julie raised her head to look at his face. "Do you mind?"

Dave's eyes widened and his mouth crooked into the grin she adored. "Mind. Oh, God. *Mind*? I feel like I just won the lottery! I'm almost embarrassed to tell you how much I enjoyed that. It's different. It's kinky. It's cool. It's so much fun I doubt I'll ever stop feeling like the kid set free in the candy shop."

"Nick?" she asked.

Air fluttered against her shoulder as he laughed. "I'm so blessed I can't believe it's possible. I'm amazed, thrilled and incredibly grateful you and Dave let me share this with you."

When Dave released her from the cords, she half-fell into Nick's arms. She turned to face him. It felt odd to embrace him, skin to skin, an intimacy she'd have sworn was impossible a few days ago. Now it felt right. She tipped her head up to kiss him on the lips, putting all her gratitude and newfound love for him in the gesture.

She worried it would upset Dave, but instead he put his arms around both of them, drawing them into a group hug.

After a moment, though, he left, saying he'd be right back. He disappeared into the bedroom, leaving Julie still leaning against Nick. Seconds later, he returned, one hand held behind his back.

Instead of embracing her again though, he held out a jeweler's box. She took it from him and flipped up the lid to find a beautiful solitaire diamond ring.

Nick released her and backed away while Dave went down on one knee. "Will you marry me, Julie?" he asked.

Shock sent chills running up and down her body. "Omigod, omigod! Yes, yes!" As he stood, she jumped into his arms, kissing and embracing him. Sharing her life and her future with Dave was a dream she hadn't dared consider when she feared herself sexually frigid. What a turnaround the last few days had brought.

Joy was like a balloon inside her, filling her up until she didn't know if she could stand it. It broke free in wild laughter and some jumping up and down. Dave watched her with an amused grin for a moment then looked around for Nick.

When they didn't see him, Dave called, "Nick! Where the hell are you? Get in here!"

Nick wandered out from his bedroom. "Wanted to give you two a bit of privacy. It's not every day you get engaged. Congratulations."

"Thank you," Dave said. "You will be my best man, won't you?"

Nick grinned. "Damn right I will."

"And a part of the family we create with this marriage?"

The grin disappeared. "Are you sure? I don't want to intrude between the two of you. And there's no telling what the future will bring."

"We're sure," Dave said. "It's still our marriage, but we want you to be part of us too. Of course things will change. There'll likely be other members of the family coming along. And you'll meet your special person and we'll have to adjust to whatever that means. Nothing stays the same. But our friendship and love for each other should. We want you to continue to be a part of that with us."

Nick grinned. "I'd be honored then. Now let's get dressed and break open that bottle of champagne I just happened to stick in the back of the fridge."

Also by Katherine Kingston

Binding Passion
Daring Passion
Equinox (*anthology*)
Gargoyle's Christmas
Glimmer Quest: Bronzequest
Glimmer Quest: Silverquest
Healing Passion
Holiday Heat (*anthology*)
Pleasure Raiders (*anthology*)
Ruling Passion

About the Author

Katherine welcomes comments from readers. You can find her website and email address on her author bio page at www.ellorascave.com.

KNOCKOUT

Hannah Murray

Dedication

For Shannon – my hetero life partner, my say-anything friend, the sister of my heart. Love you, little.

Trademarks Acknowledgement

The author acknowledges the trademarked status and trademark owners of the following wordmarks mentioned in this work of fiction:

Yankee: New York Yankees Composed of Howard Z. Steinbrennen Limited Partnership

Chapter One

❧

Nina Bowes sighed in relief as the door swung open. "Finally," she muttered, dropping her duffel bag inside the door and shaking the rain out of her hair as the screen door slammed behind her. She stripped off the raincoat, hanging it on a hook by the door as she toed off her soaked sneakers. The summer rainstorm had goose bumps rising along her flesh and she shivered in her skimpy tank top. She went to shut the door but the musty, closed-in smell of the house was making her nose itch so she left the door open and dug in her duffel bag for something with long sleeves.

She was just pulling a worn sweatshirt over her head when her phone rang. She dug it out of the front pocket of her jeans. "Hello?"

"Hey, Neen. Make it to the house okay?"

Nina grinned and tugged the sweatshirt into place. "Julie, hi. Yeah, I just got here." She looked around. "This place is great."

The living room was one big open space with hardwood floors and very un-beachlike furniture. Most houses on the Jersey Shore had a wicker and seashell motif—this one had leather couches, mahogany end tables and a plasma TV on the wall.

"I owe your friend a big hug," she said, and Julie laughed in her ear.

"He was happy to do it. He's got some big merger keeping him in the city for the next several weeks and it was either loan it out or let his ex-wife use it."

"Bitter divorce?"

Julie's voice was wry. "That's the understatement of the century. Since the divorce decree prevents either of them from profiting off the property, he loans it out a lot."

Nina laughed, brushing dusky blonde curls out of her eyes. "You were his lawyer?"

"If I had been, he'd have gotten the cottage outright."

Nina chuckled. "I love your arrogance."

"Confidence," Julie corrected, and Nina could picture her grinning. "It's only arrogance when it's undeserved."

Nina wandered over to the front door to look out the screen at the boardwalk. "I wish you could've come with me."

"I do too, doll. But I snagged three more cases this week and they're all going to be nasty. Besides," she continued, her voice going sly, "for what you're there to do, you don't need me hanging around."

Feeling her face flush, Nina forced a note of bewilderment into her voice. "What do you mean? I'm just here to relax—"

"—before summer classes start. Uh-huh, I've heard this song. But you sing it in the big fat liar voice. You're there to see Tony Capriatti."

Nina opened her mouth then shut it again. Finally, she said, "It's just not fair how you do that."

She should have known Julie would figure it out. After all, she'd been there in that Trenton dive five years before when Nina had first seen Tony. He'd been performing with a rock band doing an Elvis cover and her heart had all but leapt out of her chest to splat on the stage at his feet. Something about him had pulled to her and the entire bar had disappeared around her. His voice like dark velvet had thrilled her, and when he'd looked up from the microphone into the audience, his chocolate brown eyes had held her spellbound.

After the concert, she'd leaned against the stage, watching with bemused adoration as they packed their gear and he'd looked at her. Just a sideways glance, no more than a flick of the eyes, but her stomach had flipped over and her knees had gone weak.

She'd racked her brain for something to say. He was nearly done packing his gear and if she didn't say something soon, he was going to walk off the stage and out the door and not remember her at all. She had to say something!

As he'd stood to leave, she'd opened her mouth to speak. To her everlasting horror, the only thing that came out of her mouth was a sighing, "Thank you."

He'd grinned at her and winked. "You're welcome," he'd rumbled, his voice shivering through her, and by the time she'd gathered her wits to say something else, he was gone.

Since then, she'd managed to go to almost every show within driving distance, but had never managed to find a way past the fan girl crush to talk to him. He'd stopped touring a couple of years ago, the band's website had gone inactive, and she'd gradually given up on the idea of seeing him play again. Until she'd checked a little-used email account and found an announcement about a show in Point Pleasant. No band, just Tony and his guitar—getting back to basics, he said. And she'd immediately started planning a little trip.

She was snapped back to the present when Julie chortled. "When are you going to learn? I am unbeatable!"

"Oh just hush," Nina mumbled. "I'm nervous enough."

"Oh darlin', I know you are," Julie said, her voice softening into the Southern drawl four years in New York couldn't disguise. "Do you have a plan?"

"Hope to run into him?"

"You mean at the show on Friday?"

"No, not there. There'll be too many people, too much going on." She shook her head. "I won't be able to talk to him there."

"So, what? You're just going to wander the boardwalk and hope to run into him?" Skepticism colored Julie's voice. "That doesn't seem very effective."

"Yeah, well." Nina breathed deep against the sudden tightness in her chest. "I'm not as brave as you are, Jules. I can't just walk up and say 'Hey, I'm Nina. I love you and want to have your babies.'"

"I'd never do that," Julie protested. "I'd at least save the babies part for over breakfast the next morning."

Nina laughed. "I'm letting fate take its course."

"Which means…?"

"It means if it's meant to happen this week, then it'll happen. And if it's not…well, then it's time to move on."

"I believe in karma and fate just as much as the next divorce attorney—"

Nina snorted out a laugh.

"—but you are going to leave the house, right? I mean, you're not expecting fate to just dump him on your doorstep?"

Nina rolled her eyes. "Yes, I'm going to leave the house. I'm going to stroll the boardwalk, lie out in the sun, shop around. I'm just not going to go searching for him like some damn groupie."

"Nothing wrong with being a groupie," Julie grumbled, and Nina grinned.

"Says the former groupie," she chortled.

"Hey, that band was *good*," Julie said on a laugh. "I was in my twenties, what did I know?"

"Nothing," Nina said with a wry smile. "None of us knew anything and it was great."

"Yeah," Julie sighed. "It really was. Okay, I have a deposition waiting for me and you have fate beckoning you so I gotta go. Be safe, okay?"

"I will."

"And call me if you get some."

Nina laughed. "I definitely will. Love you."

"Love you too." Julie blew a kiss into the phone and was gone.

Nina flipped her phone closed with a rueful grin. She should have figured Julie would see right through her reasons for coming to the Shore.

Not that the reasons she'd given for this little vacation weren't valid. Summer classes started in two weeks and after working full-time all spring while taking twelve credit hours, she was pretty burnt-out. Thankfully the money she'd been able to set aside along with her scholarships would enable her to finish her education over the next year without having to work full-time. She'd still be working part-time at the hospital, but thankfully she wouldn't have to go from graveyard shift in the ER straight to class anymore.

"So it's a perfectly valid vacation," she muttered to herself. "And if I just happen to run into the secret love of my life while I'm here, well then it's fate."

She watched the rain pound the boardwalk for a moment. The summer storm had chased away all but a few hardy souls and the boardwalk was nearly empty. She could see the short stretch of beach and the ocean beyond it, nearly as gray as the sky in the storm. Rain made some people feel sad but it had always made Nina feel calm and centered.

With a last, lingering look at the ocean, she turned to face the living room again. "This place is really something," she muttered. Hoping the bedroom would be just as fabulous, she picked up her duffel bag and padded on bare feet to the staircase off the kitchen.

The second floor was just as gorgeous as the first. Echoing the open floor plan of the main level, the stairs led directly into the only bedroom in the house. From what Julie had said, it used to be two bedrooms and a single cramped bathroom. The current owner had knocked down the walls, expanded the bathroom and turned the entire second floor into a master suite. French doors led to a small balcony overlooking the beach with gauzy curtains she imagined would flutter delicately in the breeze when the doors were open.

The furniture followed the same lines as downstairs. Dominating the room was a king-sized sleigh bed in rich cherry wood with a bureau to match and an overstuffed easy chair and ottoman in the corner surrounded by built-in bookcases.

The walls were painted a very un-beachy apple green and the duvet on the bed was a dark, rich red. "I love this guy's decorator," she said. She set the duffel bag on the bed and went to investigate the bathroom. The sight of the freestanding clawfoot tub and handheld shower massager had her grinning. "And his taste in bathrooms."

She walked back to the bedroom and unzipped the duffel bag. She put her week's worth of summer clothes away in the bureau then went to put her meager supply of toiletries in the bath. When she finished with the minor task of making herself at home, she realized she was hungry. She'd been in such a hurry to leave the city she'd skipped lunch, and the omelet she'd scarfed for breakfast was a very distant eleven hours ago. A quick glance out the French doors confirmed it was still raining.

She headed downstairs to the small kitchen to poke in the cupboards and refrigerator for a reason to not go out in the rain, but all her search yielded was a few cans of soup and a very stale box of crackers. Resigned to getting wetter, Nina went back into the living room and wedged her feet into her sneakers, grimacing as they squished. She pulled the hood up on her sweatshirt and tucked her hair, made curlier and more unruly than usual by the humidity, under the hood as best she could.

She grabbed her keys, her ID and a few bills out of her purse and opened the door. The rain was lashing hard, the storm having grown stronger in the twenty minutes since her arrival. Ducking her head against the rain, she dashed out, running down the short path to the boardwalk. She veered left, heading for the side street she'd left her car on and slammed into something solid.

She bounced off and fell backward, arms pinwheeling madly for balance, but the wood of the boardwalk was slick from the rain, the soles of her sneakers worn smooth, and she went down hard. The second before her head cracked the ground she thought she heard someone mutter, "Oh shit", and then the lights went out.

Chapter Two

ဢ

"Ow."

Nina grimaced, her eyes still closed, and reached a tentative hand up to feel the back of her head. Unsurprised when her fingers encountered a goose egg, she probed the tender area, relieved when she didn't find any blood. "Jesus, what did I run into?"

"Me."

"Ahh!" Her eyes flew open, startled to find a man standing in the doorway of the kitchen. She looked around wildly and realized she was lying on the leather sofa in the cottage's living room. "How'd I get in here?" Her eyes flew back to the man. The kitchen light was on, throwing his features into shadow. "Who're you? What the hell?"

He chuckled, the sound a deep rumble. "Sorry, I didn't mean to startle you. But I didn't want to leave you lying on the boardwalk so I brought you back in here. This is your cottage, right?"

Nina frowned. "Actually, it's a loaner. What happened?"

"You ran into me. Your head was down," he explained, coming into the room. "You didn't see me and I didn't have time to move out of the way. And since I'm a lot bigger than you," he sat down on the sofa by her hip, "you bounced off and hit your head. Fastest I've ever knocked out anyone. How does it feel?"

"Um." Nina blinked up into his face, certain fate couldn't be this cruel. It just couldn't. "My head? It hurts...but I'll live. Do you knock a lot of people out?"

"My fair share, I guess. I do some amateur boxing. You sure your head's okay?" He leaned forward, sliding one broad palm around the side of her head, wincing when he felt the bump. "You need some ice."

"Oh no," Nina stammered. "I don't think I do."

"Better safe than sorry." He winked at her. "There's probably some in the freezer. Be right back."

Nina watched him go then dropped her head back on the cushion. "Ow." She blinked up at the ceiling as her head throbbed and mentally railed at God. "I can't believe this," she whispered. "I can't believe Tony Capriatti is here, I can't believe I ran into him, I can't believe I knocked myself unconscious, I can't believe he carried me into the house and I missed it!"

She covered her eyes with her hands on a moan. The man of her dreams, the man she'd been half in love with for five years was in her kitchen getting ice for the bump on her head.

"Are you all right?"

Nina uncovered her eyes. "Fine!" she said brightly.

He frowned as he sat on the sofa next to her hip. Close next to her hip. Practically touching her hip. "You're not getting nauseous or dizzy, are you?" he asked. "You could have a concussion."

"Oh no," she said on half a laugh. *Sitting so close to her hip!* "Really, I'm fine. It's just a bump. I'm almost a nurse so I should know. Trust me, it's fine."

"Here, let's put this ice on it, just in case." He had a tea towel in his hand, folded around the ice. He cupped her neck and tugged her slightly forward to tuck it behind her head. "Almost a nurse, huh?"

"Um, yeah." She tried to ignore the way her skin tingled at his touch. "I'm going into my last year of nursing school."

"Here, keep this on there." He guided her hand to the makeshift ice pack, wrapping her hand around it and holding it in place. "I'm Tony, by the way."

"I'm Nina."

"Nice to meet you, Nina." He smiled, his brown eyes crinkling at the corners, and she felt her chest tighten.

"Likewise." She smiled back, desperately trying to think of something to say. "Sorry about the collision," she finally said, fighting the urge to roll her eyes at her own lameness. "I didn't hurt you when I ran into you, did I?"

He grinned. "A little thing like you? Nah. You were sure in a hurry though. Where were you headed?"

Still reeling from being called a little thing, it took her a second to answer. "Ah…dinner. There aren't any groceries in the house and I didn't bring anything with me. I was going to find a grocery store or some takeout."

"What kind of food do you like?"

She blinked, nonplussed by the question. "Ah…I was sort of in the mood for Italian. I was going to find a takeout or failing that, pick up some pasta at the grocery."

"Pasta?" He grinned at her, his chocolate brown eyes twinkling at her with humor. "If you want pasta, you ran into the right guy."

"I'm sorry?"

"No, keep it on your head," he urged when she tried to set the ice pack aside. He kept his hand on hers, heat from his skin wreaking havoc with her nervous system. "I mean I make a mean red sauce and I've got a brand new box of linguini at my place."

Nina's eyes went wide as she realized what he was saying. "Oh you don't have to cook dinner for me."

"I'd like to." His eyes stayed steady on hers, watchful, and the urge to fidget was almost overwhelming. "I was going to eat anyway, and this way I get to do it with a beautiful woman instead of the Yankees game. Besides," he said when she opened her mouth to protest, "it's the least I can do after knocking you unconscious."

She felt her lips twitch in a smile. "Nothing against your boxing skills, but I think it's more accurate to say I knocked myself out."

"Is that a yes?"

She laughed a little. "Yeah, I guess that's a yes. But only if we can watch the Yankees while we eat."

He grinned. "Yeah? You like baseball?"

Nina shrugged. "Some girls played with dolls, I played with baseball cards."

"The perfect woman. Okay, you stay here, keep that ice on your head. And I'll be back in ten minutes with dinner."

"Sure." She watched him rise, the loose, easy way he moved making her mouth water.

He plucked a black raincoat from the hook by the door and shrugged into it, then turned and sent her a wink. "Be right back."

"I'll be here," she managed. She waited until he walked out the door, watched him dash through the rain down the boardwalk and into a house a few doors down. As soon as the door closed behind him, she slid to the floor in a heap.

"OHMYGOD!" She fumbled for her phone, the ice pack tumbling to the floor with a wet splat as she dialed. "Answer, answer, answer!"

She nearly sobbed in relief when the line engaged. "Julie! Christ, I'm having a heart attack."

"What?" her friend hissed into the phone. "Nina, slow down. Jesus, you're practically hyperventilating. Breathe and tell me what's going on!"

"Okay." Nina drew a breath, let it out slowly then did it again. "Okay. He's here."

"Who's there? Wait—Tony? He's *there*?"

"Yeah—here. Holy shit, what am I going to do?"

"Well stop screaming into the phone, for starters. He'll hear you!"

"No, he went to go get pasta."

"He went to go get pasta."

"Yeah."

"Okay, start at the beginning."

"Okay." Nina gave a quick run-down of the collision outside the house. "He carried me back here, can you believe it?"

"Yes, I can. I keep telling you you're not as big as you think you are."

Nina rolled her eyes. "This is not the time to talk about my body issues. The point is he carried me back here, he got ice for my head and he's making me dinner!"

"What's he making?"

Nina huffed out a breath. "Linguini with red sauce—does it matter?"

"Is the sauce homemade or out of a jar?"

"Homemade." Nina frowned. "Is that good?"

"It's romantic as hell! You have condoms, right?"

"Jesus, Julie, I'm not going to jump his bones."

"You better, girlie. That's what you're there for, after all. Karma has dumped him in your lap, and if you don't take the opportunity to do something about a fantasy you've had for five long years, then you need your head examined."

Nina felt her breathing quicken just at the thought. "You're right. Shit."

"So, do you have condoms?"

"What? Oh yeah. Yeah, I have condoms. I'm just thinking—what if it sucks? I mean, I've been fantasizing about this—about him—for five years. What if it's completely lame and awful and horrid?"

"Well, then at least you'll know and you can stop fantasizing about it. And now I have to get into this deposition before my client's soon to be ex-wife has his balls for dinner. Spineless little weasel. Use a condom," she ordered, "and call me tomorrow."

"Okay." Nina took a deep breath. "Bye."

She clicked off then looked at the clock in the phone's display. "Fuck. He'll be back any second." Her hands flew to her hair, groaning when she found it soaking wet and matted to her head. "Oh shit!"

She flew toward the stairs, taking the treads two at a time and dashed into the bathroom. "Oh just hell," she moaned. Her hair was plastered to her skull, the curl pulled out by the rain, and what little makeup she had on was running down her face in a mascara river.

"Fucking perfect," she grumbled, and grabbed a tissue. She wiped her cheeks, cleaning off the mascara streaks, and quickly removed the rest of her eye makeup as well. That accomplished, she turned her attention to her hair.

There wasn't time to dry it completely but the great thing about having naturally curly hair was she didn't have to. She whipped the sweatshirt over her head and grabbed a towel, giving her head a brisk rub and soaking up as much excess water as she could. When it was as dry as she could make it, she grabbed a tube of gel from her meager stash of toiletries, squirted some into her palm and worked it into her hair. A quick finger fluff through the curls and she was done—her hair would dry curly and light, and Tony would hopefully want to run his fingers through it.

She made a face in the mirror at the sappiness of that thought then dashed into the bedroom for dry clothes. She stripped out of the wet shorts and tank top and yanked a dark blue sundress over her head. She gave the spaghetti straps a quick adjustment, shoved her arms into a light blue cotton hoodie to ward off the chill from the rain and dashed down the stairs just in time to hear the front door open.

"Hey, you were supposed to keep the ice pack on your head," he accused as he kicked the door closed behind him. He carefully shed the raincoat and hung it on the hook again before heading toward her.

"I needed to get out of the wet clothes," she replied, distracted by the bags in his arms. "How much food did you bring?"

He laughed, the low sound rumbling out to scrape along her nerves and make her shiver. "It's not that much food, trust me. Just some stuff for the sauce, some antipasto." He grinned and sent her a wink. "A bottle of wine."

She laughed despite the curl of lust in her belly. "Are you going to get me drunk?"

"I don't know, I guess that depends on how you like my food," he said, striding past her into the kitchen to set the bags down. She watched as he pulled out fresh romaine lettuce, cucumbers, tomatoes. And a jar of red sauce.

"Hey." When he looked up quizzically, she pointed. "You said you *make* a good sauce, not *buy* a good sauce."

He picked up the jar. "This isn't bought. No, this is homemade, one hundred percent. See, it's a canning jar, not a store jar. Paul Newman did not make this sauce."

"Something tells me you didn't make it either," she said, folding her arms across her chest and raising an eyebrow.

His eyes dipped briefly to her ample breasts, pushed up by her crossed arms, before returning to her face. "Okay, you got me," he said. "My grandmother made it."

She shook her head in mock disappointment even as she felt her pulse skip a beat at the sudden heat in his eyes. "And you said you could make it yourself. The shame."

"I can make it myself," he protested. "But it takes a while do to red sauce right."

"So?" she shrugged. "I wasn't going anywhere."

"Well, I wasn't sure. It's not every day a beautiful woman comes running right into my arms." He smiled and pulled out a bottle of wine, setting it on the counter between them. "I didn't want to waste the opportunity."

Oh shit. Nina swallowed the urge to squeal and wondered that her pulse didn't leap from her throat, it was beating so fast. "So you were planning to seduce me with your grandmother's red sauce?"

"And her homemade bread," he said, tugging a huge loaf from one of the bags.

"And a really nice bottle of wine," she observed, looking at the label.

He raised an eyebrow. "You know wine?"

She shook her head. "Not really, but this is my friend Julie's favorite. She's forever whining about how expensive it's gotten but she can't help herself from splurging on it."

"Well, if she's the one loaning you this house, she can afford it." He reached into the bag again and came out with a corkscrew. "This place is great."

"It is, isn't it?" She watched him uncork the wine and turned to search the cabinets for glasses. "It actually belongs to someone she knows through work and she got him to loan it to me for the week."

She turned back with a wineglass in each hand to find him watching her. She swallowed hard at the light in his eyes, a light that looked suspiciously like lust, and thrust out a glass.

The corners of his lips quirked up knowingly as he poured. "So how long have you wanted to be a nurse?"

"Oh. Um...well, I never finished college but I always wanted to do something in the medical field. I was thinking radiology. You know, a tech?"

He nodded, shifting the bottle to fill the second glass. "So what made you switch to nursing?"

"I was working in a hospital, on the mental health floor. I was an admin but they were so short of nurses I ended up doing a lot of the nursing duties." She shrugged. "I liked it. I liked helping the patients. And going to school for nursing wasn't that much longer than going to school for radiology."

He took a glass from her outstretched hand and lifted it to his lips. "How much longer do you have to go?"

"Just a year," she mumbled, taking a sip of her own wine. It did absolutely nothing to cool the fire in her blood. "I'm taking summer classes so I can graduate early."

"That's great," he murmured.

His gaze on her was so intent Nina was starting to feel like a bug under a microscope. "What?" she asked, rubbing her nose self-consciously. "Do I still have mascara running down my face or something?"

He chuckled and she had to brace herself with a hand on the counter when her knees turned to water. "No, nothing like that. It's just—you seem familiar to me. Have we met before?"

Nina was glad she wasn't taking a drink when he'd asked—she'd have choked on it. Never in a million years would she have guessed he'd recognize her. There were always so many bimbos around him whenever he played, she'd have bet her diamond earrings there was no way he'd have been able to pick her out of a crowd.

"Um, I don't think so," she managed, and took a fortifying sip of wine.

"Are you sure?" he asked. "There's something about your eyes… I really think I've seen you somewhere before."

She made some noncommittal sound and drank more wine. She wasn't about to refresh his memory, having no desire to remind him of the shy, overweight girl who used to gaze at him like an adoring puppy.

"Hmm." He narrowed his eyes at her then seemed to shrug. "Maybe it's just wishful thinking."

She blinked, confused. "What do you mean?"

"Well, it would have been nice to have a connection," he said. "Other than you just running into me in the rain."

She chuckled weakly. "I still can't believe I did that."

"I'm glad you did," he said, still looking at her with a knee-knocking intensity. "Otherwise, we might not have met. And that," he said, picking up the bottle to top off her wine, "would have been a shame."

Nina cleared her throat, watching the wine in her glass rise up to tease the brim. "*Are* you trying to get me drunk?"

"If you think it'd help," he said, and winked again before he turned to the groceries.

Nina felt a bubble of wild laughter rise up in her chest. "Help with what?" she asked, and he turned back at the teasing lilt in her voice.

His left eyebrow quirked up in a way that had her knees knocking again. She was always a sucker for a good one-eyebrow look. "With the seducing, of course."

"Oh." She laughed, a girlish sound that was foreign to her own ears. "You don't need wine for that."

Chapter Three

Nina thought she'd swallow her own tongue when he turned to face her fully.

"Is that so?" he murmured.

"Pretty much," she sighed, shivering in anticipation as he moved towards her. "You had me at 'oh shit'."

He chuckled again, coming to a stop in front of her. He was so close, his feet were practically on top of hers and she could feel the heat of him through their clothes. "You're funny. And you're cute and sexy and adorable." He reached out and put his hands on her shoulders, and even though the hoodie covered her skin, she shuddered in reaction.

"Tony?"

"Hmm?"

It was now or never and she'd hate herself if she didn't say it. Nina took a deep breath. "Were you planning on kissing me anytime soon?"

He was standing so close, looking right at her, so she saw the lust flare bright and hot in his eyes at her words. "As a matter-of-fact," he murmured, and lowered his head to hers.

She held herself perfectly still, barely daring to breathe as his lips touched hers. Once, twice, he brushed over them lightly, almost delicately, leaving a delicious tingle in their wake. She couldn't help the slight whimper or the way she swayed toward him, following his mouth. She vaguely heard him groan and answered it with one of her own when she felt the tip of his tongue flicker over the corners of her lips.

"Damn," he rumbled, and his hands tightened almost painfully on her shoulders.

"Yeah," she breathed, and rose up on her toes. She brought her hands up to his chest, gripping his shirt in her fists as she tried to get closer. "More," she moaned, and in a sudden blur of movement, he obliged her.

His head twisted, his mouth slanting over hers and forcing her lips apart. She whimpered in relief when his tongue slipped past her teeth, the more forceful caress both soothing and inciting her lust. She curled her tongue upward, sucking on his, and with a curse, he wrenched free.

"What?" she gasped. "Did I do something wrong?"

He shook his head. "No," he said, his voice harsh with desire. "But if you want to eat, we have to stop."

"I'm not hungry," she said, and leaned forward to lick at the skin of his throat. He was salty with sweat and went to her head faster than whiskey. She groaned and, using her grip on his shirt, bounced once on her toes and boosted herself up into his arms. His hands moved automatically, sliding from her shoulders to grip her ass as he took her weight. She thought briefly she was too heavy to do this and should jump back down, but then his hands dug into her ass, kneading and pinching and stroking, and she forgot all about the last ten pounds she couldn't seem to lose.

"Oh Jesus," he hissed when she nipped him with her teeth. He took two steps forward, making her shriek when she felt her ass slam against the butcher block. With the counter supporting her weight, he took one hand off her ass and tangled it in her hair. He tugged her head back, his fingers tangling in her hair tight enough to make her scalp sting deliciously, and she whimpered involuntarily.

"Nina." He groaned her name and she opened her eyes. He was looking down at her, his eyes narrowed and his lips peeled back in a sensual grimace. "Be sure."

"I'm sure," she whispered, licking her lips and tasting him on them. "I'm really, really sure. I want you like mad and if you don't fuck me, I'm never going to forgive you."

He laughed but there was no mirth in the sound. "I don't have any condoms with me."

"I do." She leaned forward, straining at the grip of his fist in her hair to nip at his neck again. "A whole box. Upstairs. Are we done talking now?"

"Just one more thing," he said, and she groaned as he tugged her hair back again.

He waited until she was looking at him. "I just want you to know, I don't do this. I used to do this—I used to do it a lot. But not anymore. I just wanted you to know that."

"Neither do I," she managed. "But I really want to do it with you."

He slammed his mouth down on hers, his tongue delving into her mouth and stealing her breath in a kiss that left her tingling and panting for more. "Me too," he said, and pulled her away from the counter, dropping her back on her feet. "Me too. Where's the bedroom?"

She pointed vaguely in the general direction of the stairs and he turned her to face them. "Move," he rasped, encouraging her with a slap on her ass. "Before I fuck you on the kitchen floor."

I'm fine with the kitchen floor, she thought giddily, but then his hand landed on her ass again and she moved.

He was right behind her on the stairs, his hands roaming all over her back, her hips, her ass. By the time she hit the top step, her pulse was pounding in her ears and her body felt like it was on fire.

She turned around, intending to say something clever and sexy and enticing, but he was already pulling his shirt over his head and every single thought went right out of her head and her mouth went too dry to speak. He had a boxer's build, thick and muscular, with just a smattering of hair across his pectorals and his arms looked like they could bench press a car.

"Oh," she breathed, all her focus going to that expanse of flesh. Her fingers itched to touch and she found herself reaching out blindly.

"Yes," he growled, catching her hands and pulling them to his chest. He flattened her palms against his skin, holding them there for a moment as if he wanted to be sure she wouldn't take them away. He needn't have worried.

She slid her hands over the hard arch of his pecs, purring with pleasure as the muscles leapt under her hands. He growled in response, his hands coming down hard on her shoulders.

"You're overdressed."

Nina swallowed hard, the knots of anticipation in her stomach tightening predictably at his words. She was so aroused, so ready, that her skin felt tight and her clothes were an annoyance, so the thought of getting out of them was on one hand a welcome relief. On the other hand, this was the man she'd fantasized about for five years and there was a tiny piece of her that cringed at the prospect of him seeing her naked and finding her wanting.

She wasn't given a lot of time to angst over it. His hands were already moving, sliding the hoodie down and off to puddle at her feet. He flicked at the straps of the sundress, letting them fall off her shoulders to dangle against her upper arms. He slid his hands to her back, feeling for the zipper, and she found her voice.

"There's no zipper," she managed, her voice little more than a whisper. The wanting was threatening to swamp her, swallow her whole, and speaking was almost too difficult. Her tongue flicked out to wet dry lips. "It just pulls off," she explained, her voice only slightly stronger than before.

If possible, his eyes went even darker, his cheekbones flushing and his breathing growing harsher. Holding her gaze, he sank to his haunches in front of her and gathered the skirt of the sundress in his hands. Slowly, without taking his eyes off her face, he gathered the fabric in his hands, drawing it up her body.

Nina's chest grew tight as he slowly straightened in front of her, pulling the dress up as he went. The intensity of being undressed, of watching him watch her as he did it, was almost overwhelming. She drew in a shaky breath as the fabric cleared her hips, her waist, automatically raising her arms as he drew it up over her chest and head. For a brief moment her face was hidden, shielded by the fabric, and she took a deep breath to try and center herself.

Then the dress was over her head and off, and she stood before him in nothing but a tiny pair of panties that hid absolutely nothing. Not the curve of her belly she wished she had the money to get sucked out, not the faint white lines on her hips that were her trophy for losing the weight. Not the cellulite she imagined made her ass look like a golf ball. She kept her eyes closed tight, feeling cowardly for not wanting to see his face as he looked at her. But after a few seconds she couldn't stand it and opened her eyes.

The look of lust and awe on his face nearly brought her to her knees. She struggled to breathe, to stay on her feet as his hands ghosted over her almost reverently.

"You're so beautiful," he breathed, his fingers dancing over her breasts, her shoulders, her belly. "Look how full you are, how lush. God, I could just sink into you and stay there for days."

She laughed, the sound bursting out of her with pure joy and relief. He looked at her and grinned, his hands settling on her hips with comforting firmness.

"That's funny?" he asked, stepping into her and ducking his head to trace her shoulder with his lips.

She shuddered as his lips left a trail of tingling skin in their wake. "No, that's amazing," she managed, forgetting in the heat of the moment to censor her words.

"It's true," he murmured, his hands tightening on her hips. She groaned and he picked up his head. "You like that," he said, and did it again.

"Yes," she sighed, her hands coming up to grip his wrists. Following her instincts, praying it didn't backfire on her, she drew his hands up her torso to cover her breasts. He took the hint immediately and squeezed, her ample flesh spilling out of his hands, and her head fell back on a deep groan. "Oh yes."

"You really like that," he rumbled, squeezing hard enough to leave fingerprints. Nina closed her eyes in bliss and felt the room start to spin. She realized he was walking her backward toward the bed and felt her knees hit the mattress. She let herself fall back into the giving softness of the mattress, her hands still clinging to his arms, and pulled him down with her.

Her eyes flew open in time to watch him come down on top of her. He braced his hands on either side of her shoulders, his face lowering to hers. He nibbled at her lips, teasing her with little flicks of his tongue and nips of his teeth, and within moments she was whimpering. She tried to capture his lips, tried to make him kiss her the way she needed him to — deep and strong and never-ending — but he continued to elude her.

The frustration built until she couldn't take it anymore. Forgetting she was trying to be girly and demure, she reached up with both hands, grabbed his head and dragged his mouth to hers. She took his mouth the way she wanted him to take hers, in a deep, drugging kiss that had both of them moaning. Frantic to get closer, to feel more, she let go of his head and reached for his jeans, thumbing open the button closure. He hissed when she dragged down the zipper, his teeth biting into her bottom lip hard enough that she tasted her own blood. The tangy, metallic taste sent her libido into overdrive, and with more eagerness than finesse, she delved into his pants and pulled out his cock.

"Oh Jesus," he groaned, his head dropping to her chest as she stroked and pulled at his turgid flesh. He pulsed in her hand, feeling impossibly hard, the tip already weeping fluid. She brushed her thumb over him, gathering the moisture there and swirling it around.

He lifted his head to look at her, his eyes narrowed in lust and his breath coming in short pants. "Where are those condoms?"

Nina had to swallow twice before she could answer. "Bathroom," she managed. He leaned down to kiss her hard once, twice, then pushed himself off her to dash into the bathroom.

She lay there sprawled spread-eagled on the bed and tried to get some sort of grip on the situation. She was getting ready to fuck Tony Capriatti, man of her dreams. The reality of that was so overwhelming she could barely wrap her mind around it, the way her pulse was pounding and her pussy was dripping not helping her powers of concentration at all.

She turned her head when he came back into the room. He'd stripped off the rest of his clothes in the bathroom and was gloriously, mouth-wateringly naked. Her eyes automatically zeroed in on his cock. He'd already sheathed it with a condom and she looked back up into his face.

"I wanted to do that," she protested mildly as he climbed onto the bed. He slid on top of her, her legs automatically parting to make room for him. He settled on his elbows, his hips fitting into the welcoming cradle of her pelvis. He slid forward, dragging his cock along her clit and making her gasp.

"You wanted to do what?" he asked, and did it again.

Nina struggled to think past the sparks of pleasure exploding in her clit. "The condom," she managed, blinking the clouds out of her eyes to stare up at him. "I wanted to put the condom on you."

"Next time," he promised. He took her mouth, stroking his tongue across her lips and into her mouth. She clung to him, whimpering as he continued to grind the shaft of his cock against her cunt.

He moved his lips to her cheek, trailing kisses to her ear. He nuzzled her hair aside and licked the sensitive spot behind her left earlobe and she thought the top of her head might fly right off. "Tell me what you want," he demanded, tangling his fingers into her curls and holding her head in place when she would have turned to face him. He licked the spot again, scraping his teeth against her skin this time, and she felt the growl rumble up in her chest.

"Fuck me," she hissed. She dug her nails into his shoulders, using her grip as leverage to boost her hips off the bed. She wrapped her legs around his waist and tilted her pelvis, the action causing him to slip inside her the scantest inch. They both moaned, the sound echoing in the quiet of the room. The storm continued to rage outside, rain pounding on the roof and hammering the windows, but neither one of them noticed.

"God, you're so wet," he muttered, teeth gritted against the sensation. "So fucking wet and hot, I can't stand it."

Nina's head was tossing on the pillow, frantic now to feel him all the way inside her. But he wasn't moving, was holding himself still, and a strangled cry erupted from her throat. She pushed her hips up again, taking more of him in a desperate attempt to get him to move, and finally he did.

With a snarling growl his hips plunged, driving deep into her in one thrust. The breath left her lungs on a scream, everything inside her exploding with color and light as he hit bottom. He didn't give her time to recover from the orgasm, just kept going, holding himself fully inside her, grinding against her, rubbing against her clit and pushing deeper until she exploded again and the pulsing, drawing pull of her cunt pulled him into orgasm with her.

* * * * *

"Holy shit."

The words reached her ears as if from a great distance and could barely be heard over the pounding of her own heart. She exhaled shakily, keeping her eyes closed, and savored the warm, sweaty weight of him on her body.

She moaned in feeble protest when he moved, shifting his weight off her torso to his arms. The motion dragged his chest across her sensitive nipples and she gasped, her pussy clenching involuntarily at the sensation, and he groaned in response.

"I'm sorry," he gasped, his breath tickling her cheek, and she fought her eyes open.

"For what?"

"For lasting—" he looked over at the clock on the bedside table "—eight minutes." He grinned down at her. "I'm usually much better at taking my time."

"If you'd taken any more time," she managed, "I think my heart would have exploded."

He chuckled, the sound reverberating through his body and into hers. He was still hard inside her, her legs still wrapped around his lower back, and she shivered in renewed arousal.

He noticed the shiver and one eyebrow went up. "Really?"

She laughed, a little self-conscious. "Yeah," she admitted sheepishly. "Sometimes, once I get going, I don't want to stop."

"Is that right?" he murmured, and gave a lazy, twisting thrust of his hips. When she arched her back and gasped, his eyes lit up like a little boy on Christmas morning. "Wow, look at that," he marveled, watching the flush of arousal infuse her skin. It spread from her tight nipples up into her face and he couldn't resist pressing his lips to the hollow between her breasts.

"I can't believe I neglected these," he said. He shifted his weight to one elbow and cupped her left breast with his free hand. He squeezed lightly, experimentally, and the flush deepened.

He shifted so he could do the same with the other, smiling when she moaned. "You have beautiful breasts," he murmured, and lowered his head.

Nina watched, fascinated, as he touched his tongue to her nipple. It was light, barely heavier than a butterfly's kiss, and the sweetness of it made her sigh. The sigh caught in her throat a second later when he gripped the hardened tip between his teeth and tugged.

"Oh God," she moaned, her fingers sliding up to clench in his hair. The silky strands, slightly damp with sweat, slid between her fingers and for some reason the sight of it had the bottom dropping out of her stomach. "More," she begged, tugging him harder to her breast and he obliged, pulling her into his mouth and sucking hard.

"Jesus, you taste amazing." He licked his way across her chest, peppering kisses on the cluster of freckles across her sternum to her other nipple. He gave it the same treatment, lavishing attention on her until she was squirming, desperate to feel him harder, deeper, stronger.

She started to lurch up, to drive her cunt on his cock and force him to move, but her legs had been wrapped around his waist for a while and when she moved, her hip spasmed in pain and she cried out.

Tony's head came up immediately, releasing her nipple from his mouth with a wet pop. "What is it?" he asked, pushing himself up on both hands to look down at her fully.

"My leg," she said, unlocking her ankles from behind his back and lowering them to the mattress. Immediately the cramp began to ease and she sighed in relief.

"This one?" he asked, putting his hand on her right hip. She nodded and he rubbed his hand over her flank in a firm circular motion, soothing the cramped muscle.

"Better?" he murmured, and she nodded. The stroke of his hand changed, going from soothing and massaging to arousing, his fingers sliding up and down the outside of her thigh in a lingering caress.

"You have strong legs," he said, giving the muscles a testing squeeze. "Runner's legs?"

She shook her head. "Martial artist's legs."

"Really?" She nodded. "What discipline?"

"Tai chi."

"Are you any good at it?"

She grinned at the teasing light in his eyes, loving this silly, playful side of him. "Oh I can hold my own."

"Oh yeah?" He grinned back and lowered himself back down. He grasped her hands, pinning her wrists against the pillow on either side of her head as he settled his full weight on her. "Think you can flip me?"

She giggled and flexed her hands under his. "Sure you want me to try?"

"Oh yeah," he growled, masculine confidence stamped all over his face. "I'd love to see you try."

Nina shrugged. "Okay then."

She started trying to shift her weight, rocking back and forth underneath him and tugging at his hold on her hands. He held her easily, chuckling at her ineffectual attempts. "Oh honey," he said, shaking his head in mock despair. "You're going to have to do better than that."

"I'm just a girl," she said, pitching her voice deliberately high. "I guess I just couldn't possibly flip a big ole manly man like you off me."

He tossed his head back to laugh and she made her move. Quick as a snake, she twisted her wrists, popping them out of his grip with astonishing ease. She turned her hands so she gripped his wrists, shifted her legs, twisted her hips and pushed. In a flash she'd reversed their positions and was laughing down into his astonished face.

"Like I said," she said, tossing her hair back and giving him a triumphant grin. "I'm just a girl."

"I never met a girl like you before," he said, relaxing back into the pillows. "Pretty slick moves, sweetheart. I thought tai chi was for meditation and relaxation."

"It is," she assured him, "but it's also a martial art and like any martial art, can be used to defend."

"So I see," he said.

"And besides," she murmured, her voice growing husky. "I like this position."

"Do you now?" he asked.

"Mmm," she murmured. She let go of his hands and let her knees slide forward along his hips. The motion settled her even more firmly onto his erection, wringing a gasp from her and a groan from him. "Oh, I like it a lot."

"I can see the benefits to it," he said. "But before you get too carried away..." He grasped her waist, lifting her to her knees and making her squeal as he slid out of her. He quickly dealt with the used condom, returning to her side sheathed with a new one. "Now, where were we?"

"Right here," she murmured, and slid back down his cock in one slick thrust. He grasped her hands, linking their fingers and pushing her arms back. She instinctively sat up straighter, the motion driving her down his cock to the root and she gasped again at the sensation.

"Oh yeah, like that," she murmured. Still holding his hands, she drew them to her breasts. He took the hint and started playing with her nipples, rolling them between his fingertips and tugging. She looked down, the intent look on his face as he stared at his hands working her nipples making her pussy spasm. He felt it and looked up, capturing her gaze with his.

. She moaned at the naked lust in his eyes, her pussy clenching down on him in pulsing flutters of arousal. She began to ride him, slowly at first then with increasing speed until she was practically slamming herself down on his cock with every thrust. He was pushing up to meet her, his hands clamped down on her hips to help her as they raced toward orgasm together.

Nina could feel the coil of tension in her belly winding tighter and tighter, but the orgasm hovered frustratingly just out of reach. She braced her hands behind her on his thighs and the deeper angle nearly pushed her over the edge. But it wasn't enough and she started to sob with frustration.

Tony was gritting his teeth with the effort to hold back, wanting her to come first. He could feel the telltale flutters in her cunt, the tiny pulses that told him she was close but it was taking too long. He was going to explode soon, the heat and wet and tightness of her too much for him to hold out against. Determined to take her with him, he slid one hand from her hip to the curve of her belly, sliding his thumb down to the top of her slit in search of her clit.

He found it, a tiny pearl button hidden in the swollen folds of her cunt. Knowing it was likely too sensitive for a direct touch to feel good, he slid his thumb just above it, feeling the ridge of flesh under her skin that was the root of her clit. He pressed hard, rotating his thumb in tiny circles, and with a scream, she convulsed.

He watched her eyes go blind with the stunning pleasure of it as he felt her go off. All the muscles in her pussy clenched down on him with a viselike grip, pulsing and pulling and milking his cock, and with a roar, he let himself follow.

* * * * *

"Holy shit."

Tony chuckled. "I thought that was my line."

"I stole it. Sue me." Nina lay panting, her head against his chest, the sound of his heart pounding in her ear oddly soothing. "That was…" she trailed off as words failed her.

"Yeah." His hand stroked lazily up and down her back and she gave in to the urge to snuggle in closer. They lay there for a few moments, content to just listen to the rain pound on the roof. Nina felt her eyes drifting shut, the pleasant lassitude of the moment lulling her to sleep when her stomach let out a rumbling gurgle.

There was a moment of startled silence, his hand frozen on her back in mid stroke. Then he started to laugh, a deep rumbling belly laugh that made her blush even harder.

"Stop it," she muttered, smacking his chest lightly and grinning despite herself.

"I'm sorry," he gasped. "I guess I should have fed you earlier."

"Hey, I haven't eaten since breakfast!" she protested. Her stomach chose that moment to rumble again, sending him into fresh bouts of laughter.

She slid off his chest—he was laughing so hard he was going to dislodge her anyway—and sat beside him, arms crossed. She raised one eyebrow in what she hoped was a stern manner. "Are you quite finished?" she asked in as prim a voice as she could manage and he grinned at her.

"I don't know," he chortled. "Are you?"

"Shut up!" she cried, smacking him on the thigh.

"Okay, okay." He held out his hands in a gesture of peace. "I'm sorry."

"Humph," she mumbled, glaring at him out of the corner of her eye. He sat up, folding his arms around her and nuzzling her cheek.

"You're adorable when you're angry," he whispered, his brown eyes twinkling at her, and she couldn't stop the laugh from bubbling up.

"Jackass," she said without heat, and sighed when he captured her mouth with his.

"I am a jackass," he murmured, pressing kisses along her jaw. "A cad, a rogue and unforgivable bastard." He worked his way to her neck, pressing his lips to the sensitive spot under her ear.

"All of that and more," she sighed.

He chuckled again, the sound sending shivers down her spine. "I want to make it up to you."

"What'd you have in mind?" she asked, tilting her head to give him better access. He took advantage, scraping his teeth along sensitive flesh and making her shiver again.

"How about dinner in bed?"

"Oooh, really?" She grinned at the ceiling. "Pasta, with Grandma's famous homemade sauce?"

He picked up his head and scowled. "You're never going to let me live that down, are you?"

"Nope."

He nodded. "Thought not." With a last kiss, he slid off the bed and ducked into the bathroom. She heard the toilet flush and the water running in the sink then he popped back out, tugging his jeans over bare skin.

"You stay here," he pointed at her. "Linguini with red sauce coming right up."

"With garlic bread," she said, giggling when he frowned.

"Demanding woman," he muttered, but he grinned when he said it and trotted down the stairs whistling.

Nina lay there grinning like a cat that just ate her weight in canaries, listening to him putter around the kitchen. She settled deeper into the pillows with a sigh, her body relaxed and stress free for the first time in weeks. She must have dozed off because the next thing she knew the spicy scent of marinara sauce was tickling her nose and she opened her eyes to find Tony waving a plate of pasta in front of her face.

"Still hungry or too sleepy to eat?"

"Starving," she said, the smell of the food making her stomach rumble again as she sat up. She glared at him, daring him to say anything, but he just grinned and handed her the plate.

"Oh wow, this looks great," she enthused, her rumbling stomach forgotten. The plate was piled high with pasta smothered in meat sauce, a fat chunk of warm garlic bread perched precariously on the side.

"Be right back with the wine," he said, heading back down to fetch it. She was already eating when he returned.

"Your grandmother," she said around a mouthful of pasta, "is a saint."

"I've always thought so," he said. He sat cross-legged on the bed across from her and dug into his own pasta.

"This is amazing," she mumbled then stopped talking altogether in favor of eating.

They munched in silence, pausing only to refill their glasses until there was nothing left on the plates but streaks of tomato sauce.

"That was fabulous," she sighed, and handed him her plate. She lay back against the pillows with a groan, feeling more content and satisfied than she had in months. "Tell your grandmother thanks for me next time you see her."

"You can tell her yourself, if you're planning to stick around for a while," he said. He set the plates on the floor next to the bed and shucked off his jeans, stretching out beside her.

She turned her head to watch him settle in. "What do you mean?"

"The entire family is coming to hear me play on Friday night at this little club on the other side of town. It'd be great if you could come."

"Really?" she asked, insanely pleased he would ask. She started to say she'd love to since she was planning to go anyway and then she remembered he didn't know she knew who he was. "You're a musician?"

"Yeah." He propped his head on his fist to smile down at her. "Yeah, I am."

She turned so she was lying on her side, facing him. "What kind of music do you play?"

"Blues mainly. Some rock. I used to write a lot of angry stuff, hard, edgy songs with a lot of angst. My stuff's a lot more introspective these days. More 'what's going on with me' rather than 'I hate the world'."

She stared up into his eyes. "What happened to change your style?"

He shrugged. "I grew up mainly. Stopped being so mad at everyone, started taking responsibility for my own life."

"That's great," she said. "I'd love to hear you play."

"Yeah?" he grinned down at her. "Awesome."

They lay there for a moment, grinning at each other when a thought suddenly occurred to Nina. "We forgot to watch the baseball game while we ate."

"We had other priorities," he said with a chuckle. "And the game's probably over by now."

"Darn," she sighed. "I guess we'll have to find something else to do then, huh?" she said, peeking up at him through her lashes.

He threw back his head on a shout of laughter. "You're insatiable!"

Nina could feel her face flushing hot and buried it against his shoulder. "I know, I know, it's terrible!"

"Terrible's not the word I was thinking of," he said, and startled her by ducking under the covers.

"What're you—oh!" she squealed when she felt his tongue snake out and tickle the crease of her thigh. She grinned and settled back into the pillows. "Somehow terrible isn't the word I'm thinking anymore either."

Chapter Four

🔊

Friday afternoon Nina unlocked the front door to the cottage. "Tony?" she called out, dropping her keys on the table by the door and taking the bags of food into the kitchen. "You here?"

"Upstairs," came the reply, and she dropped the food on the counter and trotted up the steps, giddy with happiness to find him waiting for her.

He'd spent every night since Sunday with her, going back to his own place whenever he needed to change clothes or rehearse for Friday's show. He'd finally brought his acoustic guitar back with him and started doing his rehearsing in the bedroom upstairs. He said the high ceilings and open floor plan made for great acoustics, and he'd spend hours up there working through one song after another.

"Hey," she said, feeling her stomach clench at the welcoming smile he gave her. "What're you working on?"

"Something new," he said, holding out a hand. She went to him automatically, linking her fingers with his and bending down for a lingering kiss. "Do you want to hear it?"

"I'd love to," she said. She perched on the side of the bed, tucking her legs up Indian style and resting her chin in her hands.

"Okay," he said, rubbing his hands together. He picked up the guitar and settled it on his knee. He flexed his fingers before settling them on the strings and she realized with some surprise he was nervous.

Before she could wonder at the reason he began to play, and within moments she was too caught up in the music to think of anything else. It was a ballad, haunting and sweet. There weren't any lyrics but he hummed the melody, his whiskey voice lending a harsh note to the gentle notes of the song and making it all the more poignant.

When the last note had faded, she sighed. "Wow."

He smiled, shy and boyishly hopeful. "You think?"

"It's beautiful," she said. "Does it have lyrics?"

"Not yet," he admitted, setting the guitar aside and reclining back in the club chair. "I just finished the music today. I've got a couple of ideas about lyrics but nothing solid yet."

"Well, it's stunning," she said. She rose from her perch on the bed to straddle his lap, looping her arms loosely around his neck. "Really, it's one of the loveliest things I've ever heard. Thank you for sharing it with me."

"Well, you inspired it, it's only right you should hear it."

Nina felt her eyes go round with shock. "I inspired it?" He nodded and her heart just fell at his feet. She all but heard the splat. "Oh that's just the sweetest thing," she murmured, pressing a kiss to his lips.

"Mmm." She felt his arms come up, his hands spreading across her back, and the kiss quickly grew heated.

"You feel so good," he murmured, trailing his lips down to the sensitive spot behind her ear. "Warm and lush and hot."

"You feel hard," she whispered, running her hands across his chest. "Especially here." She drew her fingertips down the length of his erection, teasing him where he strained against the fly of his jeans. "My, someone is happy to see me, aren't they?"

"Someone would be happier to see you if these jeans weren't in the way," he mumbled, and she giggled.

"Well, why don't we just take care of that," she said, and slid out of his lap to kneel on the floor at his feet.

She went to work on his belt buckle, peeking up at him from beneath her lashes. He was watching her with the stark intensity she'd gotten used to over the last week, his eyes dark and his cheekbones flushed dark with lust. She grasped the tab of his zipper and drew it down slowly, the rasp echoing his own husky groan. She smiled with satisfaction when his cock sprang free.

"No underwear today?" she murmured, wrapping her hand around his throbbing length. "Naughty boy."

He chuckled. "Naughty, huh? Does that mean I get punished?"

"Oh yeah," she whispered. She flicked out her tongue to lap at the pool of moisture already weeping from the head of his cock. She suppressed the wild giggle threatening to burst free when he groaned, and did it again.

"Your punishment," she said, rising to her knees and taking a firmer grip on him, "is to just sit there and take it."

"Whatever it takes," he said, sounding as if he were being strangled, "to make it up to you."

She lapped at him again, teasing both of them with dainty little licks. She kept up the light touches and teasing flicks until his hips were surging toward her face with every stroke and pre-come coated her hand, then took him into the warm cavern of her mouth with one deft stroke.

"Jesus," he groaned. She felt him tangle his fingers into her hair to hold her head in place as his hips started to thrust frantically. He was already close, his balls drawing up tight at the base of his cock. She began a strong suction, working to make him come, but his hands tightened painfully in her hair and drew her off him.

"Why did you stop me?"

"I want to be inside you," he panted. He dug in his pocket for a condom, ripping it open with his teeth. He gritted his teeth and struggled to put it on with shaking hands. She

142

watched for a second, her own arousal fuelled by his frantic need then took the condom from him.

"Here, let me," she said, and lifted it to her lips.

"What—?"

She winked. "Just watch." She placed the tip of the rubber between her lips, applying a light suction to hold it in place. She lowered her head, pressing her lips around the head of his cock through the condom and, using the pressure of her mouth, slowly rolled the condom down his shaft.

She pushed it the final inch with her hands, pulling her mouth off him and stood with a grin. She fell back with a squeak of surprise when he surged to his feet. He clamped his hands on her shoulders, spinning her around and pushing her forward. He stopped when her knees hit the edge of the bed and she moved to turn to face him.

"Uh-uh," he said, one hand diving into the hair at the base of her neck to hold her in place. "Stay."

She did, shivering in anticipation. Her skin pebbled with goose bumps when his hands came around her hips to work on the fly of her cutoff shorts. They fell to the floor to puddle at her feet and she felt more than heard his growl of masculine approval.

"No panties today?" He ran his hand over her bare ass, giving her left cheek a light squeeze.

She had to swallow twice before she could speak. "Haven't had a chance to do laundry."

"I like it." His mouth was right behind her ear, his voice sending shivers racing over her skin. "I like it a lot. It's very…accessible." He slid his hand between her thighs from behind, delving into her wet cunt with one broad finger.

"Jesus," she gasped, reaching out blindly to brace her hands on something as her knees buckled and he took the opportunity to push her forward onto the bed.

"Oh I really like that," he murmured. He draped himself over her back, twisting his fingers inside her and making her moan. "I like that a whole lot. How about you, baby? You like this position?"

"I'd like it…a lot better if you were…inside me," she gasped. She braced her hands on the bed under her shoulders, pushing back, and he chuckled.

"I am inside you, baby." He twisted his fingers to illustrate the point, eliciting a squeal.

"Want more," she panted, twisting her head to look over her shoulder. He loomed over her, his face so close she could feel his breath. "I want your cock inside me."

"That's what you want?" he asked, his voice a near growl.

"Yes, please!"

The words were barely out of her mouth when he slammed into her, hitting bottom and pushing her into the edge of the mattress. He didn't give her a chance to catch her breath, to adjust to the sensations, but set a driving rhythm that had her gasping for breath.

"Oh Jesus," she moaned. She could feel the knot of tension in her belly tightening, her orgasm barreling down on her with an almost frightening intensity. "Oh *fuck*!"

"Yes, baby," he urged, his voice in her ear and his breath on her neck. His hands moved, sliding up her stomach to push her tank top above her breasts. He gripped them hard, rotating his hands and abrading her nipples with his rough, calloused palms. She felt him bite into the sensitive curve of her shoulder, gripping the tendon with his teeth and tugging, and with a hoarse scream, she came.

Light and color exploded in her vision as she pulsed and quivered around him. He kept fucking her through the spasms, driving her higher and harder until she thought her body might simply fly apart at the seams. Dimly she heard him shout, felt his cock expand even farther inside her as he followed her into orgasm.

He collapsed on top of her, draping himself over her and crushing her into the mattress. Nina lay there panting for air, relishing the warm and sweaty weight of him against her back.

"I love that you scream 'fuck' when you come," he said, and she giggled.

"I can't help it."

"Why would you want to? It's sexy as hell," he rumbled, pressing a kiss to her shoulder then another. "So is this tattoo."

She smiled sleepily. "My chain of butterflies?"

"Mmm. Girly and sexy." He kissed the butterflies again. "Don't move, okay? I'll be right back."

"Hmm." She fluttered her fingers at him and he slowly pulled free of her before heading to the bathroom.

She lay there, floating in a post-sex haze while she waited for him to come back. She idly thought she should scoot up on the bed to ease the cramps starting to form in her calves but it seemed like too much trouble. She was drifting off to sleep when she felt herself being lifted.

"What?" she murmured, blinking her eyes open. She smiled up into Tony's face then closed her eyes again with a happy sigh. "Hi."

"Hi, yourself," he murmured. She felt him settle her onto the pillows and strip the rest of her clothes off. He curled up beside her, folding her in his arms when she turned into his warmth. "Sleep," he whispered, and she did.

* * * * *

Nina stretched and yawned, feeling rested and limber. She knew he wasn't beside her any longer, could hear the shower running in the bath. Glancing at the bedside clock, she saw it was nearly five. He had a sound check at the club at six, even though he didn't go on stage until ten or eleven. She stretched again then climbed out of bed.

She padded across the room to the open bathroom door, snagging her robe from the closet as she went. Belting it around her, she tapped on the door and stuck her head in. "Hey."

His head popped out from behind the shower curtain. "Hey, you're up. How'd you sleep?"

"Fabulously."

He winked. "You're welcome."

She laughed. "Braggart. You hungry?"

"Starved."

"I picked up a couple of burgers on my way home earlier," she said, barely suppressing a giggle at how cute he was with shampoo piled on top of his head. "I can warm 'em up for you."

"Oh that'd be great," he enthused. "I'll be out in five minutes."

"Meet you in the kitchen." She blew him a kiss and headed down the stairs.

In the kitchen, she dug a bottle of water out of the refrigerator, taking a big gulp as she retrieved the bag of burgers off the counter. She dug through the bag, pulling out the one container of French fries and tossing them in the trash.

"Can't reheat fries," she muttered. "They get all soggy." She peered back into the bag at the three burgers in their shiny wrappers then tossed the whole bag into the microwave. Punching a minute and a half on the clock, she hit Start and leaned against the counter to sip her water and worry about the coming evening.

Tony's entire family was coming to this show and he wanted her to meet them. Which normally would have been great—nerve-racking and nausea inducing, but great. But she hadn't even figured out a way to tell him she knew him from before and she knew she had to do it soon. She'd caught him looking at her curiously several times over the last week and once after she'd beaten him at checkers and was laughing at him, he'd asked, "Are you sure we haven't met somewhere before?"

She'd distracted him with sex—he was easily distracted with sex but then so was she—and he hadn't brought it up again. Still, it was going to have to be said. She just hoped she could get the words out without choking.

She sipped her water and berated herself for a coward. What kind of a woman was she that she could sleep with a man for a week and lie to him all the while? "A horrible one," she muttered, "and a fraidy-cat."

Fraidy-cat was actually pretty accurate. No matter how much fun they had together, no matter how much he seemed to like her, she was still afraid if he knew who she was, it would all end. Which was ridiculous. She knew there was very little chance he would connect her to the chubby girl who used to show up at all his concerts. And even if he did, it would likely have no bearing on his current feelings for her.

Which was another problem. Because even though they had fun together and he seemed to like her just fine, she really had no idea what his feelings for her actually were. He'd only known her a week, after all—or so he thought—so to expect him to declare undying love at this stage was ridiculous. She didn't even really want him to, since it wouldn't mean anything. but it might be nice to hear some kind of declaration.

"Of like?" she wondered aloud, rolling her eyes at herself. "Jeez, get a grip."

She was going to have to tell him tonight, that's all there was to it. She took another drink, searching her mind for the best way to say, "Hey, by the way, I used to hang around the stage and undress you with my eyes," when she heard a muffled thump.

She frowned and turned toward the living room. Thinking someone was knocking on the front door, she took two steps toward it when she heard it again, this time from behind her and she turned back to the kitchen.

"Oh my God!" she shrieked when she saw the microwave. Blue sparks were flaring inside and with a whoosh the fast food bag caught on fire.

Footsteps came pounding down the stairs and then Tony was rushing past her. She watched stunned as he punched the button to open the microwave door and reached in to grab the flaming bag.

"Be careful!" she cried when he cursed and shook his fingers. He snatched a pair of barbeque tongs from the utensil drawer and used them to pull the bag from the oven and fling it into the sink. He turned on the faucet, putting out the fire and filling the room with steam.

The fire out, he turned to face her. "You're okay?" She nodded. "What happened?"

"Well. You know how sometimes burgers from fast food places come with paper wrappings and sometimes foil?"

He was watching her warily. "Yeah."

"Well..." she bit her lip, fighting not to laugh. "I sort of forgot these were wrapped in foil."

"You put foil in the microwave." She nodded, and he started to laugh. "God, it's a good thing you're pretty."

She gasped in mock outrage. "Shut up!" she said, smacking his shoulder. He ducked the blow, diving in for a swift kiss.

"I'm going to head down to the club for sound check. And since dinner appears to be ruined—" they both contemplated the sodden bag in the sink "—I'll just get something on the way." He pressed another kiss to her mouth. "You're coming down later, right?"

"I'll be there," she promised, and he kissed her again.

"Good. I can't wait for you to meet my family."

"Me neither," she said, smiling as her stomach curled into knots. "Can't wait."

Chapter Five

છ૭

It was after midnight when the knock came. The sun had set hours ago and Nina hadn't bothered to turn on the lights. She sat in the dark, her stomach in knots and tried to think of something to say.

The knock came again, impatient this time, and she rose to answer the door. "Hi, Tony."

"Nina." He stepped inside, concern stamped on his features. "What's wrong? When you didn't make it to the show, I thought something had happened to you. You didn't answer your cell phone, I was worried sick."

"My phone?" She looked around absently. "I think it's still charging in the bedroom. I'm sorry, I didn't mean to worry you. I needed some time to think and I sort of lost track of time."

"Here, come over here." He took her by the hand, drawing her into the living room. He flipped on the light then sat with her on the couch. "What's going on?"

Nina folded her hands in her lap and struggled with a way to begin. "I did come to the show tonight," she said. "I don't want you to think I didn't. But by the time I got there, you were just getting ready to go on and I didn't want to get in your way so I left."

"I wish you'd come up and told me you were there," he said. He folded his hand over hers, stilling her fidgeting fingers.

She shrugged. "You had your family around you, I didn't want to interrupt."

"Interrupt?" He frowned. "I told you I wanted you to meet my family. My mom, my grandma. I told them all about you, they were wondering where you were."

"Oh God, I'm so sorry." She buried her face in her hands. "It's just… I have something to tell you and I don't think I can do it."

"Nina, you're really starting to spook me." He peeled her hands away from her face and she reluctantly opened her eyes. "Just tell me—you're married, you're dying, you're really a man named George?" She gave a watery laugh and he squeezed her fingers. "Whatever it is, just say it."

"Okay." She drew in a deep breath, closed her eyes and it all came pouring out in a mad rush of words. "I used to come watch you play. I used to come to every show and I was bigger than I am now and I doubt you even noticed me at all but there it is. And I know this is really weird but I didn't want you to know I used to be sort of like one of your groupies because I didn't want you to think I do this a lot or that I just like you because you're a musician because I don't. Like you just because you're a musician, I mean. I really like you a lot, I could possibly, maybe, probably, be in love with you but I'm not sure because it's only been a week and I don't know where this is all going but wherever it's going, it's not because you're a musician. Or because I used to be a groupie. Kind of."

She ran out of breath and out of words and just sat there trying to breathe with her eyes still closed.

"Wow," he said, and she winced because she couldn't tell by his tone of voice if it was a good wow or a bad wow. "You've been holding that in all week, huh?"

She nodded. "Pretty much."

"Feel better now that it's out?"

"Sort of," she said. "I'm still pretty nauseous, but that's probably because I ate the burgers that caught fire in the microwave."

He chuckled. "Yeah, that might do it. Nina, look at me."

She did, reluctantly opening her eyes to peer up at him. He was watching her with amusement. *Well, at least it's not revulsion,* she thought. "What?"

"I recognized you the first day when you ran into me and knocked yourself out in the rain."

Her eyes flew wide open at that and her jaw dropped. "What?"

He laughed, tapping her under the chin, and she snapped her mouth shut. "I remember you coming to the shows, bringing your girlfriends."

She finally found her voice, although it came out scratchier and squeakier than usual. "You do?"

His expression softened and he reached up a hand to cup her cheek. "Of course I do. I remember packing up in this hole in Trenton. You were leaning against the stage, your blue eyes staring up at me and you said 'thank you'." He smiled. "How could I not remember that?"

"Oh God," she moaned, and closed her eyes again. "I'm so embarrassed."

"Embarrassed?" he asked, the surprise in his voice enough to have her opening her eyes again. "Why? I love that memory. Those years were so hard, playing gig after gig in dive bars for peanuts. Knowing people liked what I was doing made it easier to keep going."

"But..." She fumbled for something to say. "But...I didn't think you knew who I was."

"I knew." He smiled. "You never seemed to hang around long though. Every time I went to find you after a show, you were gone."

"I just...never thought you'd be interested." She waved her hands vaguely. "There were always all these women hanging around, throwing themselves at you."

He shrugged, sheepish. "I was twenty-six and stupid. I thought the bigger the boobs, the better the girl."

She rolled her eyes, feeling the knots in her stomach loosening at the humor of the moment. "Boy, were you wrong."

"Oh I don't know," he mused. He eyed her chest lasciviously. "These are pretty substantial and you're the best girl I know."

She giggled, smacking him on the shoulder. "Jackass." Then she sobered. "Tony?"

"Hmm?"

"It really doesn't bother you?"

"What, that you knew me before?" He shook his head. "Not in the least. Does it bother you that I'm not the big rock star I planned to be?"

"Of course not," she said. "I like you for you."

"I like you for you too." He took her hands again. "Look, I don't know where this is going either. But I know we're good together and I know I want to keep seeing you. I want to see if we can make something more out of this. And I still want you to meet my family."

"Really?"

"Absolutely," he said.

"I'm sorry I bailed on you tonight." Her lips twisted wryly. "I guess I just got scared and insecure, thinking if you knew I had hung around like a lovesick puppy five years ago, you wouldn't find me attractive now."

"Well, you were wrong," he said, taking her lips in a soft kiss. "I find you amazingly attractive now. And I found you amazingly attractive then. Sexy," he kissed her cheek. "Adorable." He kissed the other cheek. "Loveable."

She sighed, settling into his embrace and twining her arms around his neck. "This is one time I can say I'm so glad to be wrong."

He chuckled. "I wish you'd stayed to hear the show. You missed your song."

She pulled back, frowning in confusion. "My song?"

He nodded. "The one I played for you this afternoon? It has lyrics now. I was hit by inspiration while I was waiting to do the sound check. It's called 'Nina's Song'."

"Oh." She blinked back tears. "Oh that's the sweetest, most romantic thing anyone's ever done for me. Will you play it for me?"

"Now?" he asked, pulling her closer and nuzzling her neck.

"Well, maybe later," she sighed, tilting her head so he could reach the sensitive spot behind her ear.

And much later, he did.

Epilogue
Four Years Later

ഇ

Nina kicked open the door of the beach house with her sneakered foot and dropped her bags. "Wow, this place hasn't changed at all," she said. She started to step inside then squealed with surprised delight when she was snatched off her feet.

"What're you doing?" she gasped, her hands coming up to grasp Tony's neck as he swung her up into his arms.

"Carrying my bride over the threshold," he said, and did. He let her slide slowly back down once they were inside, keeping her within the circle of his arms and taking her mouth in a lingering kiss.

When he lifted his head, she shook hers. "Babe, I was your bride three years ago. Now I'm just a wife. The old ball and chain, the old lady—"

He laid a finger on her lips. "You'll always be my bride," he insisted, and she felt herself go all gooey inside.

"Aww." She rose up on her toes to kiss him, moaning when it turned heated. "I should check on the kids," she murmured, and felt his lips curve against hers.

"I called home when we stopped for gas," he said, chuckling. "Jack was running around naked and Ginny was telling Auntie Julie he was just following his bliss and would get dressed when his bliss got tired."

She laughed. "Julie will never want to watch the twins again after this."

"She did mention renewing her prescription for birth control," Tony said, and Nina laughed again. "But enough about Julie, and as much as I love the kids, enough about them too." He pulled her in close. "This weekend, I just want to think about what a wonderful, sexy, wife I have."

"That's all, huh?"

His smile turned smoky. "Maybe not quite all," he rumbled. He hoisted her back into his arms and headed for the stairs. "I hope you've been taking your vitamins, woman. You're gonna need them."

Nina giggled, so full of love and lust she thought her heart might burst with it. She reached back and pinched his ass, laughing out loud when he nearly dropped her in shock.

He scowled in mock sternness. "Sass like that might get you a spanking," he growled.

"Really? Well, just in case one wasn't enough," she mused, and did it again.

"This is going to be a hell of a weekend," he said, and took the stairs two at a time.

It's a hell of a life, she thought. *And I'm a hell of a lucky girl.* Then she was flying through the air to bounce on the bed, her very determined husband coming after her, and she stopped thinking altogether.

Also by Hannah Murray

∞

The Devil and Ms. Johnson
Jane and the Sneaky Dom

About the Author

∞

Hannah Murray started reading romances in junior high, hoarding her allowance to buy them and hiding them from her mother. She's been dreaming up stories of her own for years and finally decided to write them down. Being published is a lifelong dream come true, and even her mother is thrilled for her—she knew about the romances all along. Hannah lives in southern Texas in a very small house with a very large dog, where the battle for supremacy rages daily. The dog usually wins. When not catering to his needs, she can usually be found writing, reading, or doing anything else that allows her to put off the housework for one more day.

Hannah welcomes comments from readers. You can find her website and email address on her author bio page at www.ellorascave.com.

WILD OATS

Nikki Soarde

Trademarks Acknowledgement

§◌

The author acknowledges the trademarked status and trademark owners of the following wordmarks mentioned in this work of fiction:

Corolla: Toyota Jidosha Kabushiki Kaisha TA Toyota Motor Corporation

Jacuzzi: Jacuzzi Inc.

Chapter One

හ

"Thanks, Celia!" Samantha waved from the landing outside her townhouse. A flight of wrought iron steps curved gracefully from the second-story entrance down to the street.

Celia leaned out the window of her Corolla that she had pulled up to the curb, and squinted up at the darkened windows. "You sure you don't want me to come in? It's late and I hate leaving you on the doorstep alone."

As much as Sam hated walking into a dark, empty house, she hated the appearance of insecurity more. "I'm fine, and Trent will be home any minute."

"Any minute, eh?" Celia's eyebrows waggled. "Sure I couldn't come in and keep you company until he gets here?" She fluttered her long blonde lashes. "I worry *so* much for your safety."

"Uh-huh." Sam arched one meaningful eyebrow. "Why does the fact that my maid of honor lusts after my fiancé not fill me with warm fuzzies?"

Celia giggled. "Maybe because you're a very smart woman?"

"True. I am a chemical engineer at one of the largest firms in Canada." She grinned, still basking in the glow of landing such a plum position. And she was soon marrying Trent Macey. Life just didn't get any better.

"And you graduated in three years instead of four," continued Celia. "Smart, sweet, gifted and beautiful too. If I didn't love you so much, I'd have to kill you."

Sam laughed aloud and waved to her friend. "Go on, get out of here. All that mushy stuff will *not* get you inside this door."

"Drat," cursed Celia as she revved her engine. "Foiled again." But she grinned and the next moment she was waving out the car window as her taillights disappeared down Rue St. Denis.

Sam's gaze lingered for a moment on the long row of neatly kept townhouses, some with grand, sweeping staircases, and others with elaborate faux façades. The quaint Montreal neighborhood brimmed with texture and tradition and she felt blessed to call it home.

She had moved to Montreal to continue her schooling and had fallen in love instantly. The fact that it had been Trent's home and that he already had established a successful investment counseling business had nothing to do with her decision to stay. Absolutely nothing.

Smiling at herself, she stuck her key into the lock and prepared herself to walk into a cold, empty silence.

Instead she stepped into soft, flickering candlelight and the subtly enticing aroma of something cooking in the kitchen. "Trent?" she whispered, surprised. "Are you—" He cut off her words with a kiss.

He sealed his mouth to hers, his lips hot, his tongue eager. Her purse thudded to the floor as his body pressed against hers, sandwiching her between the hard planes of his chest, and that of the solid oak door. He tasted pleasantly of wine and spices, his hands on her cheeks were warm and possessive.

The door snapped shut and he broke the kiss.

A pair of mischievous brown eyes gazed down at her— even as he secured the deadbolt.

She swallowed thickly, her heart pounding a ragged rhythm against her chest. "You surprised me. I didn't think you were home."

He skimmed a finger down her cheek. "You weren't meant to."

She flushed with pleasure. "You were trying to surprise me?"

"No." Abruptly he swept her off the floor, and up into his arms. "I *did* surprise you." And then he began to ascend the stairs toward their bedroom.

She wrapped her arms around his neck, savored the way his muscles moved against her as he climbed the stairs. She nibbled on his ear. "But what about dinner?"

"The lasagna has another forty minutes in the oven."

"You made lasagna?"

He granted her a withering look. "That's what I said, didn't I?"

"But what's—"

Again her words were cut off, but this time by a high squeal as he tossed her onto the bed. The scent of vanilla laced the air, and the room glowed faintly with the light of a dozen more candles.

It was just bright enough for her to make out his bowlike mouth as it curled into a smile, and the way his brown hair hung rakishly over one eye. "Enough talking." He peeled off the black T-shirt he'd been wearing, revealing a set of well-defined shoulders and abs. "Let's get to fucking."

As always, the word sent a shiver racing through her and she reached for the buttons on her blouse.

"No." The word was a command. He stepped out of his jeans, leaving only a pair of skin-hugging boxer briefs. It was too dark to see his erection well, but she didn't need to. She knew it intimately.

He reached for her hand and drew her up to stand before him, bent to breathe in her ear. "I'll undress you."

He grasped the lapels of the blazer that she wore to shield her from the early spring chill, and slipped it from her shoulders. His hands skimmed down her arms, sending shivers skittering over her even through the thin cotton of the blouse. "You've had this blouse for a while, haven't you?"

She frowned. "I guess so."

"That's what I thought." He grasped the front and tore it from her body.

Buttons clattered to the hardwood floor and she sucked in her breath in shock.

His smile turned mischievous. "I've always wanted to do that. Did you mind?" His fingers skimmed the curve of breast that swelled over the top of her bra.

"No," she breathed, watching him. "I liked it."

"Good. So did I." He bent and traced his tongue along the same path that his fingers had followed a moment earlier.

She rested her hands on his shoulders, as much for support as to enjoy the subtle bunch and play of the muscles beneath the skin. Trent may sit at a desk all day, but he made up for it by working out five days a week. It showed.

He unhooked the clasp and her bra fell to the floor, allowing him to devour her breast. His tongue circled her nipple lightly, laved her breast hungrily. Her fingernails dug into his skin and she let out a small moan of pleasure when his hands slid under her skirt and pushed the thong to the floor.

She swelled beneath his fingers, moved against his hand, willing him to go further, move faster, but preferring not to ask. Trent moved at his own pace—fast or slow, it was his decision, his call. But somehow he always fulfilled her desires, drew out her pleasure, and never left her wanting. After five years, he knew her intimately, was thrilled to pleasure her and knew how to do it well.

His fingers were inside her, his mouth doing sinful things to her breast. "Trent," she said, grinding herself against him. "Please."

"Oh, sweetie, don't be in such a rush." But then he nudged her back onto the mattress, pushed up her skirt and spread her thighs. He studied her pussy and then rested his eyes on her face. "Fuck, you're gorgeous."

She touched herself, spreading her wetness and hoping it made her glisten for his pleasure. "Am I?"

He laughed, low and softly in his throat. "Vixen." He stared at her, his enjoyment obvious. "Do more. Finger-fuck yourself."

And she did. Her breathing quickened as her pleasure built. She arched her back, seeking something she couldn't quite give herself.

"Open your eyes, babe."

And when she did she saw that he had shed his briefs. His cock was full and hard and she wanted to taste it.

Holding her gaze with his own, he grasped her hand that was still massaging her pussy and brought it to his mouth. He licked her fingers and drew them deeply into his mouth, sucking them clean before placing her hand on his cock. "Touch me."

She wrapped her hand around him, stroking softly at first, touching the tip and spreading his own moisture down its length.

"Mmm." His hand found her pussy once more, and he slipped two fingers inside her, pumping her hard and seeking out her G-spot. His eyes closed in pleasure as her touch grew more firm in response. "That's it. That's my girl."

She felt an orgasm looming but wanted to experience it with him. "Trent?"

"You want it? You want it now?"

"Yes," she breathed. "Please!"

And then in one quick motion, he grasped her wrists, pressed them to the mattress, and thrust inside her with enough force to send her senses spiraling. She arched her hips, matching his movements and thrilling to the sheer physical power of him.

He kissed her, pressed his lips to hers and assaulted her tongue with his as his thrusts accelerated and his chest became slick with sweat.

He broke the kiss and the look in his eyes was the final straw, the thing that sent her over the edge. The climax hit and she arched her back, driving him even deeper. He released her wrists and entwined his fingers with hers, allowing her to squeeze his hands as wave after wave of pleasure broke over her.

As the orgasm ebbed and the last of the contractions clutched at his cock, she sensed his body tense, felt the quickening of his heart and heard the low moan of his own release.

She opened her eyes again to see him hovering over her, an odd expression haunting his features. "I love you, Sam. You know that, don't you?"

"Of course I do." She let go of his hands and stroked his cheek, shadowed by a day's worth of beard. "What a silly question."

He smiled and nodded.

"And I love you, too."

"I know." He kissed her quickly. "Okay, let's get our robes on and go eat dinner. There's something I need to talk to you about."

* * * * *

Trent sipped from his wine and watched the love of his life stuff another huge bite of lasagna into her mouth. Sex always made her ravenous.

He watched her eat for a moment, enjoying the way her lips moved, the way her long brown hair tumbled over her shoulders, and the way her robe gaped open revealing an enticing bit of skin. Damn it, he wanted her, was infatuated with her, couldn't get enough of her! He loved her so much, and that was going to make this that much harder because he knew exactly what it would do to her.

She scooped up another forkful and grinned, her blue eyes twinkling. "I don't know, Trent. A man who knows how to crunch numbers *and* blend spices? Next thing I know you'll be doing the laundry and having babies, and *then* where will I be?"

He just stared at her, his mind a flurry of words and impressions.

She laughed. "Hey. Where's my witty retort?"

He said nothing.

"Trent?" She set down her fork. "What is it?"

He swallowed, surprised by how hard this was. "Sam, I —"

The ring of the phone cut him off.

"Rats." With an apologetic glance, she folded her napkin and headed for the phone on the counter. "Hello?" She rolled her eyes. "Hi, Mom."

Trent couldn't help but smile to himself. Sam loved her mother and they got along great—at a distance. Planning a wedding, however, had brought them closer and given them more to talk about than Sam cared to acknowledge.

At least they'd gotten past the big issue of the difference in Trent and Sam's ages. The fact that he was twelve years her senior had been a huge brick wall for Sam's family and one that he'd had to pound at constantly to make a dent. They'd finally broken through a year earlier, thus paving the way for his proposal, and hopefully a happy and angst-free wedding.

He tuned out their conversation and concentrated on his food.

At last she plunked herself down beside him and reached for her fork.

"Everything okay?"

"Little problem with tulle and mini-lights, but nothing a fuse and a little dynamite couldn't fix." She smiled sweetly. "I don't want to talk about that. Tell me what's going on."

He raked his fingers through his hair and dove in. "Do you think we have good sex?"

Her eyes went wide and he cursed himself for sounding like an imbecile. "Well," she said slowly, "I'm not really sure. Why don't we do it again and I'll pay more attention this time. I'll get back to you in a week or so."

"Sam, this is serious."

"No, this is ludicrous. What kind of question is that? Of course I do." She winked. "You're the best lover I've ever had."

"Exactly."

"What?"

"I'm the *only* lover you've ever had, Sam." When they'd met five years ago, Sam had been twenty and although she'd had a couple of boyfriends, had not yet lost her virginity. Trent had been thrilled and honored to be the one to initiate her into the wonderful world of sex and intimacy, but now he was realizing that what had once been a plus, could just as easily turn into a big red mark in the debit column. "You have no basis for comparison."

She reached for his hand. "I don't *need* a basis for comparison. I love you, and I enjoy being with you. I want to be with you forever, and that's all that matters."

"That's all that matters *now*, but what about five years from now? Ten years from now? You never got to sow any wild oats, barely got to flirt or date anybody else. What if you get restless? What if you get curious?"

She released his hand and sat back in her chair, arms folded across her chest and eyes blazing. "Jeez, Trent. We're not even married yet, and you've got me having an affair."

"I just don't want to wake up one morning and find your side of the bed empty because you had an urge to find out what you missed out on."

"I love you, Trent, and I'm not missing out on anything." She picked up her plate and stomped to the sink. "This is crazy. I don't want to talk about it anymore."

"We have to talk about it, and it's not crazy. It's realistic." She opened her mouth to speak but he continued. "It happened to a friend of mine."

She blinked. "What?"

"A good friend of mine married his college sweetheart. They started dating when he was twenty and she was seventeen. He'd had several experiences by that point, but she hadn't. They got married and after eight years together he thought they were happy. They bought a house and were starting to talk about kids, and then one day he woke up and she was gone."

She came back to the table and sat down. "Oh, Trent. I'm sorry."

"He discovered that she'd been having an affair for almost a year, and she had decided she wanted to expand her horizons even further. She blamed him for scooping her up and plunking her down in the middle of domestic tedium before she had really lived, and she confessed that she'd begun to wonder what it was like to be with other men. Once she got a taste of it, she wanted more. The divorce was final a year later." He studied Sam intently. "It devastated him, Sam. He barely pulled himself together and eventually left the country because he couldn't bear to be on the same continent as her."

She grasped his hand. "That's not me. That won't happen to us."

He squeezed her hand. "You're damn right it won't. It won't because I'm not going to be the only man you've ever slept with when we get married."

She stared at him, blinked and let out a strained laugh. "What are you talking about? Of course you will be."

"No, I won't." He withdrew his hand from hers and walked to the small desk they kept in the corner of the kitchen. He opened the top drawer and withdrew an envelope. He handed it to her. "Open it."

·   Frowning, she did as he asked and examined the contents. Her mouth dropped open. "Hedo? You're taking me to *Hedo*?"

"No. I'm *sending* you to Hedo. And when you get there I want you to take part in all the activities. Take advantage of *everything* the resort has to offer. I'll come down to spend the last weekend with you but until then I want you to be wild. I want you to pretend you're single and available and free."

"What? What are you saying?"

He sat down again and clasped her hands between his own. "I want you to experience other men, Sam. I want you to know what sex is like outside our bedroom. I don't ever want you to wonder what could have been, and I want to know that you *chose* me. I don't ever want to wonder if you would have stayed with me if you'd actually been with other men. I don't want to be the one you took just because I was the first guy to give you an orgasm."

She tugged her hands away. "That's insane." She stood and paced to the other side of the room. "This whole thing is insane."

"It's not insane. It's the most sane thing I've ever done in my life."

"Don't you want me, Trent? Is this some twisted way to get me to leave you? Don't you care if I'm with other men? Aren't you worried that some other man will sweep me off my feet?"

"Of course I want you. I want you more than I've ever wanted anything. But I want you to keep, and if it's that easy to lure you away from me then we don't belong together. This is sex we're talking about, not love. I think that's another lesson you need to learn."

"Lesson? You may be older, but you're not my teacher. And I resent being treated like some freckle-faced sex-student."

"I'm sorry. I didn't mean it to sound that way."

She folded her arms and glared at him. "Whatever. It doesn't matter anyway because I'm not going."

"Yes, you are."

"You're not my boss, Trent! You can't force me to go."

"That's true. I can't force you, but let's put it this way." He took a deep breath and said what he had to say. "If you don't do this—if you don't go and sleep with at least one other man—the wedding is off."

Chapter Two

❧

Sam sat on the beach and stared out across the water. The vibrant blue of the Caribbean glittered in the late afternoon sun, the sparkle so intense it hurt her eyes. She dug her toes a little deeper into the silky white sand and closed her eyes, concentrating on the pounding of the surf and the caress of the breeze, and trying to tune out the chatter and laughter that surrounded her.

The beach was abuzz with activity. People drank and laughed and splashed. Back behind the row of palm trees, the circus school was in full swing, teaching people to do flips on the trampoline and to fly on the trapeze. There was snorkeling and scuba lessons, two beautiful pools with swim-up bars. There were nude areas and flagrant sexual frolicking everywhere. But she barely noticed any of it.

She'd been in Jamaica almost four days, and although the sun had already kissed her skin and she had drifted on the waves, her heart remained among the chilly breezes and budding trees of Montreal. She didn't want to be here. At least, she didn't want to be here alone.

Oh, she had fought him tooth and nail on this. She had argued half a dozen angles, and finally suggested she go through with it, but that he come along. He could help her find someone. She'd be more comfortable with him there. Perhaps they could even try a threesome.

But through it all he'd held fast, as stubborn and ornery as a mule whose feet had been embedded in concrete. She had to go alone. If he went she'd be even *more* inhibited.

She rolled her eyes. "Blah, blah, blah."

"Pardon me?"

She jumped at the sound of a man's voice. She swiveled her head to find him sitting no more than four feet from her, butt planted in the sand and toes dug in deep just like her.

"I-I'm sorry," she stuttered. "I didn't realize I spoke aloud."

He smiled and she found herself staring at him, blinking dumbly as she took him in.

Wearing nothing but a pair of ragged denim cutoffs, with deeply bronzed skin, Caribbean-blue eyes and sun-bleached blond hair, he looked more like a castaway than a guest at an exclusive and somewhat elitist resort. But then she rethought that impression. Castaways tended to be underfed and scrawny. Few boasted those broad shoulders, a six-pack, and thighs that looked like they could crack coconuts.

"Too bad," he was saying. "I was hoping you were finally going to talk to me."

She blinked, frowned. "Finally? What does that mean?"

He chuckled, shook his head and turned his gaze back out to sea. "I've been sitting at bars near you, and trying to catch your eye at the beach grills for the past two days. But apparently you didn't see me." He turned back to look at her. "In fact it seems to me that you're not seeing much of anything here. Your mind is somewhere else entirely."

"Oh." She chuckled. "That's a very uncanny observation."

"Is it?"

"Yes. I'm really not *here* at all."

"So tell me…" He shifted a little closer to her on the sand, and she shifted away. He sighed. "What could possibly be so important as to keep you from immersing yourself in paradise?"

She cocked her head, studying him once again and considering. "Do you want to know the truth?"

"Always."

She arched one skeptical eyebrow.

Apparently he noticed. "You don't believe me? You don't think I want to know the truth?"

"Frankly? No. I think most people prefer things to be simple and easy. And the truth is *always* complicated and hard."

His gaze turned intense. "That's awfully cynical, isn't it?"

She shrugged. "I don't think so. It's just the way things are."

He shifted sideways, propping himself up on one sinewy arm and facing her directly. "Okay, then. Believe it or *not* I do want to know the truth. I'm a big boy and I can take it. So, lay it on me."

She pursed her lips. He was attractive, one of the most attractive men she'd seen here so far. Mouthwateringly so, if she was honest with herself. Also he had yet to look at her chest, or compliment her on her ass. He seemed intelligent and sincere. At any rate he was the best candidate so far, and maybe—just maybe—she could see herself taking things further with him.

However, while she would do her best to fulfill her promise to Trent, she refused to resort to underhanded tactics in order to do it. If the truth scared off all the likely candidates then surely she couldn't be held responsible. She'd do her part, but if it didn't work out Trent would have no choice but to accept her efforts and toss out this ridiculous notion. The wedding would be back on and they could get on with their lives.

"Okay." She crossed her arms and looked him in the eye. "I'm here under duress. My fiancé sent me here because he wants me to sleep with other men, but I don't want to. He's the only man I want and I have no interest in anyone else, but I have to do this or he won't go through with the wedding." She spread her hands. "So, here I am."

He took a deep breath, nodded slowly, his eyes never leaving her face. "I see."

She laughed. "Do you now? You hear this kind of thing all the time? About men trying to pawn off their fiancées onto other men?"

"Well, no. I confess it is a new scenario for me. But I highly doubt this is a case of being 'pawned off'. If it was, you wouldn't be here, you'd be out somewhere tossing your engagement ring into a fiery furnace. I suspect there's a little more to it than that."

She stared at him, surprised by both his insight and the fact that he had yet to run away screaming.

"So? Is there?"

She blinked, as if waking from a dream. "Is there what?"

"More to it?"

"Well, yes."

"So, lay it on me."

"You like that phrase."

He stared at her for a moment and then let out a short laugh. "Yes, I guess I do."

"You really want to hear all about this?"

"I really, really do." He held up a hand. "However, how about we get a couple of drinks and a couple of loungers and let the waves lap at our feet while we talk. Just because we're digging into the secrets of life and love doesn't mean we can't be comfortable while we're doing it."

"Umm."

Abruptly he stood. "Good. I'll be right back."

Sam drained the last of her rum punch and allowed her head to loll on the back of the lounger. The water was warm as it splashed over her legs, and the waning sun had cast everything in shades of coral and gold. She had little doubt that the rum had something to do with her good mood, too. As did her companion.

She glanced to her left. "Why are you still here?" she asked lazily.

He drained the last of his beer and laughed. He had a nice laugh, she'd noticed. Warm and sincere, much like him. "What?"

"I've talked your ear off for the last hour and a half, and I just told you that even if I do sleep with someone else I have no intention of enjoying it. So why are you here?"

He nodded solemnly. "Fair enough. I'm here because you are easily the most attractive, intelligent and *fascinating* woman at this resort, and even if I never hear you scream out my name in ecstasy, I figure my time is much better spent with you rather than with some horny minx who doesn't know her ass from a hole in the ozone."

She laughed in spite of herself and then stopped abruptly. "What *is* your name, by the way?"

He extended a hand. "Ben. Ben Jarvis at your service."

"Sam. Samantha Walker." She shook it hardily. "Pleased to meet you." She set her glass in the sand. "So I think I've talked enough. Who are you, Ben Jarvis? Tell me what brings you to Hedo."

His grin was mischievous. "I'm here for the same reason as everybody else—to get laid."

"And here I thought you were a gentleman."

He shook his head. "I never said that. A gentleman would have walked away the moment he heard you were engaged."

"True."

"What you need is a cad, my dear. A sweet, sensitive, intelligent cad."

"And you fit the bill?"

"I do."

"I still don't want to sleep with you."

He gave her a look that said he didn't believe her, but to his credit he chose not to voice that opinion. Which was a good thing because she was beginning to have doubts about it herself. And she didn't want to face that. Yet.

"How about swimming? Would you like to swim with me?"

She scanned the beach and realized it was all but deserted. "But isn't it suppertime?"

"Are you hungry?"

"Not overly."

"Good. There's always food available here. We can eat later."

She found it interesting that he assumed they'd be together for the rest of the evening, but didn't have a chance to comment. She was too busy gaping at the fact that he'd stood and shed his shorts, leaving behind nothing but skin and muscle and unbridled sex appeal.

He wasn't erect, and she found that strangely comforting.

She licked her lips. "But this isn't the nude beach."

"There's nobody around. Trust me, no one will care."

When she made no move to get up, he grasped her hand. "Come on. The water's warm and it will relax you."

She wasn't sure she should get any more relaxed, but she relented and stood. "Okay, but I'm keeping the suit on."

"All right."

A moment later he was leading her into the surf.

The breeze had settled for the evening, leaving the water calm and glassy with only the occasional soft swell lifting them off their feet. Sea birds called to each other and the sun almost touched the horizon. The colors had intensified and the world had taken on an almost dreamlike quality.

"It's so beautiful here," she mused.

"Yes. It is." She turned to find him standing very close to her, close enough that she had to lift her chin to meet his gaze. What she saw there made her blush. And made her heart pound.

She started to move back but he caught her hand. "Are you comfortable with me, Sam?"

"Y-yes," she stammered.

"Are you attracted to me?" Before she could answer he touched a finger to her lips. "Be honest, now. No evasions."

She took a deep breath, met his gaze. "Yes," she said, her lips moving against his fingers. He tasted salty, like the sea.

He cupped her jaw, whisked a thumb across her cheek. "Then may I kiss you?"

Yes and *no* warred in her head. But if she didn't take this opportunity she only had two days left to find someone. And what if she only met sleazeballs after this? And would Trent really accept her explanation if she didn't go through with it? Ben was sweet and intelligent and she felt an innate trust of him. He also knew the score, and hadn't run away screaming. And that sealed the deal.

Her heart pounding with a strange and unexpected excitement, she nodded.

To her surprise he didn't kiss her immediately. Instead he studied her for several moments, his eyes traveling over her face, taking in every detail, like a hungry connoisseur who has just been served a gourmet meal. He slid his fingers into her hair, cupping the back of her head as his other arm encircled her waist and drew her in tight.

He was erect now, no question about it. Beneath the water, his full, hard cock pressed against the skin of her tummy and that, together with the strength of his embrace, served to feed her desire. By the time he bent his head to kiss her she was already flushed with heat, her pussy heavy with excitement.

He sipped at her lips, tasting them lightly and then cruising over them with his own. The touch was torturous in its tenderness, and she opened her mouth in search of more. His tongue laved her bottom lip and then slipped inside her mouth, only to retreat again to tease the corners of her lips.

Frustration mingled with excitement and she wrapped her arms around him, seeking purchase and some control over a situation that was slowly driving her mad.

Apparently that was what he was waiting for.

His grip on her tightened, and he ground himself against her, even as his mouth took possession of hers. The kiss became eager, voracious, his tongue sinking into her and dominating her own. A low moan rumbled in her chest and she tilted her hips against him, seeking fulfillment of the need that had begun to pound in her pussy.

Without breaking the kiss he released her head and slid his hand between them. His fingers dipped beneath the hem of her bikini bottom and sought her clit. He massaged her lightly, enough to heighten arousal, but not nearly enough to bring her to climax.

His mouth left her, and in one quick motion her bikini top was gone, his hand cupping her breast, his thumb caressing her nipple. She blinked in surprise, watched the tiny piece of material float away. "What if I lose that?"

"I'll buy you another one."

She lifted her eyes and met his hungry gaze, swallowed. She could barely breathe. "What if I tell you to stop?"

"Are you?" he asked, his hand leaving her breast and wrapping around her waist to support her as he intensified his attention to her pussy. Two fingers slipping inside her. Deep. "Are you asking me to stop?"

"Mmm," she moaned, as that was the only word she could find in her brain. Her eyes drifted closed and her head fell back, his arm around her waist the only thing keeping her from floating away on the waves.

He took it as an invitation and she felt his lips on her throat. Gently at first, tracing her collarbone with his tongue, nipping at her earlobe. He nuzzled her neck, nibbled on the tender skin and sent shivers skittering down her arms despite the warm evening air. Just when she thought her senses couldn't possibly take any more, he moved lower, his mouth covering her breast and teasing her nipple until it throbbed. He lifted her to allow him to feast on her breast more completely. Her feet left the sandy sea floor, his arm around her holding her firm. The strength of his grip on her was as arousing as anything he could possibly do to her pussy.

But that didn't stop him from trying.

He pumped her pussy harder, deeper. "You're so wet," he said against her skin, and she laughed even as her arousal spiraled. She reached out, gripping his shoulders and squeezing, savoring the play of muscle and the smoothness of his sun-baked skin. Her hands skimmed down his chest, disappeared under the water and found what she was seeking.

She wrapped her fingers around his cock, felt the reassuring throb of his desire for her. He was big, perhaps not quite so long as Trent, but thick. Surprised that thoughts of Trent did nothing to curb her desire, she acknowledged that she wanted him. She wanted this man whom she had met barely an hour ago.

"Is that what you want, baby?" he asked, his fingers still buried in her pussy. "Do you want me to fuck you?"

"Yes." She stroked his cock, massaged it. "Please."

His smile was slow, but his actions quick. Her bikini bottom was pushed to her ankles and he lifted her, wrapping both arms around her and impaling her on his shaft. She wrapped her legs around his hips and let him take her for a ride.

"Oh. Fuck," she breathed. She'd surprised herself. She loved to hear that word during lovemaking but rarely used it herself.

"Is that good?" he asked, his voice breathless and shaded by laughter. "Is that a good 'Oh fuck'?"

"Oh yeah. It is." He held her hips and pumped himself into her. The pressure was exquisite, the rhythm slow and scintillating. Somehow the presence of the water and the waves added to the eroticism, filled her senses to bursting. "That was a world-class 'Oh fuck'."

His rhythm increased. "Jesus, you're hot." His words drove her higher, the pressure in her pussy building.

"Am I?"

"Mm-hmm. You're hot and sweet and one of the sexiest women I've ever met."

She closed her eyes, sinking into his words and losing herself in her own body. "Fuck me," she pleaded, barely even aware of what she was saying. "Fuck me harder."

And he did. And when one hand cruised over her hip and his finger teased the edges of her anus before sinking into her, that was all it took.

She arched her back and pushed her hips forward as the orgasm seized her and shook her to her core. He continued his thrusts, driving himself deep as her contractions pumped him to his own climax.

When she was spent she wrapped her arms around him and wilted, resting her head on his shoulder and trying to catch her breath. "Thank you. That was amazing."

"Yes, it was." Then he added, "But don't thank me yet."

She lifted her head and drew her eyebrows together. "Yet?"

"Right." He turned and with her still wrapped around him, started toward shore. "You can thank me later. When we're finished."

"Y-you mean we're not finished?"

He shook his head. "Not even close."

Chapter Three

ဆ

Ben watched her eat. She'd told him she was famished and insisted on grabbing a bite before they did anything else. She stabbed a hunk of steak loaded down with mushrooms and Madeira sauce and wrapped her lips around it, chewing greedily.

He chuckled. "When you said sex made you hungry, you weren't kidding."

She shook her head. "I never kid about food."

He set down his fork and took a sip of wine, never taking his eyes off her. Despite the short notice, he'd been able to get them a table at one of the resort's premiere restaurants. Conversations buzzed and waiters bustled about them, taking orders and delivering food. Linen tablecloths and soft candlelight gave the room an intimate, romantic atmosphere despite all the activity.

Not that it would have mattered. With her windblown hair and bright eyes, delicate cheekbones and willowy figure clad only in a wisp of a sundress, she was completely captivating. He was so glad she was beautiful. It made his job so much easier.

He set down his wineglass and tore off a hunk of bread. "How do you do it?"

"Hmm?" She tore her attention away from her plate. "Do what?"

"Make gorging yourself look delicate and sexy."

She crinkled her nose. "Very funny. I know I eat like a pig, but—"

"No, no. I'm serious. Watching you eat is..." He took a deep breath. "It's damned arousing."

She arched her eyebrows, apparently pleased by the notion. "Really?"

"Let's just say I'm glad I've got the tablecloth over my lap at the moment."

She took another bite and chewed slowly, thoughtfully. Sexily. Her smile told him she was completely aware of the effect she was having on him. "No one's ever told me that before."

"Well, it probably doesn't have the same effect on everyone. Your fiancé may get turned on by...other things."

"Oh yes. He does. It doesn't take much. In fact, sometimes—" She stopped herself. Her expression startled, set down her fork and reached for her wine.

"What? Why did you stop?"

"It's not appropriate, is it? Talking about another lover to you?"

He shrugged. "If I had a diamond ring in my pocket it would be in poor taste, but as it is, I don't see a problem. In fact..." He leaned forward, bracing his elbows on the table. "...it's a turn-on." In truth he had another reason for asking but he felt his purposes would best be served by keeping such things to himself. He hated secrets, but it was all necessary. He had no choice.

"Really?"

"Really." His appetite rekindled by a renewed sense of purpose, he picked up his fork and dug into his baked potato. "For example, what kind of lover is he? What does he do that turns you on? What does he do that doesn't? I'd love to hear details, but whatever you're comfortable sharing with me is fine. It's up to you."

She considered that for several moments. "Well, okay. I could tell you a little."

And then she did. She told him exactly what he needed to know.

And he knew exactly what he needed to do.

* * * * *

Sam leaned against the railing of the balcony and gazed out over the water. The evening air was cool, but the breeze kind. And the moon seemed to hover mere inches above the horizon, golden and enormous and so close she fought the urge to touch it.

Ben stood beside her, and she could feel his eyes on her. A moment before she felt the warmth of his skin as his knuckles brushed her cheek.

She closed her eyes and allowed him to draw her into his arms.

She was expecting him to kiss her, but instead he asked, "So, what would you like to do, Sam? I'm in your hands."

The question startled her. "Hmm? What do you mean?"

"Well, we have this beautiful room complete with king-size bed and Jacuzzi." The spa tub bubbled just a few feet away on the balcony. Lounging there would afford them a beautiful view as well as relaxing them with hot water and frothing bubbles. Trent had spared no expense in his efforts to give her the ultimate erotic experience.

"We have champagne chilling and a romantic ocean view," continued Ben, "not to mention an assortment of erotic toys and massage oils at our disposal. But what we do next is —"

"Pardon? Toys?"

"Yes."

"I didn't order any toys."

He laughed. "You didn't have to. All the luxury suites come with them. They're in the cupboard in the bathroom. Didn't you see them?"

"No, actually. I didn't notice a cupboard."

"You didn't?" He frowned. "It's beside the shower? In the corner?"

Then she understood. "Oh, that! It's labeled 'supplies', so I assumed it was for the cleaning staff."

He stared at her for a moment and then looked away, muttering something under his breath. She thought he said, "I knew that was a lousy idea," but couldn't be sure. But to her he finally said, "Well, trust me. They're there." He grinned. "And don't worry," he said, apparently reading her mind, "they're all brand-new and in their packages. You open one, you bought it." He tilted his head. "Have you never used toys?"

"Actually, no. Trent's mentioned it, but I never felt the need. I have quite enough with just him." She felt herself blush and her face heated further at the embarrassment of that.

He leaned back against the rail and studied her. In fact it went on long enough to make her uncomfortable. "What?"

"Well, since we're in this just for the sheer debauchery of it, why don't you go into the bathroom and pick out one or two. I'll be waiting in the Jacuzzi and we'll take it from there." He bent and kissed her, slowly and deeply. "And *where* we take it will be completely up to you."

He moved away from her, heading for the hot tub.

She remained rooted to the spot, hesitant and uncertain.

He removed his shirt. "Is something wrong? If you really don't want to try out the toys we don't — "

"No, no. I want to." She whirled on her heel and headed inside. "Just give me a minute."

A few moments later she found herself in the bathroom, staring at a cupboard stacked almost to the ceiling with everything from double-ended dildos to fur-lined handcuffs, to scented oils and lubricants. She stood there, more than a little overwhelmed and completely uncertain as to what to pick or even what she really wanted.

She wasn't used to thinking about her needs. She'd been with Trent so long that he seemed to know instinctively what to do. She'd never really had to focus on what she wanted because her needs were met so completely, so had never verbalized or asked for anything. And she'd certainly never felt the need for *enhancements*.

But Ben barely knew her. He didn't know what she liked, enjoyed, needed, and so she'd have to tell him. And that meant she had to look at herself and figure it out in order to communicate it to him. Also, if she was honest with herself, the whole "toy" idea did hold some level of fascination for her. But to pick something in the context of her desires and preferences—now *that* would be the challenge. And, she hoped, the fun.

She stared at the cupboard for a long time, examining the choices, sifting through everything in her mind. At last she came to a decision. It wouldn't be what Ben would expect and strangely that pleased her.

When she returned Ben sat up and set his wineglass on the side of the tub. "Good. I was just about to come looking for you."

Sam just smiled, her hands hidden safely behind her back.

Ben's eyebrows arched. "So you took your time and found something interesting?"

She shrugged.

He chuckled. "Okay, I give. What have you got there?"

She brought her hands into view and held up her prize.

And Ben frowned. "That's it? All you want to use is a pair of handcuffs?"

She walked to the side of the tub and held them out to him. "Actually, I want *you* to use them on me, along with whatever else you decide to try. I want you to surprise me. I want to put myself in *your* hands."

He took the handcuffs and examined them thoughtfully for a moment before lifting his gaze to hers. "You want to be dominated."

She tilted her head. "Well, I don't know much about the whole formal Dom/sub scene, and I really can't see myself being into collars and punishment or anything, but I do know I like when Trent really takes control." She smiled, shyly. "I like it very much."

Ben studied her for a moment and then nodded slowly. "Okay, that's fine with me." And by the slow, savvy smile that spread across his face she could tell just how much he liked it. "But you have to answer a few questions for me first." He erupted out of the water. "And then we'll see just how far to take this."

* * * * *

Sam stood in the middle of the room, and although she was fully dressed she felt strangely exposed. Vulnerable.

Ben had been sitting in the large wing-back in the corner, studying her for the last several minutes, and she had gradually come to feel as if he was stripping away her clothes with his eyes alone. He had donned a pair of skintight briefs, but other than that remained nude, one foot propped on the opposite knee. He looked sexy and serene, casual and relaxed, yet an intensity crackled about him like static electricity. She cleared her throat. Straightened her dress. Decided she couldn't take it anymore. "Ben, what—"

"Quiet." He said the word softly, but the command in it was unmistakable. He took a sip of the brandy he'd poured for himself. "I like looking at you. I wasn't lying when I said you were one of the most beautiful women I've seen."

She blushed again at the compliment.

"Now, turn around. Slowly. I want to see your back."

She did as he told her, feeling even more vulnerable because she couldn't see him. She almost jumped out of her skin when she heard him whisper very close to her ear. "Lovely." He skimmed a finger down her arm and a parade of goose bumps followed his touch. She started to turn around, but he stopped her. "No. Stay still." Trailed a finger down her other arm. "No matter what I do, don't react. Don't touch me and don't move away." He lifted her hair and kissed her neck. "All right? Can you do that?"

"Yes." She closed her eyes, took a deep breath. "If you want."

"I do. I want that very much." His hands left her body, and she sensed him move away. When he returned, he stood very close, close enough that his chest brushed her back. "Now, remember. Don't move." And then something dark and soft covered her eyes. Her hands jerked in surprise, her first reaction to reach up and rip the blindfold away, but she caught herself in time and kept her hands at her sides.

"Is that all right?" he asked when he was finished. "Is it too tight?"

"No. It's...it's fine."

"Good." And then his hands were on her again. They settled on her shoulders and squeezed, the contact was gentle, but the weight of his touch held an unmistakable message. He was in control, and that knowledge made her shiver with anticipation.

With slow, torturous precision he undid the zipper but left the dress hanging loosely from her shoulders. "One thing, before we continue." He combed his fingers through her hair, let it drizzle over her shoulders. "If you ever become uncomfortable with what I'm doing you just have to say one word and I'll stop." He trailed a finger down her spine, tracing each vertebra with a featherlight touch.

She took a shuddering breath. "Okay. What's the word?"

"The word is Trent."

She started in surprise at the mention of her fiancé's name.

"If you ask for him, I'll know that I've gone too far, or that we need to talk about what's happening, and we'll decide where to go from there. All right?"

He followed the same path down her back with his tongue. From the nape of her neck he left a trail of wetness and little shivers all the way down to the small of her back, finally stopping at the waistband of her thong.

She let out the breath of expectation she hadn't even realized she'd been holding. "All right."

"You have a very sexy ass," he said, reaching for the shoulder straps of her dress. "I'd like to see it better."

The dress fell, forming a puddle at her feet. Her thong followed, leaving her nude since she hadn't bothered with a bra. He reached around to fondle her breasts, tracing their outline lightly before cupping them and thumbing her nipples.

He was close enough that she could feel his erection pressed against her backside. Even through the briefs it was exciting and she had to curb the urge to rub herself against him.

"Mmm," he said, his voice vibrating through his chest and into her back, his lips against her shoulder. "You're like candy." He nipped at her skin, licked her earlobe. "And I could just eat you up."

She said nothing, merely smiled as a trace of heat crept into her cheeks.

His hands left her breasts, skimmed her lowest rib and flattened against her belly, giving him leverage to press his cock more firmly against her. "Mmm. That ass is tempting." One hand slipped lower, toying lightly with her pussy and making her so wet that she felt a bead of moisture slip down her inner thigh. "So very tempting."

Suddenly he left her, but only for a moment.

When he returned he grasped her elbow. "Now move forward. The bed is one step in front of you. I want you to lie on it, facedown, but let your legs hang over the edge."

He helped her find the position he wanted. The bed was low enough that her knees touched the floor.

"Perfect." His hands cupped her bottom and began massaging her. His fingers were slicked with oil and the spicy aroma of patchouli filled the room. She almost swooned at the subtle pressure and how he worked the muscles of her lower back and ass, and felt every muscle in her body turn to liquid as she sank more deeply into the mattress.

"You like that." It was a statement, not a question. "Then you'll love this." His oil-slicked fingers slid into her crease and toyed with the edges of her anus.

She tensed, sucked in her breath. "Relax, baby. I won't hurt you. This will be amazing, but you have to trust me." He added more oil, dribbling it directly onto her ass, and continued to massage her.

"Do you trust me?"

"Yes."

"Good. That's it." His hands were so warm and strong, and somehow reassuring. "That's my girl." His finger slipped inside and she arched her back in pleasure.

"Good." He kissed her back, flicked out his tongue. "Very good. Now trust me a little bit further."

The pressure on her anus changed, and something slipped inside, something soft and smooth and pliant. To her surprise it felt good and she let out a soft moan. "What's that?"

"Anal beads." He inserted another, pushing deeper. "They're silicone, so they're soft and safe." Just when she was feeling full and on the edge of discomfort, he stopped. "How's that? Are you comfortable?"

"It's...strange." She shifted slightly. "But good."

"Good." He licked her ass. "Stay there. I'll be right back."

She heard water running and knew he must be washing his hands. While she waited she listened to the sound of the waves hitting the beach outside the window and the soft sigh of the breeze as it blew in through the open patio doors. It caressed her skin, the touch as silky as a lover's.

"How are you feeling?" He straddled her hips, his hands massaged her shoulders. "Relaxed?"

"Mmm," was all she could manage.

"Well, I think it's time to get your blood pumping." He wrapped his arms around her waist and lifted her, hoisting her up and all but throwing her onto the bed. She let out a little yelp when she landed on her back in a nest of pillows. She felt the mattress shift when he joined her, chuckling. "What's life without a few surprises, eh?" And then he grasped her wrists, putting her hands together in front of her just as she felt something soft wrap around them. A lock clicked into place.

"Handcuffs?" she asked, surprised. She'd completely forgotten the cuffs, and now the reality of them was a little overwhelming. "But—"

"No buts." He shifted her on the bed until she was positioned as he liked. "No words at all." He straddled her, his hot thighs brushing the sides of her breasts as his lips caressed her mouth.

Reflexively, she opened her mouth. "Just stay still and take what I dish out." His tongue tasted hers. "If you can."

It was a dare and she was ready for it. She nodded.

He caught her chin in his palm and held her firm as his mouth took possession of hers. He kissed her long and deep, his lips firm, his tongue aggressive.

"Mmm," he said. "I take it back. You're sweeter than candy. And I want those sweet lips on my cock."

She couldn't see, but she could sense his movements. Her tongue flicked out to taste him, and found him hard and ready for her. She licked the bead of cum from the tip and her hands came up to wrap around him, but he grabbed the cuffs. "No. Just open your mouth and take me."

He controlled the action, holding her as he liked and pumping his cock into her at his own pace. It wasn't too hard or too fast, the movement gentle, his hold on her subtle but firm. It was at once infuriating and exciting to have so little control over what was happening. Instinct warred with conscious effort, as frustration built into arousal.

"Jesus," he groaned, his rhythm increasing. His excitement heightened her own. She increased the pressure of her lips and the action of her tongue, eager for his climax, already tasting his cum. "Oh. Christ!" His body tensed as he pumped himself into her, and she swallowed every bit greedily, pleased that she'd given him so much pleasure.

"Fuck, that was amazing." He withdrew from her mouth and lavished a long slow kiss on her. "So, now it's your turn."

He shifted downward, grasped her wrists and secured the cuffs somehow to the wrought iron headboard. "Now, that's a picture," he said. "Naked and bound and mine to do with as I please."

She shivered slightly at his words, and then jumped when his tongue touched her clit. "Hey there," he chuckled, pressing her thighs further apart and holding her down. "Take it easy." He blew softly over her pussy, his breath moist and warm. "And stay still. You're mine, remember?" He massaged her clit between two fingers. "For tonight, you're mine."

And then he proceeded to torment her with his mouth. His tongue was soft and sweet, teasing and light, and then suddenly firm and commanding. He flicked her clit rapidly with his tongue, bringing her to the brink of orgasm before retreating and changing to long, slow licks that made her crazy with need. She shifted her hips, seeking more, but was punished with the withdrawal of his tongue.

"None of that," he warned. "I'm in control here, remember?"

She nodded, wishing she could touch herself and bring some relief to her aching pussy. His tongue touched her again, and two fingers drove inside her, pumping deeply and then retreating before thrusting deep again.

"Damn, you're wet," he said, his voice reverberating against her pussy. "Let's see if we can get you wetter." The vibrator touched her and the orgasm shot through her like a bullet. She screamed, arching her back and pressing her pussy more firmly against the source of her pleasure. The contractions seized her and just when she thought she couldn't take any more he slowly pulled the beads from her ass.

"Oh. *God!*" The added stimulation sent her spiraling. Her body jerked so hard she was surprised she didn't rip the headboard off its moorings.

Wave after wave of pleasure washed over her and she broke out in a sweat, struggled to catch her breath.

"That's my girl." He kissed her and his cock slipped inside her just as her heart rate began to calm. He tore the blindfold away. She blinked, her eyes adjusting to the golden glow of the warm tropical evening. He was staring at her, his eyes so blue and his smile so wide—at that moment she wanted to eat him up just as surely as he had wanted to eat her.

"I want to touch you," she breathed as he stroked her pussy slowly with his cock, building arousal all over again.

His answer was the click of the lock as the cuffs came undone and her hands were freed. She wrapped her arms around him, noting that his back was damp with sweat his skin hot with passion. She kissed his shoulder and dug in her fingers, tasting his saltiness and savoring all that muscle and raw energy.

"Can you come again for me, baby? Can you?"

"Yes. I...maybe."

His rhythm increased, his thrusts deepened. "Wrap your legs around me. Tight."

She wasn't sure where she found the strength, but she managed it, wrapping her legs around his hips and squeezing.

"Oh yeah. That's—" He cried out, his climax matched her own. While not as intense as the first, it was a thrill to share it with him and when he collapsed beside her on the bed and drew her to him, she felt sated and dreamy.

"Are you going to be okay?" he asked, stroking her back.

"Oh yeah." She snuggled in tight. "I'm going to be just fine."

* * * * *

Ben sat back in the hot tub and watched her. The sun had set leaving the sky a soft blanket of midnight blue dotted with stars, and the glow from the half-moon lit her in a silvery silhouette. She was so beautiful. And so young. Sometimes it hurt his heart just to look at her.

She sipped from her wine and laid her head back on the cushions surrounding the tub. But a moment later she lifted her head. "What is it? You're staring at me."

He set down his glass. "I wonder…"

"Yes?"

"I wonder if you enjoyed…" he waved back toward the room, "…that."

Her smile and the blush on her cheeks would have been answer enough, but she said, "Yes. Of course I did."

"It was a new experience for you. The toys. The way I played you. In fact I might be so bold as to suggest that was probably one of the most intense orgasms you've ever experienced."

She frowned, nodded.

"That was nothing, you know. Only a beginning. The tip of the iceberg."

Her frown deepened. "What are you getting at?"

He set his glass down and leaned forward to enhance the earnestness of his plea. "You need to make a decision, Sam."

"I do?"

"Yes. Are you willing to give all that up in order to settle down with Trent?"

She stared at him, wide-eyed. He could see the way her pulse pounded in the base of her throat.

"I know you care for him, but you're still so young, and there's a whole world out there waiting for you." He leaned back again, picked up his glass and sipped. "And I'd be more than happy to lead you through it."

"Are you asking me to leave Trent? After all I told you, you have the nerve to ask me that?"

He shook his head. "All I'm asking is for you to consider all the options. Go into this marriage with your eyes wide open, Sam. Or don't go into it at all. And if you don't, I'm here for you." He drained his glass and set it down before erupting from the water and reaching for a towel. "It's your decision. If you need me, just ask at the front desk. They know where to find me."

She blinked in disbelief. "You're leaving?"

"Yes. I think you need some time alone to think about this." He moved to leave but then stopped abruptly and turned to face her. "But I'll stay if you like. I'll stay and sleep with you and share breakfast with you and be your lover. All you have to do is ask."

He hardened himself to the stunned look in her eyes, and the way it changed to anger and finally embarrassment. "No, you can go." She lowered her eyes. "And the sooner the better."

He nodded and without another word, left her alone with her demons. And her decision.

Chapter Four

ॐ

Sam sat at the table at the edge of the patio and stared out over the water. She stirred her drink, the plastic swizzle stick clinking gaily against the glass. It had been a day and a half since Ben had left her room, and this was the first time she'd ventured outside since. But she'd made good use of the time holed up in her room alone. It hadn't been easy, but she'd done a lot of thinking, and come to some important decisions.

She felt quite sure that they were the right decisions, but for some reason that didn't lessen the anxiety she felt about seeing Trent and sharing them with him. Of course it was his bed, and he'd forced her to lie in it, but that didn't mean he'd like it when faced with the reality of his fiancée having slept with another man.

"Sam!"

At the sound of his voice her eyes flew open and she almost jumped out of her skin. Strange, but the moment she saw him all her anxiety melted away. No matter what happened, he loved her, and she had faith in that. If she didn't she wouldn't have come here at all. "Trent!"

She stood and fell into his arms for a long embrace, followed by an even longer kiss. He pulled away from her and cupped her face in his hands, gazing at her intently.

"You did it, didn't you?" he asked softly. "You found someone."

"Yes." She tried to read his expression but his smile seemed ambiguous. "But could we talk about it somewhere else?"

"Of course. Let's head down to the water."

He took her hand and led her past the crowds and the boardwalk until they found a secluded spot under a nest of palm trees. The waves lapped at the beach just a few feet away and the sun beat down on the sand making it almost too hot to walk on. But in the shade of the palms the sand was cool, the air comfortable.

They sat down together, side by side, their legs spread out, the blue of tropical infinity surrounding them. "So tell me. Tell me everything."

She laughed. "Everything? You want a blow-by-blow account?"

He jerked his head back in surprise. "No, no. Of course not. But I'd like to know who he is, and how he treated you. I'd like to know if you enjoyed it and..." He shrugged. "And whatever else you'd like to tell me."

"Okay." She took a moment to formulate her words. "His name is Ben and he treated me wonderfully. We spent a day and an evening together and it was some of the most incredible, mind-blowing sex I've ever experienced."

Trent's eyebrows arched as he stared at her. "Really."

"Yes, really." She tilted her head. "Do you feel threatened by that?"

"Well..." He shifted on the sand and she allowed herself to enjoy the fact that for once she had the upper hand. "I guess I'd be lying if I said no."

She smiled and laid a hand on his arm. "I'm glad to hear you admit it, but in all honesty, you have no need to feel threatened."

His eyes twinkled. "I don't?"

"No. You don't." She turned her gaze out to the water. "At first I was so angry with you for putting me in this position, Trent. I felt like you didn't trust me and that you were asking me to prove myself to you when I've spent *the last five years* proving myself to you."

"I'm sorry, Sam. I didn't—"

She squeezed his hand. "But then I tried to put it in the context of who you are and what that friend of yours had experienced, and it helped me to understand a little bit better. And now that it's all over I've decided I should thank you."

He laughed, the relief in his voice apparent. "You should?"

"Yes. At first I was confused by the way Ben made me feel. I wasn't lying when I said the sex was amazing, and then when he offered to continue seeing me, that really confused me and got me thinking."

"He offered what?"

"Does that surprise you? Did you think it would be so easy for a man to walk away from me?"

"No! Of course not. I…I just…" He shook his head as if to clear it. "Forget it. That involves my ego and that's not what this is about. Tell me what you were going to say."

A seagull landed just a few feet in front of them and studied them as if trying to discern if they had any goodies for him. Sam picked up a stone and tossed it, frightening the bird away. "His proposal made me really look at what I had been feeling and what I wanted, and it made me realize that although the sex was great, it was just that. Sex." She turned to face Trent. "There was no love, no caring. I mean he was good to me and I trusted him to not hurt me, but it was a purely physical experience. It was good and fun but…"

"It was hollow? Empty?"

"Yes. And what I have with you is so much more than that. It's an expression of things that words can only begin to convey. And that's what I want to experience for the rest of my life."

His smile widened. "So, this is a good thing."

"Uh-huh." She snuggled into his arms. "It's a very good thing. Your methods may be a bit unorthodox, but I gotta tell you I'm impressed. Not many men would be secure enough to give me that kind of freedom."

"Well, you know what they say. If you love something set it free."

"Yeah." She sighed, rested her head on his shoulder. "I guess they do."

Trent was silent for a time, and although there seemed to be little left that needed to be said, she became vaguely aware of a tension in the air, and tightness of his muscles.

"Uh…" She felt him swallow. "They also say that honesty is one of the most important things in any relationship."

She sat up and turned to face him. "Yeah. I suppose."

He nodded and she didn't think she'd ever seen him look so nervous. "Trent, what is it?"

"I have something to tell you, Sam." He raked his fingers through his hair and blew out a long, slow breath. "And honestly, I don't think you're going to like it."

* * * * *

"I wish you'd tell me what this is about." Sam's confusion was warring with a rare bit of temper at Trent's mysterious behavior.

"Don't worry. It'll all be clear soon enough." He raised his hand to knock at the door of the small seaside cottage.

When the door opened she was, once again, face-to-face with Ben. Clad in nothing but a pair of navy-blue swim trunks, a tan and a smile, he looked as sexy as ever. And her tummy did a little flip-flop the moment she saw him.

"Hi, Sam." His eyes remained hooded, as if unsure what her arrival meant, but then his gaze shifted to Trent and his face lit up. "Trent!"

Sam watched in mute wonder, and growing confusion, as the two men shook hands and then embraced.

"I wasn't sure if I'd get to see you," Ben was saying. "I mean, considering—"

Sam's confusion erupted into fury. "You mean you two *know* each other?"

"Oh." Ben's gaze shifted from Trent to her and back again. "You haven't told her?"

Trent cleared his throat. "Could we talk about this inside?"

"Yes." Sam kept a laser-like gaze on her fiancé. "Let's talk about this inside."

With a soft chuckle that Sam decided to ignore, Ben ushered them inside.

They found themselves in an airy, spacious room. The cottage was small, but very open concept with the bed, living area and kitchen all opening onto the same space. A set of gauzy white curtains billowed into the room and the surf crashed against the beach just a few feet away. It was lovely and she wondered that such cottages weren't advertised in the literature, but decided against asking. She had other, more pressing matters to address.

She stopped in the center of the room and whirled to face the two men who were both standing there looking a little sheepish. "So, how do you two know each other? And what the hell is going on?"

Trent stuffed his hands in his pockets, and damn if he didn't look even sexier with that little-lost-boy look on his face. But she hardened her heart to it and crossed her arms.

"Sam, Ben is a very old friend. We've known each other since high school."

She was already stunned. "You have?"

"Yes. You remember that friend of mine I told you about? The one who married a young woman only to have her walk out on him a few years later because she'd never been with anyone else and became curious?"

"Of course I do. But what does—" And then it hit her. She looked at Ben, her mouth gaping. "You're *him*?"

Ben saluted her. "One and the same. Sir Cuckold at your service."

Her heart sank at the thought of his heart being broken so callously. "Oh, Ben. I'm so sorry."

He shrugged. "Shit happens. But it was all the more reason to say yes when Trent asked me to help him out."

That was enough to bring the rage back and set her blood to boiling. "You *planned* this, Trent? You set me *up*?"

"No, Sam. You don't understand. It wasn't like that."

She crossed her arms and plunked herself down on the bed that just happened to be behind her. "No? Then how exactly was it?"

Ben stepped forward. "He just asked me to watch you, and see how things went. He was hoping you'd find someone on your own, but—"

"But to be blunt, I wanted a backup plan. I knew and trusted Ben. I knew he'd treat you well, and I trusted him not to push himself on you if you weren't interested. I was just afraid that you'd be too uptight to find someone on your own and…"

She sighed. "And you were right."

Trent knelt in front of her, his hand on her knee. "I'm sorry, babe. I didn't intend for it to be a deception." He grasped her hand, cradled it in his palm. "I was just so scared."

She brushed her fingertips through his hair. "Scared? Of what?"

"Scared that you wouldn't go through with it and I had no idea what to do if that happened. Scared that you'd have a horrible experience and blame me for it. But most of all, scared of losing you."

"You thought I'd leave you because of another man?"

"No. I was afraid you'd leave me because you didn't think I trusted you. But more importantly I was scared of losing you five years down the road. I saw what it did to Ben. I couldn't face that, Sam. I just couldn't."

She looked at Ben to find him watching them, an enigmatic smile on his face. "I was so devastated I left the country and became a professional beach bum."

At that Trent laughed. "Some beach bum. He manages the whole fucking resort."

Her eyes went wide. "You do?"

He shrugged. "I was hanging out here so much they decided to give me something useful to do."

Trent just rolled his eyes and shook his head, but then he looked at her, his face a question mark.

She cupped his chin in her hand and spoke her heart. "I suppose I should be furious with you, and I *was*." She sighed. "Right up until the moment you admitted to being so afraid. How can I turn down a man who shows me that kind of vulnerability?"

Trent laughed. "So you like your men vulnerable, do you?"

"Well, yes, but…" She shifted her gaze to Ben. "But not in the bedroom."

Trent nodded and drew her up to stand beside him. "Right. You've discovered the joys of submissive sex."

Her mouth fell open. "What? You know about that? You had already talked to Ben?"

"Shit. Don't get all mad again. This is a good thing!"

She had to work at tamping down her anger. "How's that?"

"It eased another worry I had about us."

"Whatever it was you could have talked to me about it, instead of Ben."

Trent's fists clenched. "But I did. I tried repeatedly over the years to get you to talk about it but you wouldn't."

"What? What are you talking about?"

"I've asked you many times what you do or don't like in the bedroom. And you always say that whatever I do is fine."

"It was the truth."

"But it wasn't *enough*, dammit! It sounded like an evasion to me. How was I supposed to know those few cryptic words meant you actually liked to be dominated?"

She considered that, weighed it. "Well, I guess I didn't know that either. Not until I had to deal with someone else..." She glanced at Ben. "Someone I didn't know as well, and who didn't know me."

"So you admit it? You admit that you took things for granted with me? And that maybe we need to communicate better about what we want in bed?"

She nodded slowly. "And maybe outside of bed, too. I know it's crazy, and I know I'm an intelligent, independent woman, but I think, because you're older, I just tended to assume that you knew better. Even when it came to my personal needs."

"Or especially when it came to those."

"Yeah." She moved in closer to Trent, close enough to feel the warmth of his body. "Especially then."

He broke into a smile. "So... Wow." He glanced at Ben too. "This is really good, right? It accomplished what I hoped it would and more."

"I don't know..." She shrugged, tossed a coquettish glance at Ben. "I think there might be one more thing left to accomplish."

Trent shrugged, obviously puzzled. "What do you mean?"

"Since we're being more open about what we want, I have a little request."

A slow, sly grin spread across Trent's face. "Oh, you do, do you?"

"Uh-huh." She turned around, nestled her bum against Trent's middle and drew his arms around her waist as she gazed at Ben who had been watching them with frank interest the whole time. "And I think I know just the men who can fulfill it."

Chapter Five

ஐ

Hair still damp from her shower and eager to see what the men had come up with in her absence, Sam stepped out the back door of the cottage, directly onto the cool sand of Ben's private beach. The sun had set, leaving behind a balmy tropical evening, a legion of stars and the glitter of moonlight on the water.

A bonfire crackled a short distance away and she started toward it, the soft cotton of her skirt swishing about her ankles. As she drew closer she heard the unmistakable echo of men's laughter.

She stopped beside the fire, propped her hands on her hips and glared at them. "So, what are you two plotting?"

Trent snickered and leaned back on his elbows, the fire casting his lean, chiseled body into golden relief. "Nothing."

"Uh-huh."

"Actually," contributed Ben as he poured a glass of wine. "He was commending me on my genius."

She accepted the glass he offered her. "Genius?"

"Yes. The offer I made was my idea. I figured you needed a little…motivation to think about everything."

She took a sip, decided not to get angry. Manipulative or not, he was right. It had been exactly what she needed to hear and there was no sense in denying it. However, there was no reason she couldn't turn it to her advantage.

She took another sip and savored the way the wine went to her head and warmed her blood. "Perhaps. But you played me, Ben. You both did. You owe me, and I think it's time you paid up."

"You speak of this little request of yours."

"I do." She gazed at him over the rim of her glass. "So when do we get started?"

Ben looked at Trent who shrugged. "I don't know, Sam. We're having second thoughts about this."

Rage instantly flooded her cheeks. "What? You promised! You can't go back on your word like that." The wineglass dropped soundlessly to the sand. "I swear, you two are the most irritating, fickle, self-important—" Her squeal cut through the night as Ben scooped her up off the sand and started toward the water with Trent hot on his heels.

"Hey! What are you doing? You can't just—"

He threw her mercilessly into the water, clothes and all. It wasn't deep, but by the time she struggled to her feet she was sopping wet, every bit of clothing she wore clinging tightly to her body. She was surprised the water didn't boil off her skin. "You guys are so—"

"Shh." Trent had moved in behind her, and when he wrapped his arms around her she was surprised to realize he'd shed his swim trunks somewhere along the way.

As had Ben who stood directly in front of her. "You have to be quiet now." He ran a finger down her cheek. "And do as we say. You're ours to do with as we please. Do you understand?"

Instantly aroused by his words and by the strong presence of Trent behind her, she nodded.

"You must be chilly," observed Trent, cupping her breasts, and tracing the outline of her nipples through her clothes.

Although the water was warm, the air had cooled, but the shivers that passed through her had nothing to do with temperature. She didn't respond, however, sensing that she wasn't expected to.

Ben joined the exploration by tracing the V of skin that peeked out of her blouse. "She must be. She has goose bumps."

Trent palmed her breasts a little more firmly. "It's the wet clothes."

"Yes. We should do something about that."

Ben glanced at Trent and at a slight motion of his head, Trent grabbed the lapels of her blouse and tore it open, ripping it from her body like it was tissue paper.

She sucked in her breath in surprise and felt her nipples tighten further at the cool air hitting her wet skin.

Ben shook his head, watching as Trent caressed her bare breasts, tweaked her nipples. "I thought you were just going to open the buttons."

"I was in a hurry."

Ben smiled, admiring her. "I can see why." And then he reached for the hem of her skirt that floated lazily on the surface of the water around her knees, and tore it in two, from bottom to top.

"What's this?" said Ben, chuckling and sliding a hand between her thighs. "No panties?"

Trent shifted her wet hair aside and nuzzled her throat. "You sinner."

"I'll say." Ben parted her lips and massaged her clit briefly before sliding two fingers inside her. "She's got a lot of nerve, depriving me the fun of ripping off her thong again."

"Nervy little wench." Her legs had gone weak, but Trent wrapped a hand around her waist to support her. He nipped at her throat. "What are we going to do about it?"

Ben withdrew his hand from her pussy and left her aching as he cupped her chin. He held her gaze. "I think we need to teach her some manners." And then he kissed her. There was nothing tender about that kiss. It was hard and deep, commanding and possessive. And she melted beneath it.

And then he tore his mouth away and she was spun around, allowing Trent an opportunity to claim her. His arm still around her waist, he pulled her in so tight she could barely breathe, and then stole what remained of her breath with his kiss. It was as hard and commanding as Ben's, but touched with something else. A passion that she knew could only come from an enduring sense of love and devotion.

He broke the kiss but his lips still brushed against hers as he whispered. "I love you so much, Sam." He kissed her lightly. "Now more than ever."

She met his gaze and felt something flutter deep inside just as Ben shouted, "Bring her up here!"

Trent swept her into his arms and carried her up the beach to the blanket they had laid out beside the fire.

Ben had laid down on his back, his wet skin gleaming in the firelight. He spread his legs slightly and motioned her forward. "On your knees."

She crouched between Ben's legs, studying his cock that seemed somehow bigger in the flickers and shadows of the firelight.

He stroked it, enhancing an already intimidating erection. He frowned. "No, no. On all fours. Ass in the air."

She felt Trent kneel behind her, grasp her hips and lift, positioning her as he liked. He began stroking her pussy — and she had to work at staying upright.

"Is she wet?" asked Ben.

"Oh yeah." Trent dipped his fingers inside her and spread the moisture over her pussy before pumping her deeply. "She's ready."

"Good." Ben held up his cock in blatant offering. "Now use those sweet lips on me, baby. While Trent uses you."

Her tummy tumbled as she bent to take Ben in her mouth. She let out a soft groan as Trent grasped her hips and eased his cock inside her.

Since she needed both hands to support her weight and keep her balance, Ben held his cock for her. She took him as deep as she could, teasing him with her tongue, and massaging him with her lips. He stroked her hair, gently guiding her movements and offering soft words of encouragement that turned her insides to jelly.

Trent's thrusts remained soft and slow, stroking her arousal as surely as his fingers stroked her clit. Massaging her toward climax and then easing off, only to draw her close once again.

She groaned in frustration, pushed her hips back in search of the added pressure she needed for climax.

"Oh no," said Trent, gentling his touch on her clit. "Not yet."

"Is she ready?" asked Ben.

"Oh yeah, she's ready," replied Trent, his voice breathless. "And I'm way *past* ready."

"Okay, baby." Ben stopped her, cupped her face in his hands and directed her to look at him. "We're going to try something. You have to trust us, but if you become uncomfortable or it doesn't feel good, just say so, okay?"

She frowned, confused. "Okay."

He brushed wet hair off her forehead and drew her forward until her breasts touched his chest. Trent followed, his cock still buried inside her. "Have you ever had two cocks in that sweet little pussy of yours?"

Her eyes widened. "No."

"Well, you're about to." She saw him reach for a tube of lubricant that had been lying near the edge of the blanket. She hadn't noticed it until that moment.

"I...I don't know."

"Trust us, baby." It was Trent, his hands firm on her hips as he positioned her. "Relax and trust us. It'll be amazing."

"You almost sound like you've done it before."

"Well, Trent hasn't but I have." Ben's smile was almost shy. "This *is* Hedo, you know. And I'm not exactly a priest."

"No. Not exactly." She rewarded him with an answering smile. "Okay." She nodded, closed her eyes, and trusted.

"That's our girl." Ben's tongue teased her lips as he applied the lube to his cock. She made a conscious effort to relax when the tip of his cock nudged her pussy. "Mmm." He groaned as, with help from Trent, he slipped inside her.

"Holy Jesus," moaned Trent, "that's tight."

And it was. Deliciously so.

"Are you okay?" asked Ben, his eyes glazed.

She nodded. "Yeah." Arched her back, thought she'd never felt so full, but ironically wanted more. The two of them were in deep. So deep they nudged her womb. "I'm good."

At that Trent grabbed her hips and guided her, using her movement to provide the impetus for the thrusts.

Ben's hand slid between them and found her pussy, fondling her clit lightly as her motion accelerated.

The pressure was intense, exquisite, on the verge of painful, but that only added to the excitement. She groaned and her head fell forward.

"You okay, baby?"

She had no idea who had asked, but she only had the strength to nod and whisper, "Don't stop."

"Wouldn't dream of it." Trent's grip tightened and the movement of her hips accelerated, the thrusts driving her higher.

"Fuck, you're so wet," breathed Trent. "I wonder if—"

The climax hit, slamming into her and knocking her almost senseless. Her arms gave out and she collapsed on top of Ben as the sensations shuddered through her. It was only moments before she felt Ben tense and heard Trent's familiar groan of fulfillment. He wrapped his arm around her waist and drove himself into her one more time, his body stiffening and shuddering hard before he withdrew and collapsed beside Ben on the blanket.

She rolled off Ben and snuggled between them, eyes closed as she sucked in breath after breath of tangy salt air.

Trent snuggled up to her, spoon-style, his waning erection nestled against her ass. "You squirted, you know. I don't think you've ever done that before."

"Mmm. That's nice."

Ben's chest was against her lips and she felt the vibrations as he chuckled. He turned on his side, offering her his back and soon the three of them were nested together, with her wedged in between a pair of hard, hot bodies.

She sighed in contentment.

She felt Trent trace a finger down her arm and she shivered. "I love you, you know. Did I tell you that today?"

She just smiled.

"So, where do we go from here, baby? What's next?"

"We get married, silly." She kissed Ben's shoulder. "And I want Ben to give me away."

Ben stiffened in surprise. "You do?"

"Uh-huh."

"But what about your father?"

"He died three years ago, and I have no brothers. I was struggling with this problem, but this is the perfect solution."

He grasped her hand and drew it around him, kissing her fingertips. "Thank you." She could hear the emotion in his voice and it touched her. "I'd be honored."

"And I'm setting you up with my friend Celia."

"Oh Jesus." But Trent was laughing. "Now you're in for it."

"Bring it on," said Ben. "After this I can take anything."

"Yeah." Sam felt like she was floating. "I think I know what you mean."

Also by Nikki Soarde

ℬℐ

And Lady Makes Three (anthology)
Balance of Power
Duplicity
Jagged Gift
Phobia

About the Author

ℬℐ

Nikki lives in a small town in Ontario, Canada. In the midst of the chaos that comes with raising three small boys, working part-time as a lab tech in a hospital blood bank, and caring for her ever-adoring husband, she dreams up her stories. Nikki's work is an eclectic combination of romance, mystery, suspense and humor with characters that have plenty of room to grow.

Nikki welcomes comments from readers. You can find her website and email address on her author bio page at www.ellorascave.com.

UNDYING MAGIC

Ravyn Wilde

Dedication

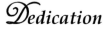

This book is dedicated to my editor, Kelli. I want to express my appreciation for helping me to strive for more, for seeing the holes in the plot and because without you…the books just wouldn't be right.

Thank you.

Trademarks Acknowledgement

The author acknowledges the trademarked status and trademark owners of the following wordmarks mentioned in this work of fiction:

Bacardi Limon: Bacardi & Company Limited Corporation

Captain Morgan: Diageo North America, Inc.

DustBuster: Black & Decker Corporation

Peachtree Schnapps: Johs De Kuyper & Zoon B.V. Private Limited Liability Company

Slurpee: Southland Corporation

Tupperware: Dart Industries Inc.

V8 Splash: CSC Brands Inc.

Chapter One

❧

Pulling out her knife, Jane stabbed the man in the heart. As she did, her vision snagged on his expression and she was transported two decades back in time.

She'd been thirteen the first time she'd seen that look of surprise in a man's eyes.

The look she now thought of as "What the fuck? How did *you* manage to do that?"

The brief flash of confusion was almost always followed by an expression of sudden comprehension that the female who looked young and fragile and consequently would be the perfect prey, wasn't so perfect after all.

She really liked that look.

Today she knew exactly what she fought, but twenty years ago she'd been damn lucky to survive. At thirteen she'd been a skinny slip of a girl enjoying a rainy, gray afternoon curled up in the hayloft of her grandfather's barn. Reading.

The attack came with no warning. All of a sudden a man in black, with a mouthful of teeth and very obvious intent, had jumped on her. She'd struggled, her hands flailing, trying to grab onto something…anything. She'd managed to find an old, broken broom handle with her fingers. In a flash she'd wrapped both hands around the splintering wood and stabbed wildly at the man sitting on her stomach just as he leaned down to bite.

Somehow she'd managed to hit the right spot.

Later the news media and police report said she was hysterical. Law enforcement officials never did find more than traces of the man who'd attacked her. Footprints in the dust, strange jewelry he'd left behind. Scratching his head, the county sheriff looked at the bruises on her body and the traces of blood on the makeshift stake she'd wielded, and decided Jane had managed to wound her attacker and he'd run through the fields to a waiting car. The incident had been reported as an attempted rape. They'd patted her on the head and told her she'd been a very lucky girl.

No one believed her when she'd said the man had simply crumbled into ash and that the blood on the broomstick was her own. She'd bled when a large splinter of wood had wedged into her palm.

They were sure she'd been traumatized and was hysterically trying to assure herself that the man was gone for good.

Snapping back to the present, she sneered. She'd left hysterical behind a long time ago. Absently wiping the knife blade on her jeans before she folded the custom switchblade and put it in her pocket, she wondered how many this made. Surely she was up to triple digits by now? When she started doing this full-time she promised herself she wouldn't count. So instead she wondered. Guessed. And shrugged the numbers off.

Numbers didn't matter. As with the first fight, staying alive one more day was the only thing she counted at the end of the battle.

The years between thirteen and her early twenties had been spent training her body and her mind. Jane researched and made tentative inquires about the existence of mystical monsters. Shortly after her twenty-first birthday a very secret society had approached her.

Supposedly the group known as CCOM had private benefactors and government sanction. It paid for rogue vampire kills and information on other mythical entities, and only those who worked for the group knew the acronym stood for Control Creatures of Myth.

Jane had been killing vampires for money for over ten years, but her latest kill was by far the most difficult—and personal. She'd killed Marcus for revenge, not payment.

She kicked the pile of ashes at her feet and resisted the impulse to let tears trail down her cheeks.

Damn, she missed Marissa.

Marissa De'Angel had taken her by surprise. De'Angel meant "of angels" in some romantic language, and Rissa had definitely epitomized her last name. It had been a nice surprise, finding a vampire with her friend's temperament. Until meeting Marissa, Jane had killed every vamp she found. Now she at least waited until they attacked her or she could determine if the vampire killed while feeding.

Rissa had been instrumental in convincing Jane of something she'd only intellectualized—the belief that vampires could be good, evil and in-between. Her friend had been a vibrant, beautiful and truly loving woman with very sharp teeth. Proof that just like humans, vampires come in all shapes and sizes and temperaments. Jane had spent decades dealing with the worst of Marissa's kind—and one very short year with a bloodsucking best friend.

It hadn't been enough time, damn it!

For Jane, the last few weeks had been the worst in long years of bad. Since the night she found Rissa murdered by her vampiric leech of a boyfriend, Jane had barely taken the time to eat or sleep. Her little apartment had become a stopping-off point. A place where she could shower off the sweat of her labor and close her eyes for a few moments. She'd been consumed with her quest to avenge Marissa's death by chasing after Marcus.

Tonight she finally managed to drive her knife into the bastard's heart.

Once the deed was done, her emotions plummeted. Leaving Marcus' ashes to drift in the wind, she dazedly climbed into her car and drove home. She knew she was weary and hurt. But the minute she forced her aching body to walk through the front door of her apartment, Jane realized she'd reached a breaking point. Spending her life fighting things that went bump in the night and falling into bed at the break of dawn wasn't fun anymore. She couldn't remember the last time she'd seen more than the first golden fingers of a sunrise.

Even more than craving sunlight, she needed time to grieve for her friend.

She definitely needed a break. Recognizing the signs of burnout, Jane knew she was mentally and physically exhausted. She needed a change of scenery and some relief from the sad reminders of Marissa. The Colorado Mountain cold bothered her. She was tired of icy roads and seeing her breath in the air.

She was damn tired of fighting the monsters.

Jane pulled off her boots and then threw the leather bomber jacket, black tank top and leather pants onto the bed. Her gaze caught the white body reflected in the mirror over the dresser. She almost didn't recognize herself. Tired blue eyes peered back in astonishment. Her body and face were paler than the killers she'd been hunting. Her once glorious mane of dark hair now hung lifeless and stringy. The circles under her eyes were just a tad lighter than the spreading multicolored bruises on her butt. Bruises she'd acquired when Marcus knocked her on her ass just before she drove the thin, wood-coated piece of steel into his black heart. Her custom switchblade was a modern innovation in vampire hunting. It was really nice that she no longer had to lug heavy stakes around to make her *point*.

Ha, ha.

Marissa was the only person Jane had ever known to get her rather macabre sense of humor. And Rissa wouldn't be laughing anymore.

Marissa made Jane swear a blood oath to take her ashes and spread them over an ocean if she died while Jane was still alive. It should have been a safe pact...Rissa was supposed to be immortal, for Christ's sake.

The thought of carrying out her end of the deal while taking a vacation full of sun and sand formed, and she couldn't shake the notion that she needed this.

The decision to put monster hunting on hold for a short time resonated in her soul with the solid surety of being the only choice she could make. If she didn't do something right now, she'd become vampire bait. Too tired, too angry...too overwhelmed to see the fangs headed for her throat.

Hawaii was her first choice of destination, but Jane realized it wouldn't be that easy. She couldn't—or wouldn't—fly. Not because she was afraid to, but because she couldn't leave her weapons behind. The assorted knives and guns serving as her arsenal would never make it through airport security. Sure, she wanted a break from the life she'd been living since she realized the world's evils were more complicated than most humans knew. But she wasn't foolish enough to believe trouble wouldn't somehow find her in paradise.

Never one to waste time after she'd decided to do something, a quick fifteen-minute cruise on the Internet found her a private bungalow at an exclusive Florida Keys resort. She could drive to it within three or four days. The exotic-looking option advertised coffeemakers with gourmet beans in each room, a spa specializing in alien treatments like "Bali spice rituals", and a beachside bar. It even boasted eleven miles of private white beach with gorgeous panoramic views.

* * * * *

Jane walked onto the sparsely populated Florida beach and breathed a sigh of relief. She'd made it. In this wonderful tropical paradise the sun seemed like a living thing, caressing her from the top of her head, stroking the expanse of skin left uncovered by the string bikini she wore. She curled her bare toes in the sand and her flesh covered in goose bumps. It felt *so* good.

Stretching her body out on a woven mat in the sand, she signaled a waiter for the first drink of many and stared out at the ocean. For a moment she got caught up in the steady rhythm of the waves lapping at the shore.

She couldn't drink enough alcohol to forget what led her here.

Jane looked down at the small sarong she'd worn to cover her hips. As much as she wanted the sun to bake every inch of her pale body to a crisp, she couldn't leave her bungalow without making sure the black-and-blue marks were hidden. The bruises were so severe, someone would be sure to ask questions. Questions she wouldn't answer.

She would spend the first day doing nothing more than sitting on the beach, listening to the primal rhythm of the ocean and soaking up the heat. Because she was so pale, she alternated between slathering her lily-white skin with sunscreen and spending time in the shade of a cabana. She sifted the powdery sand between her fingers and refused to allow other guests to engage her in conversation. Paring her vocabulary down to wordless motions, she lifted her empty drink in the air and waved it toward the bartender. He understood her perfectly and quickly refilled her Tropical Storm.

Studying her glass, she was mildly disappointed that the resort didn't put paper umbrellas in its drinks. Instead it used little plastic picks in the shape of palm trees to hold the slice of strawberry and kiwi fruit that accompanied each frozen beverage. She'd decided to drink Tropical Storms because of Rissa. The combination of two kinds of rum, strawberry-kiwi juice and peach schnapps blended into a pink Slurpee seemed like something her peach-obsessed friend would have appreciated.

Thinking of Marissa and peaches reminded Jane of her conversation with Ricardo.

Before leaving Colorado, Jane realized she couldn't just take Marissa's remains without notifying her friend's family. Marissa had two brothers who lived in Europe. Jane knew their names were Franco and Ricardo, but she'd been unable to find a phone number or location to contact them about Rissa's death.

That little problem had been rectified after staking Marcus. In the short moments she had before he turned to dust, she'd gone through his pockets and been surprised to find Marissa's little red address book. Why Marcus had it would remain a mystery since the dead couldn't talk, but Jane could no longer delay notifying the next of kin.

The conversation remained etched on her memory in excruciating detail.

Sitting on the bed, Jane braced herself for the conversation to come. When the phone rang several times she started to relax. No one was home and she wasn't about to leave a message on an answering machine. Just as she started to hang up, a deep masculine voice cut through her musings.

"Hallo."

Shit. In one word, the male on the other end managed to convey both irritation and unswerving command. This man was definitely an alpha male with a big shot of testosterone running through his veins.

"Um. Yes. I'm trying to locate either Franco or Ricardo, brothers of Marissa De'Angel." Just saying Rissa's name out loud threatened to have her in tears, and Jane forced a swallow around a lump in her throat.

"This is Ricardo." The flat voice filled with both suspicion and questions.

"My name is Jane. I hate to do this, but I need to make sure you're her brother. As a teenager, what was Rissa's favorite thing to eat?" One night when she and Rissa shared several bottles of wine

and ended up talking about mindless cravings, Jane said hers were all tall, blond and had bulging muscles…Rissa's had been entirely different.

"Jane? Rissa has written us about her friend Jane Nichols. Are you this Jane?"

"Yes, I am." It warmed her heart to know Rissa had mentioned her.

"Is Marissa okay? Does she need our help?"

And the earnest question just about killed her. "I can't answer that until you name her favorite food. Please?" Her throat started to close up again and she swallowed hard to prevent the emotion from showing in her words, but this time she couldn't help the tears that started to flow.

"Peaches. In any form. From the trees or in what you would call sorbet. She also liked them in cobblers and muffins and even with her meat. Franco and I teased Ris that she would wake up one morning with fuzz covering her body if she didn't stop eating them. Is that enough? What is wrong?"

The man didn't have any patience and she couldn't blame him. "There isn't a good way to say this and I'm sorry I have to break the news to you over the phone. Two and a half weeks ago, Marissa was killed by her boyfriend, Marcus."

To say there was dead silence on the phone would be an understatement. Closing her eyes she scrambled to fill that silence. Tried to think of what Ricardo would want to know. "I didn't have your phone number until tonight. I'm sorry I couldn't call earlier."

"You are sure she is dead and not just missing? How do you know this?"

She tried to explain without actually saying the words. "I don't know if Rissa told you anything about Marcus, but they shared the same blood type." Translation — as a vampire, he had the strength and knowledge to kill Rissa. "I know she's gone because I held Rissa in my arms as she died."

"Do you know what happened?"

Jane didn't think he wanted a play-by-play of what Marcus had done to Rissa before he killed her. She knew she couldn't talk about that, it was bad enough not being able to close her eyes without seeing her friend's injuries.

"When Marcus and Marissa started dating, I think the attraction was based on the fact that they were polar opposites. Rissa's blonde and bubbly appearance was the perfect foil for Marcus' dark and brooding sophistication. He managed to hide his chauvinism for a while, but eventually it became obvious he wanted arm candy, not someone with opinions and attitude. Or morals. They had a few arguments about how he expected her to act. And then Rissa discovered he…well…Marcus' dining habits didn't agree with her. Do you understand what I'm saying?"

She couldn't just say that Marcus killed the humans he fed from in case anyone was listening to their conversation. Homeland Security and spy satellites needed to be figured in.

"You're saying he ate like a glutton, one who left nothing behind?"

"Yes. Rissa planned to end the relationship. I'm sure he killed her after the rejection."

"I understand Rissa didn't keep secrets from you. And she told us some of what your life is like. I will be leaving once we finish this conversation. I would like to help with any details that need to be seen to." His voice was heavy with emotion and absolute need for revenge.

So he knew she hunted for a living. Well, it was too late for his assistance, although she hated to disappoint him. "The reason I couldn't call you earlier is because Marcus took Rissa's address book. I retrieved it tonight." *Translation –* I've already taken care of the problem. Sorry.

"Rissa and I made a pact of sorts, to scatter the other's ashes over the ocean. I just never figured I'd be the one doing the scattering." Taking a deep breath she continued. "I think we decided on the ocean because of living for the last couple decades in the middle of the United States. We both loved the beach and never spent *enough time there. I'm actually on my way to Florida to honor her wishes, but if you'd rather I send her home to you, I understand."*

"You have her ashes? Were you able to collect all of them?" His voice rose in disbelief and hope.

And wasn't this a weird conversation? "Well, yeah. I think I got everything"

"I can't tell you over the phone why this is important. But do not scatter her ashes. Give me the address where I can find you in Florida," he demanded and she answered automatically. Then he confused her by saying, "What a great location, it's the perfect place to find everything I'll need. Keep Marissa safe and I'll be waiting for you at the resort."

And then he hung up the phone. In disbelief she'd looked down at the receiver in her hand.

She wasn't finished with him.

Chapter Two

After the first three drinks, Jane went back to her room and unpacked the container holding Rissa's ashes.

She hadn't been thinking very clearly the night Rissa had been killed. Vampires disintegrate to chunky dust within a few moments, the speed of decomposition tied to the number of years they'd been "alive". Marissa had been a vampire for a few hundred years, so the transition from friend to ashes hadn't taken more than sixty seconds.

Devastated by the loss of her friend and eager to find Marcus to exact revenge, Jane still realized that she couldn't just leave the ashes to be cleaned away by the landlord. She'd searched Rissa's apartment for something to hold the remains. Initially, all she could find with an airtight lid was a Tupperware container. Since she couldn't imagine putting what used to be her friend inside the almost see-through plastic, she was really happy to find another solution.

Jane hadn't remembered seeing the urn she found on display in Rissa's bedroom. She'd figured it didn't matter where the beautiful cobalt blue pottery came from. Just that it was perfect for holding Rissa's remains. The unusually heavy urn had a lid that fastened with a wire hinge and closed with old-fashioned effectiveness. Tentatively she opened the top, hoping nothing or no one else was inside. Later she'd reinforced the seal by dipping the entire top half of the pot in wax.

She returned to the beach, placing Rissa's urn in the sand beside her chair. She held a quiet one-sided conversation with her friend, carefully making sure she wasn't overheard. As she sat there, Jane steadily surrounded the pretty blue pot with a forest of palm tree garnish holders. Pushing the green plastic picks into the sand as fast as she could consume the drinks.

The alcohol and the sun did their jobs. Jane relaxed completely, her grief deadened and her thoughts centered on remembered fun and secrets shared with a best friend. Thinking about ordering another drink and staying on the beach to watch the stars come out, she turned her head a little and realized someone stood right behind her lounge chair.

Too close.

She never went anywhere unarmed. It was a simple thing to slide her hand into her beach tote and wrap her fingers around the handle of the six-inch knife.

After jumping up and whirling to face the intruder, she tripped over her own feet. When she finally untangled herself, Jane waved a long roll of candy in the man's face. Even in her present state, she felt embarrassed. The knife remained in her bag…probably a good thing.

Once she actually focused on the man, she had to work hard to keep her mouth closed. Gorgeous didn't even scratch the surface. Unless the alcohol turned ugly into appealing, this blond and muscular man was a contender for craving of the year. Starting at his bare feet and taking note of his long toes, she shifted her gaze upward and catalogued the man's many and varied assets along the way. He wore long shorts, so the muscular calves were well displayed, his thighs were covered and unfortunately the shorts weren't tight enough to get any idea of the size and breadth of his manly dimensions.

But his bare chest with its small V of golden hair could win awards. This man defined ripped and she crossed her fingers he wasn't a steroid user. She didn't want to touch and have him completely uninterested or unable to return the favor. She definitely wanted to offer her services as tanning lotion applier before anyone else at the resort got the chance. As she glanced up and met his gaze, she sucked in a breath of surprise.

One look into his ageless, mossy green eyes and she knew without doubt who stood before her with a slight smirk on his face.

"Ricardo?"

At his nod she exhaled a sigh of relief. She wouldn't be joining Rissa in death tonight.

Either from the booze or maybe because his eyes reminded her so much of Rissa, she started to chatter. "You're lucky my reflexes are a little off after all the Tropical Storms I've been through today. Pick your sister up out of the sand, I'm afraid in my condition I might drop her. Good piece of advice, never sneak up on a vampire hunter. Unless the vampire hunter has consumed close to a dozen Tropical Storms, in which case you might be safe. I don't know. I think I had almost a dozen, count Rissa's forest for me, will you?" She waved at the urn and watched him turn and tilt his gorgeous head to one side. His hair fell to his shoulders in a slight wave, definitely worth a glance or two. He frowned at her.

When he didn't say anything she continued. "I need a shower, food and maybe a power snooze. I definitely need at least a gallon of black coffee. Follow me home and you can stow the urn and we can talk. Fair warning—if you don't put a shirt on I'll be exploring your skin with my tongue before the night is over. Isn't it a little hot out? I never drink this much. I have a limit of two beverages a night. But I'm on vacation. My butt hurts, my heart hurts and I really don't care if some nasty creature is out there waiting for me to turn it to dust. I'm on *va-ca-tion*." Her voice had gone singsongy.

Concentrating very carefully on putting one foot in front of the other so she wouldn't weave during the walk from the beach to her front door, she didn't keep any brain cells in reserve to monitor her mouth.

Suddenly she started to sniffle. "Rissa turned to dust. I knew I couldn't hold on to her for long so I laid her down on the hardwood floor, and when she disintegrated I swept her up with a makeup brush and the dustpan I cleaned. Oh, and for some of it I used Rissa's DustBuster. But I washed the inside first. Here's my bungalow. Come on in. I'm headed for the shower."

Her bungalow sat back from the beach just enough so the tropical foliage provided a sense of lush privacy. Thirty secluded villas on stilts made up the resort. Each thatch-roofed retreat offered palm-framed ocean views, tropics-inspired furnishings, verandas, outdoor showers, king-size beds with gauzy netting and tempting hammocks slung between shady palm trees.

Intent on making it into the shower without falling on her face, she started stripping off the sarong and her bathing suit the second she walked in the door. She'd kept the sarong wrapped around her hips all day, arranging it to allow maximum sun exposure, yet hiding the bruising that covered all of one hip and extended down and around her left thigh. It looked as if someone had beaten her with a baseball bat.

She ignored Ricardo's quick inhalation of breath. Assumed it was in sympathy for her injuries instead of lust-inspired awe, as she knew her naked ass would warrant pity — not heat.

Turning the shower on full blast, she left the water temperature a little chilly and stepped under the spray with gritted teeth. Within minutes she lost the alcohol glow and started trying to replay the one-sided conversation she'd had with Ricardo. As she shampooed her hair and washed her body with some papaya-mint body wash, she couldn't quite fill in the blanks. All she knew for sure was that Ricardo hadn't uttered so much as one word.

Frowning, she remembered making an *offer to explore his skin with her tongue*?

Shit!

The first time she'd walked into the bathroom in the bungalow, Jane's eyes had about fallen out of her head. The shower stall was about the size of her entire bathroom at home. With glass walls and a ceramic bench, she figured at least five people could shower at the same time and never touch. In her current condition, having somewhere to sit was really important. Carefully lowering herself to the bench, she leaned back against the glass and closed her eyes. The cold water ran over her shins and feet, and she let the enervating sensation labor to clear the rum from her system. She debated staying in the shower long enough for Ricardo to get bored and leave.

As she tried to recreate her ramblings and figure out what else she'd said, she caught a whiff of strong coffee. Opening her eyes, she found Ricardo at the open shower door. In his outstretched hand was a steaming mug of dark nectar.

Either his room was close to hers or she'd been in the shower longer than she thought. Not only had he made coffee, but he'd pulled on a short-sleeved white shirt. The buttons down the front were thankfully undone, so he'd only made a halfhearted attempt to cover the skin she'd offered to lick. Mentally she winced. She was not a subtle person by nature, but normally she wasn't quite that blunt.

"I've ordered a selection of food from room service. I wasn't sure what you'd like, but figured whatever you don't eat you can store in the refrigerator anyway. I also asked the manager of the spa if he stocked any natural ointments for severe bruising. He gave me some cream. It has witch hazel for the pain and ferns, comfrey and a few other things to help you heal. After you eat, I'll apply it and tuck you into bed. If you like, I can stay in the living room while you sleep, in case some of those creatures you mentioned are lurking in the dark."

Jane took the cup out of his hand and nodded sheepishly. When he turned and left, she didn't understand the disappointment. He was just being a Good Samaritan, taking care of his sister's friend in her time of need.

Well. There were needs…and then there were *needs*.

227

Ricardo paced the small confines of the bungalow while Jane finished her shower. His body and mind warred with each other. Part of his mind wanted to start working on gathering the supplies he needed. The other half was incensed that she'd been hurt, the bruises testament to a beating she'd taken, probably while killing his sister's murderer.

His body sent a clear message. It wanted him to do one thing. Rub Jane's tender flesh with the pungent cream he'd collected for her and let her use her tongue to ease the lust surging through him as she'd threatened to do.

The woman and her sun-blushed skin—with a multicolored ass he'd have to be careful not to hurt as he spread the lotion across the tempting globes—was a distraction he didn't need. He had until the full moon to complete the ceremony. Three days. His cock and its urgings would have to wait.

Room service chose that moment to make the delivery and he answered the door, bringing the cart inside. When he turned, Jane stood in the doorway dressed in a short, red silk robe. The color was perfect for her, accenting the deep blue-black of her hair and the vivid blue of her eyes. The robe stretched tight across ample breasts, teasing him with the hint of taut nipples pressed against the thin fabric. The hem brushed just below her crotch, and he wondered if she wore anything at all beneath the skimpy covering.

When she walked closer he got a tantalizing whiff of aroused woman and mint cleanser. She was dangerous. It had been a very long time since he'd felt such an instant attraction to a woman.

"Ten," he informed her.

When she turned expressive blue eyes to him in question he elaborated. "You told me to count the grove of trees around Rissa's urn. There were ten, not quite the dozen you'd imagined."

She winced and moved her head as if it was too heavy for her shoulders and he empathized with her pain. "Headache?"

"Yeah. Sun, alcohol and too little sleep don't help. But I've had a headache ever since…" She trailed off.

"Ever since you fought Marcus?" He wanted her to be honest with him.

Her chin came up. "Yes. Since Marcus threw me across a room. Didn't do him any good though." She smirked sadly.

He couldn't help but smile. This woman was irreverent and tough. She wouldn't be hunting out-of-control vampires if she wasn't.

"I wish I'd been there to see that. But let's work on making you feel a little better. Eat, take a couple aspirin and I'll treat you to a Ricardo Body Massage. I'm told they are to die for." He didn't miss her heightened arousal at his throaty laugh.

"Just keep your fangs to yourself," she mumbled.

Ricardo frowned in surprise. Fangs? Evidently his little sister hadn't explained the quirky dynamics of their family.

In record time Jane downed four cups of coffee, took three aspirin and finished with the conch chowder.

"That's all I can eat," she argued after he complained that she hadn't consumed enough food.

He watched her intently as she stored the rest of the food in the room's refrigerator. When she finished, he rolled the room service cart out the door and turned toward her. "Come on, time for that promised massage." His voice turned husky. He wanted her to hear the promise in it. He knew she wanted him, almost as badly as he wanted her. He would give her the massage and sleep on the couch if he had to—but sleeping alone was not what he wanted.

Ricardo justified delaying his search for supplies by telling himself Jane wouldn't be up to chasing through the Everglades collecting materials tonight anyway.

Jane let him take her hand and lead her into the bedroom. Silently she watched as he pulled back the bed covers and exposed crisp white sheets. The sight of this gorgeous man standing beside a bed covered with white mosquito netting provided a romantic and erotic fantasy she wanted to fully explore.

"Take off your robe and lay facedown. Make sure you're comfortable."

Inwardly Jane sighed. A really fine-looking man was about to put his hands on her naked body for the first time in over a year — to rub some almost certainly foul-smelling cream on her butt.

Oh, goody.

Well, she could just lie there on the fancy bed and fantasize about other uses for those strong, long-fingered hands. And wonder if the old wives' tales were true. Did the size of a man's fingers and toes have *any* correlation to other body parts? She could only hope she had a chance to find out.

Settling herself on the bed, she arranged the discarded silk robe across her hips while Ricardo disappeared into the bathroom.

"I only want to use the cream where you have bruises. For the rest of your body I'll use the after-sun lotion the hotel provides." He turned the lights off in the bedroom, a soft glow filling the room from the moon outside.

The first touch of his strong, lotion-coated hands on her shoulders had Jane moaning in delight. Ricardo started by gently rubbing the lotion across her back to help her relax. She could feel her headache and the tension of the last few weeks melting away. Oh Lord. His massage *was* to die for and she'd been a good girl and gone to heaven. She couldn't ever remember being so relaxed and pampered — or so aroused by the simple stroke of hands. His strong fingers and the heat of his touch turned her into a warm puddle of need.

She couldn't help her little mewling sighs as he reached her lower back, slowly working his way down to the rounded globes of her butt. A raging inferno built deep inside her when he brushed the silk robe away to bare her ass. He stopped for a moment to change from the lotion to the cream for her bruises.

She should have felt exposed, or at least a little embarrassed. But she didn't. She just waited in anticipation for more of his touch. She could smell the slightly medicinal scent of witch hazel, but the cream carried a more earthy fragrance that seemed to add to her arousal. He spread the cream over her bruises with gentle strokes and then kneaded the muscles with restrained force, very careful not to cause her pain.

Shifting restlessly on the bed, she moaned and whispered hoarsely, "A little harder. Please." She'd beg if she had to.

But she didn't. Ricardo increased the pressure for several long moments then ran his fingers down between her thighs to cover the bruises there. She knew he wasn't trying to seduce her, but she couldn't help but part her legs to give him easier access to her battered flesh.

Jane rolled her eyes at her mental rationalization. *Yeah right.* She just wanted him to put cream on her boo-boos — spreading her legs wasn't meant as a blatant invitation at all.

Jane strained and held her breath, disappointed when those long fingers didn't accept her silent plea and slip further up her leg and into her heat. *Damn!* The alternating warmth of his hands and the shivers of anticipation he created in her body caused conflicting emotions. She pushed her thoughts away, locking her mind on the physical response to his caresses. She didn't want to think, she only wanted to feel and experience. No matter the reason for this massage, she planned on enjoying every sensual second of it.

It took her by surprise when he moved his hand upward to brush the tips of his fingers teasingly over her slick folds. When he started to retreat, she arched her back and pushed her ass upward. "Don't stop. Please."

He growled his pleasure at her demand and fit his body over hers, bending to kiss and nibble his way down her spine, careful not to put any pressure on her bruises. She writhed under him as his mouth suckled bits of her flesh and his fingers continued to play in her damp moisture. He slipped those long digits up and down in her juices, flicking her clit and driving her crazy.

Finally his mouth trailed velvet-soft kisses over every inch of her ass. When he pulled back and stood she moaned in protest.

"Turn on your back, Jane." Ricardo's voice came out gruff. Demanding. The sound a wicked, rumbling caress over every nerve ending in her body.

Jane rolled over and took a sharp breath as the feel of warm night air shifted in a tantalizing slide over her damp skin. Ricardo made her sweat. This wasn't a soft tumble into arousal. Her heart hammered in her chest and she felt the growing buzz of excitement spiraling out of control within her body.

Ricardo didn't waste any time arranging her thighs in a position that seemed to suit him. As he moved her around he watched her face, and she felt certain he looked for any signs of pain. It surprised her when he didn't just fall on her and dive in.

It was what she wanted.

Instead he stood there naked—at some point he must have magically stripped and secured his long hair back in a ponytail—and he simply looked at her with passionate heat in his green eyes. The man's body was fantastic, his cock long and thick and ready for her.

Ricardo allowed himself a moment to look at Jane. To see how beautiful she appeared in the moonlight coming through the bedroom window as it painted her naked skin in silver. Raking his gaze down her body, he sucked in a silent breath. There were small triangles of paler skin over each breast where her bikini had shielded her fair complexion from the sun. Moving his eyes lower, he felt his cock twitch in anticipation. The hair on Jane's mons had been shaved down to a short rectangle running only the length of her nether lips. As she moved and shifted her legs he saw moisture glisten on the soft, hidden flesh of her pussy. The thought of tasting her there brought a heated rush of urgency to his shaft.

Jane's succulent body and her sensual responsiveness hypnotized Ricardo. He loved the feel of her sun-kissed skin under his fingers. He could imagine the soft give of her breasts, the beaded, blush-colored nipples thrusting demandingly into his palms. Could barely wait to have her inner muscles milking his cock.

He wouldn't be able to restrain himself if he stopped to enjoy the sight of her spread before him any longer. His control had already slipped past retrieval. Adding more lotion to his hands, he put his palms on the outer side of each breast and slid his slick hands up and around them. He gently teased the edges of the dark pink rings of color, not allowing himself to touch those nipples. Even though they'd hardened into teasing pebbles. His mouth watered as he thought of tasting her. Sucking on her.

Jane sucked in a breath. "Ricardo."

Meeting her gaze, he could see the need flare within her heavy-lidded eyes. Her eyes shifted downward. He followed her gaze and became caught in the vision of his dark hands against her pale skin as they moved with insistent persuasion, kneading her breasts, causing her to moan in arousal and desperate need.

He liked Jane needing his touch.

"Your skin is so dark. I'm the one who looks like a vampire."

Ah, she still worried about his fangs. Well. Explanations could wait. Slowly he moved one hand to the top of her right breast and pinched the nipple between his thumb and index finger. He rolled it and she pressed into his hands as he continued to pinch and release the hard bud. Pinch. Release. Pinch. Release.

"Ah, God. Please. Your mouth, please!" Jane begged.

He bent over her to capture her whispered demands with his lips.

Jane immediately reached up to wrap her arms around his neck, pulling him closer. Their mouths met. Merged. He drew back and used his tongue to trace her lips and then spear inside. In. Out. A parody of what he wanted to do with his cock. Her warm mouth tasted of coffee and spicy aroused woman. The response to his kisses a wild, uninhibited joy. As he ravaged her mouth he tugged again at her nipple, and she gasped and threw her head back.

He could no longer resist the mouthwatering temptation of her breasts.

Trailing his mouth down her chin, he laved his tongue down her throat, nipping and sucking on her skin. She tasted like sunshine and minty papaya. Tropically sweet. With deliberate hesitation he followed a path down her chest, finally taking the nipple he wasn't using his fingers on into his mouth. He moved his hand to plump up her breast as he suckled the tip and pulled on it with his teeth, releasing it to blow warm air over the top.

Jane hissed, "Oh God, Ricardo!" She struggled with him, the sharp tug on his hair demanding he put his mouth back on her flesh. Jane was frantic. Strung so tight she felt like she would break into a million pieces. She went wild when he touched her core. Ricardo's fingers shaped her, spread her and caressed her into madness while he kept suckling at her breast. She didn't know if she could take any more teasing. She wanted his body over her—plunging hard and deep.

He mouthed words into her skin. "Janie, love. You taste so good."

Running his hands to her knees, he shifted to kneel between them. As his breath caressed the moist heat between her legs, Jane gasped and started to mewl. She thrashed her head from side to side as she dug her heels into the mattress and offered her pussy to him.

Ricardo had to grit his teeth and take a deep breath before he could continue. She was so wet. Slick with passion and need. He wanted to bury himself hip deep and forget the urge to taste her. The breath pulled her spicy fragrance deep into his lungs and the scent of her arousal almost undid him. Then he remembered he hadn't brought any protection. *Merde!*

"It has been so long since I allowed myself to be with a woman...I didn't think of bringing a condom," he gasped sadly. "But I can love your body with my mouth and hands, the rest can wait until tomorrow."

Jane frowned and tried to clear her lust-clogged brain. Vampires didn't need protection. Their bodies didn't hold disease and unless she'd missed something, birth control shouldn't be necessary.

Well, birth control wasn't an issue. "I don't understand. I'm on the Pill."

"Thank you God and Goddess!" Ricardo growled low in his throat and didn't hesitate to continue making love to her. "Oh, baby...you are so tight, so swollen with need for me." As he spoke, his breath whispered across her heated flesh.

"Ricardoooo..." Her strangled cry was filled with demand, and any questions as to why they would need protection fled.

Flattening his body between her legs, he positioned her knees over his shoulders and buried his face in her hot slit. He licked and suckled her sensitive folds, drawing her hard bud into his mouth, reveling in her spicy musk and then plunging his tongue into her clenching passage.

Jane cried out and sobbed. Her body shook with the intense wave of her orgasm. Not allowed any time to recover, she realized he wasn't even close to being finished with her.

The second time he played with her. Using his mouth and fingers to bring her close to peak and then letting her settle, only to start again. By the time he let her come she was wild and sobbing. Mindlessly begging him to fuck her.

Happy to oblige, Ricardo climbed up her body, his cock throbbing in agony. The feel of his swollen crown pushing against her vulva was heaven.

Jane moaned as Ricardo pressed against her. He was big and thick and oh-so lovely. He flexed his hips just enough so the engorged head of his shaft breached her, spreading her entrance. Pulsed. Just one inch in. Out. In.

"Damn, so sweet. Tight. You're killing me, Janie," he gasped.

Ricardo punctuated his approval by surging forward until he buried his long length deep inside her. Jane hissed in reaction to the mind-bending sensation of her internal muscles quivering around his flesh.

Jane groaned. Every new sensation heightened the arousal of her already sensitized body. The tantalizing brush of his chest hair against her nipples combined with the hard thrust of his hips as his shaft sank deep within her. His pubic bone nudged her clit with the forward motion and his heavy balls slapped her ass. He pulled out of her tight heat and pounded forward. And again. Faster.

"Harder! More!" Jane pleaded as she threw her head back, arching her hips to meet each demanding thrust. For a long time no sound could be heard in the room except for the slap of bodies and heartfelt groans as they came together in raw primal hunger.

As he burst within her, Jane screamed. Her body clenched tight and convulsed with his in crushing pleasure.

Within seconds she tumbled into sound sleep.

Ricardo pulled out of her and winced. He remained half erect. Carefully he moved to her side and gathered her against him. It took a while before his mind settled enough to join her in slumber.

Chapter Three

✖

Sun was streaming through the windows when Jane started to stir. Ricardo propped himself up on one elbow and ran his fingers gently through her hair, pushing it away from her face. Jane lay naked beside him. The sheets were in a puddle on the floor. The warm tropical air allowed them to sleep comfortably without any covering.

He took advantage of this opportunity to study the first woman who'd been able to get him rock-hard and mindless within quick seconds of meeting her. She was one of the most beautiful women he'd ever seen, with her long dark hair and a recent touch of color on her very pale skin. He concentrated on memorizing her supple curves, the deep rose color of her nipples and the trim strip of dark hair between her legs. Her personality was refreshing, irreverent and slightly hostile. He loved it. Too bad he'd sworn off anything more than sex with mortals a long time ago.

Using only his eyes to catalogue her body, he kept his hands off her while she came back to herself.

Jane opened her stunning blue eyes and looked at him for a minute. Ricardo waited for her to say something.

"The sun is shining on your face and you aren't erupting into flames."

He laughed. That certainly wasn't what he'd been expecting. Somehow he knew Jane would never say or do the expected. She hadn't really asked a question, but he answered her anyway. "The family De'Angel is very old and, well…complicated. Our last name actually came from a description of our father. Michael…the angel of life."

"So, are you telling me that you aren't a vampire, but an angel?" Jane didn't realize she was frowning until Ricardo lightly brushed the skin between her eyes, and she smiled.

"No, Jane. We are not angels. In the early ages if you held any magic, you were either labeled demon or angel. If you didn't want to be burned at the stake for witchcraft, it was definitely healthier to make sure you were thought to be somewhat angelic. Eventually it didn't matter what side you were on, all magical creatures were hunted down and killed. But the De'Angels are Druid-mages. Through the ages we have escaped those who would rid the world of our abilities."

"But your sister was a vampire. And after all that time Marcus could still kill Marissa," she said sadly.

"Well. It's a little more complicated than that. Do you know what a Druid is?"

She snorted at that. "I've read the history books. No one really knows what a Druid is, although popular conjecture is a priest or sorcerer of some sort. Which can also be one of the definitions for mage. So would a Druid-mage have two times whatever magic you're supposed to possess?"

"Druids can be many things. To complicate matters, within the calling there are many levels of abilities as well. As Druid-mages, our family is rather high up in the hierarchy. We have the magic and resources to become anything we wish. Every so often we revitalize our essence as a different paranormal creature. This allows us to hone new skills, to experience different lifestyles and perhaps more importantly, the change keeps us from becoming bored and disinterested in the world around us. Rissa chose to spend her last incarnation as a vampire. Right now Franco is a werewolf. And I've been studying the magic and elementals of past history in our original form. To some extent we can use magic in any supernatural body, but our abilities are stronger when we are nothing more than a Druid-mage." He stopped to think for a minute, wondering how to make her understand.

"You mean if you're a vampire or something else, your magic isn't as powerful? Is that why Rissa died?"

"Yes. She was probably caught off guard. But Rissa's death may not be a final death."

"Are you saying she may someday reincarnate?"

Ricardo closed his eyes. "Burnt to ashes, Rissa won't be able to reincarnate. But there is one hope. I have discovered an ancient ritual that could bring Rissa back to life. This is why I asked you if you had all of Rissa's remains. If you were able to gather every piece of her essence, the spell should work. I will need your help in finding the ingredients and performing the awakening. We don't have long. In two days the moon will be full, and if we can't bring Rissa back by midnight on the night of the first full moon after her death, she'll be lost to us forever."

* * * * *

Jane watched Ricardo as he maneuvered their flat-bottom boat through the swampy Everglades. Did she believe his story? Was there a way to bring her best friend back to life? Hell. Most people had no idea there were vampires or were-creatures in the world. A Druid-mage who could do some sort of ritual that would turn Rissa's ashes back into a vibrant, crazy vampire didn't seem too much of a stretch.

If Ricardo's spell worked, Jane swore she would get Rissa a vibrator and tell her to stay away from men for a while.

Ricardo seemed to know what he was doing. He'd brought the hair of a werewolf with him. Said he'd gathered it from his brother's brush. Already today they'd marked three of the other ingredients off the list.

The first two had been easy. The local voodoo shop carried grave dust and mandrake root. The crocodile tears had been a bit of a pain. But in the end they'd managed to fill a small vial with what they needed. Needless to say they'd been banned for life from the crocodile farm after what they'd had to do to make the croc cry.

Ugh!

She was a little nervous about her abilities in collecting the next item.

"This should be fine." Ricardo's voice broke into her thoughts.

She hadn't realized he'd stopped the boat next to a mound of dirt and moss topped with a lone tree. The area wasn't very big, but then she supposed they didn't need much room. It filled the requirements of being under a clear sky, and was in a location where they were pretty much guaranteed privacy from human eyes and ears. The privacy was important if they didn't want to be arrested for being naked and committing indecent acts in public. In this area of the world, that meant you went into the Everglades. The beach might be private enough for a quickie, but for what she needed to do they couldn't take the chance on someone interrupting. It would require a bit more time and effort.

Jane shuddered with anticipation of what would happen next.

The fourth item needed in Ricardo's spell sounded a little vague. *Lust-sweat taken from a captive Druid under a clear sky.*

It was so handy Ricardo happened to be one.

Now she needed to bind him and make him sweat under her tender ministrations. It certainly wouldn't be a hardship.

As she watched Ricardo strip, she gathered the ropes they'd brought with them. "Don't you have to let me chase you or something? It hardly seems like stripping out of your clothes and standing with your back against the tree while I tie you up really qualifies as *captive* Druid," Jane stated. She couldn't believe her luck. Ricardo was built like a bodybuilder, his muscles defined and tempting in the sunlight. His long blond hair framed a strikingly chiseled face. His lips were full and sensuous, his moss green eyes gorgeous.

241

"The incantation doesn't say *unwilling* captive. I believe the fact that I am tied up will be sufficient. Do you have the test tube?"

Jane held up the tube with the plastic lid. And this was why they needed the privacy of the secluded hill in the middle of the Everglades. She had to fill the small test tube to the halfway mark with his sweat.

Once she'd secured Ricardo to the tree, she spread the blanket she'd brought on the ground before him and arranged her backpack within easy reach. Slowly she peeled out of her own clothes, intent on watching the heat as it built in his eyes. She raised her hands above her head and stretched, glorying in the heat of the sun teasing her skin and the look of fascination covering his face. That look gave her ideas.

She sat on the blanket and looked around for a moment.

He must have understood her concern. "I've worked a small protection spell," he said. "Nothing will bother us in this place. None of the natural or paranormal creatures who live in this area will intrude."

Jane hadn't been thinking of anything more than snakes or crocodiles. It was good to know that for now they were safe from other things as well. She reached into her bag and took out the coconut suntan oil. She couldn't spread it on *him*, as she'd like to. The oil would contaminate the purity of his sweat. But she could rub the concoction on her body and tease him. Pouring a generous amount in her palm, she spread the oil on her chest, using both hands to work it slowly over her breasts. She tilted her head back, lowered her lashes and watched him through half-closed eyes.

His gaze focused on her hands. She pushed her breasts together and used her fingers to pinch her nipples, continuing to tug and pull and offer herself to the sun and his undivided attention. Slowly she slid one hand down her stomach, leaving a glistening trail on her skin as she slipped her fingers between her pussy lips. She parted her thighs to give him a better view and lay back on the blanket, arching her spine. With one hand teasing her breasts, she plucked her nipples and squeezed lightly. The other hand played over her pussy. Parting her folds and dipping into the juices that started to flow.

She listened to his breathing deepen. Glancing up, she saw his rapt gaze riveted on her body. The first glimmer of sweat broke out on his upper lip. It wasn't nearly enough. She traced one finger around her clit, dipping it into her vagina before pulling it out and reached over to her backpack. Taking a vibrator out of the bag, she sat up and met his gaze.

Getting to her feet, she walked over to the tree and placed the vibrator alongside his straining cock. "Watch me, Ricardo. Watch me pleasure myself and think of all the wonderful things I'll be doing to you once you've seen me have at least one orgasm with this vibrator. I'll fondle this dildo as if it were your cock, slide it in and out of my mouth. Clench it with my pussy and think of you. But it won't be enough, Ricardo. Look at it. Look how much shorter it is than you. And your shaft is so much wider. It won't be enough for me."

She watched him. Watched his cock stretch and bounce eagerly at every word and motion she made. She could see pre-come oozing from the little hole in the engorged purple head.

"I've never seen a vibrator like that before. What's that piece coming out from the base and curving over the shaft?" His voice was rough and broken and he tugged on the ropes as if wanting to escape.

She grinned at him and lifted it up so he could see. "It's a rabbit. With ears strategically placed to play with my clit."

He groaned at her explanation as she returned to the blanket. His gaze locked on her as she slid the pink plastic shaft into her mouth and did a very good job of showing him how inventive she could be when giving head. She watched a light sheen of sweat start to coat his body.

It was working.

Pulling the vibrator out of her mouth, she gave the tip one last lick and then twisted the switch to turn it on. The low purring sound seemed to echo loudly in the quiet glade.

Lying back on the soft blanket, she moved the vibrating tool slowly down the center of her body. For several moments she rubbed the rounded head over her clit. Back and forth, she kept the motion steady until she writhed from the sensations shooting through her body. When she couldn't take it anymore, she slowly positioned the tip at her entrance and pushed the pink spear inside. She became so caught up in her spiraling climb to orgasm she almost forgot Ricardo watched her. Pumping her hips, the little rabbit ears tickling her clit, she started to slam the shaft in and out of her clenching channel.

"Close. Oh, so close. I can feel it. Ricardo, I can feel my body racing to climax. And I want your hands on me. I want your cock slamming into my pussy. Not this pink thing." She rolled her head against the ground and moaned. "Fuck. Want you to fuck me, Ricardo. Harder. Need it. Harder."

And then she screamed out her pleasure and collapsed, her breath coming in quick pants.

"Dammit. Jane. Come. Here."

She took a deep breath and sat up, looking at him. Ricardo's eyes were wild. He strained against his bonds, his body covered in glistening perspiration.

She picked up the vial and crossed the few feet separating them. Standing to the side so that she wouldn't be straddling his straining erection, she leaned over to lick one of his nipples. He moaned as she used her tongue to tease the tight bud. She ran the lip of the test tube up his skin in an attempt to collect a few drops of his sweat. She leaned back and looked at the level of fluid in the glass tube. There wasn't enough.

Good.

She smiled. Well. She certainly had a few ideas about how to turn the heat up. Slowly she licked a path down his chest, eventually dropping to her knees. For the time being she slipped the vial between a strand of the rope and the tree, in order to free both her hands. Cupping his cock in her palms, she watched as Ricardo strained into her, arching his back, pushing his head against the tree. She encircled his shaft with her fingers and started to run her hand up and down his length. His deep moan of satisfaction had her smiling.

"Sweat for me, Ricardo. Come on, baby. We've got all day. I can bring you close. And then back off and let you settle. You aren't going to get any release until we fill this little bottle up. So sweat, Ricardo. And then I'll fuck your brains out," she promised.

She leaned forward and licked the little slit on the crown. Fit her mouth over his swollen head and took as much of him into her moist heat as she could manage. At his gasp, she rolled her eyes upward and met his gaze.

Watching Jane suck and fondle the vibrator had been pure torture. He'd imagined what it would be like to have her sweet mouth wrapped around him the same way, her tongue licking him from root to tip. And the reality was so much better than he could have envisioned.

And when she pleasured herself, he wanted to lick the oil off her skin and bury his tongue in the soft pink flesh between her thighs. But for now, Ricardo felt as if someone had strung him out on a rack of sensual torment. When she came to him, when she used her tongue to pleasure first his chest and then lick her way down to his cock, he thought the delicious agony of her hands and mouth would make him insane.

Hot and moist, her mouth slid over his cock, her lips creating a tight fist of erotic need. Sucking in a breath as her tongue danced along the ultrasensitive rim around the head of his shaft, he exhaled as she pulled back and waves of anticipation coursed through his entire body.

His teeth clenched and every muscle tightened while his blood pounded hot in his veins. Each stroke of her mouth and tongue had every muscle seizing against the urge to use his magic. He wanted to be free to grab her by the hair and increase the pace. Or throw her to the ground and bury his raging cock hip deep within her body.

The escalating combination of savage lust and unasked for possession hit him until very little of his brain functioned. His only focus became moving his hips the scant amount the ropes allowed, to follow the rhythm she set. Pulling him deeper into her throat, she tantalized and tormented him until the pressure in his cock built to an unbearable degree. Before he could find any satisfaction from the building eruption, she stopped. And he howled in frustration.

He felt the cool slide of glass along his body and the sensation brought him a little sanity. Glancing down, he saw the vial was nearly full. She'd definitely made him sweat. But they weren't done. He wanted to pound his cock into her until neither of them could walk.

As soon as she screwed the cap on the vial, he used his magic to untie the ropes.

Growling deep in his throat, he reached down to help her to her feet. Jane looked up at him with her eyes glazed in a sensual fog. Reaching out with one hand, he tweaked her nipple and made her gasp. Bending his head to claim her sigh, he tasted the salty essence of his pre-come on her tongue.

Taking control of her body, he checked to make sure she was ready to withstand his wild desire. Nibbling at her mouth, he simultaneously opened her thighs with his leg and slid his hand over her stomach and down to the strip of tiny curls accenting her mound. Slipping his fingers through her folds, he found her dripping with moisture. Wanting him. Sampling the hot, slick wetness by pushing two fingers into her channel, he ignored her cries of passion and pushed deeper, forcing her to ride his hand, wanting her to burn for him.

"Ricardo! Oh, fuck me. Please!" She cried out his name, her breath coming in short gasps as she tried to drag air into her starving lungs.

As she begged him, as her body bucked and her internal muscles began to clamp around his fingers, he looked around and found a fallen log that would be perfect to bend her over. Retrieving the blanket, he covered the bark to protect her soft skin. Turning her back to him, he bent her over the log so her ass was raised and ready for him. Jane braced her hands on the tree, twisting around so she could look over her shoulder and watch him. The setting sun embellished her pale flesh in a red-gold light and he saw heat flare in her eyes as he moved against her. Reveling in the sight of her spread before him, he palmed the soft, rounded globes of her cheeks and rubbed his erection along the slick fire of her slit.

Jane mewled low in her throat and wiggled her ass against him. Using the swollen head of his cock to separate her folds, he dipped into her honeyed heat.

"Ricardo! Don't tease. Fuck." She panted and pleaded with him.

The view of his shaft disappearing within the enveloping folds of her body sent him over the edge. He surged forward, his hands braced carefully on her hips as her tight sheath swallowed his shaft and her breasts swayed beneath her. He was cautious not to hurt her, not to move his hand over the fading bruises. Yet over and over he drove into her with long, fast strokes while she bucked and sobbed his name. Moving one hand between their bodies, he fingered her anus. Using the abundant moisture gathered from their secretions, he coated the little rosette and pushed one finger inside. He delighted in her frantic cries for more.

His world centered on the velvet friction and heat between her thighs. Dragging her back toward him with each hard stroke, he rode her hard and furiously. With their bodies slapping in escalating rhythm, he felt the burning pressure start in her lower back and his balls tighten in readiness.

Moments before he lost control, he felt her body tighten around his cock. As she shattered with her release, her internal muscles milked him. Demanding he follow her. With a loud roar, his body jerked violently and he stood rock still as the sensation seemed to pull at his soul. Damn, he enjoyed this woman! Maybe too much.

Finally, he slowly lowered his chest over her and rested his head on her back while their hearts settled to the same rhythm. He rode the final aftershocks of pleasure within her shuddering flesh and wondered how he'd ever lived without her.

Chapter Four

છે

Back in her cabana, Jane watched as Ricardo prepared himself for the next night. He was doing some weird meditation thing. What he called "calling down the magic". He'd told her she could watch. And boy did she get an eyeful.

He'd lit several candles around the bungalow, stripped out of his clothes and sat on the floor. His skin glowed with an inner radiance, making it difficult for her to keep her distance. She wanted to touch him.

It hadn't even been twenty-four hours since she met him and she was already dreading his return to Europe. It wasn't just that she couldn't keep her hands off his body or her mind off sex.

She liked him. Really liked him. The way his smile appeared to be just for her. He was a wonderful lover, gentle and a little rough in turn. He made her feel as if she were the only woman in the world. Every time he reached a hand out to touch her, he let her see the fascination he had with her body. And he understood her jokes. It wasn't going to be easy to give him up when this adventure was over.

"Jane."

His deep voice made her shiver in awareness. She raised her gaze to his and saw a burning need reflected in the deep green depths.

"Having you in the room while I called the magic has had an unexpected result," he gasped, his breathing labored. His skin looked flushed. Sweat appeared on his upper lip.

She glanced at his lap. *Oh!*

"With you beside me, the magic has manifested itself by filling my body with erotic hunger. I won't be able to control myself much longer. And I'm not sure I'll be very gentle. If you aren't interested in letting me fuck you senseless, you'd better run, Janie."

Run? Was he crazy?

The magic rode him like never before. It was almost as if Jane's essence had spiked the build-up, turning the magic within him toward her.

Thank the God and Goddess the ritual wasn't until tomorrow. Because there's no way in hell he could wait to take this woman. Over and over again.

Once she'd made her choice by staying in the room with him and ignoring his warning, he stood in a rush and stalked across the small distance separating them. For tonight she would be his. He refused to think about how he'd become more emotionally tied to her than anyone in hundreds of years. Or the promise he'd once made to himself. No more human mates.

His wife had been human, as had one of his three children. Their deaths after the handful of decades allotted mortal beings left a hole in his heart he'd never been able to fill.

So, no. He might like Jane, he might love sinking his cock deep within her tight pussy, but this thing between them could never be anything more than sex. It didn't matter if he would miss her when he left the States.

Right now he was beyond ready for her. His cock pointed toward the ceiling and leapt with an urgent need to find her warm, wet heat. His balls were so tight, he felt as if they would explode. And she was ready. Waiting for him to take her. The only question was how? It really didn't matter…he planned on fucking her several times tonight. So whatever position he didn't use now, he'd use later.

With every step closer to her, he felt the energy he'd called upon expand inside him. Vibrate. Push. His cock ached and grew in size, as if the magic wanted to claim her as well. He was sure he could use the magic as an extension of his body. It would be a night she would never forget.

He would be the man she never forgot.

Jealousy roared through him at the thought that someday she'd take another lover. No. She would never forget him, he would see to that tonight.

He pulled her into his arms and whispered in her ear, "Get ready to scream my name in passion, Janie. I hope you're ready for this."

She took a deep breath and it was as if something alive came with his scent. Something that filled her, made every cell in her body crawl with need. Every touch seemed like a thousand fingers stroking her skin. Immediately her pussy swelled, engorged with blood and started to trickle cream. The moisture soaked her panties within moments.

She wore way too many clothes. Dragging her mouth away from his, she spoke one word. "Naked." She didn't explain further, but he understood.

Grabbing hold of the short dress by the hem and dragging the stretchy sheath over her head, he threw it in a far corner. One tug on her bright red thong and he ripped it from her body.

Backing her against the wall, he reached his hands down to grab her ass and raised her into position over his straining shaft. Automatically she wrapped her long legs around his waist, and slowly settled her dripping cunt over the swollen head of his cock.

The magic had somehow made him bigger. Longer. It was a small struggle to get her body to relax enough to let him in. But once her passage accommodated him, she arched into him, into the building pleasure of having him slam into her and send the magic soaring.

"Holy shit! What was that!? Magic monkey sex?" She panted and tried to get comfortable on the floor.

He leaned over to suck her nipple into his mouth. "Whatever it was, we're not done yet."

Ricardo moved his hands to smooth over her waist and up to the sides of her swollen and ultrasensitive breasts. He started to use his fingers to pluck and roll the nipple he wasn't tormenting with his mouth.

Jane whimpered in anticipation as Ricardo cupped both of her breasts and licked between them. He moved his body over hers, parting her thighs with his leg and then sliding down her body. He worked his tongue over her stomach. His fingers teased her thighs, dipping to stroke small areas of her skin with a circular motion. The magic sizzled from his fingertips. She'd never realized the flesh on her legs was so sensitive.

"Are you sure you can handle me again? So soon? And the magic seems to have magnified after taking you against the wall. I don't want to hurt you, Janie." His whispered murmur against her stomach made her thighs clench around him.

"Don't stop!" she exclaimed. "You won't hurt me."

Talking became extremely difficult. She wanted to concentrate on every bit of sensory pleasure she could grab. The burning rasp of Ricardo's tongue slipping down her stomach made her want to push on his shoulders and get him settled where that tongue could do the most good.

She held her breath as Ricardo finally knelt before her, and felt her pussy spasm in preparation for what she started praying would happen soon.

"Magic."

"What?" She had no idea what Ricardo was trying to tell her.

"This magic is different. I can use it to stroke and tease you, without even a touch of my hand."

And she felt it. Oh. My. God. She felt the magic. She screamed as golden ribbons seemed to reach out from Ricardo's body and wrap her in pulsing bands of erotic need. She could feel a deep vibrating start inside her as the small strands found their way into her soul.

When she felt Ricardo part her labial folds and rub his calloused fingers through the liquid drenching her core, the blood rushed through her veins. Sticking out his tongue, he licked a burning path through her sensitized, dew-laden slit before circling her clit in a rasping caress. Fireworks exploded behind her closed eyes.

Ricardo parted her legs further, one strong hand lifting a thigh until her knee rested over his shoulder, allowing him greater access to her tender flesh. His tongue plunged inside the gripping depths of her cunt. Then he moved back to licking her folds and rubbing against her swollen nub. And again.

"Please. Ricardo, Ricardo. Please. I need you to stop teasing and fuck me!"

Ricardo ignored her, continuing the torture by pushing his tongue into her pussy with a quick hard stroke before retreating to suck at her clit, lick at her folds and lap at the syrupy juices easing from her channel.

The heel of her foot dug into his back as she lifted herself toward him, tilting her hips to allow for the deliberately brief thrusts, for the tormenting feel of his tongue licking into her. Only to have it retreat again.

And then the magic began to ebb and flow within her. It was everywhere. Filling her pussy as a slow, easy glide of heat then shooting outward, warming her breasts and making them hyperaware of every rake of teeth or tongue. There was even a slender band of power easing inside her ass, warming her…caressing the sensitive tissue until she felt the shuddering warning of imminent detonation.

"Should I stop, Jane? Shall I take my mouth and my magic away from your sweet cunt?"

"Noooo!" she cried and her body bowed.

Ricardo pushed his mouth against her clit and plunged his tongue deep. When he growled, the vibration against her flesh became the final catalyst.

Throwing her head back, she screamed mindlessly and the magic arced within her. The explosion tore through her, erupting deep within and expanding to every cell of her body.

The echo of her release seemed to fill the room. And then all fell silent.

But not for long.

The power of the spell rode Ricardo's body beyond human endurance. He surged over her and filled her still quivering pussy with his demanding cock. And his lust and arousal just seemed to increase with each dig of his hips as he pumped his shaft into her heat. Growing. Expanding.

And every time he climaxed the magic filled him again.

By the time Jane managed to make it into the shower, the muscles in her legs were wobbly and she was completely spent. Collapsing on the tile bench, she whimpered when Ricardo came in after her. Tenderly he pulled her body into the shelter of his arms and helped bathe her. "I'm sorry if I got a little crazed, Janie. Did I hurt you?"

"God, no! Promise me we can have Magic monkey sex some other time. Just don't touch me now! As soon as I can crawl over to the bed, I'm sleeping for a week."

Ricardo scooped her up in his arms and took her to bed. She was asleep before he'd gone two steps.

Chapter Five

೫

Jane had gotten a good ten hours of sleep, not the week she thought she'd need. Now it was time to try and resurrect Marissa. After last night she worried about the results of Ricardo pulling down the magic, and she watched closely as he started the ritual under the full moon. If Marissa came back and found them on the beach fucking like bunnies, she'd...well...

She'd laugh and probably go find a neck to suck.

Shrugging her shoulders, she concentrated on Ricardo. He seemed confident this would work, explaining to her that magic was very simple. *Once you had all the necessary ingredients.*

Today's "harvesting" of the remaining ingredients had been hair-raising. Who knew a zombie would get extremely pissed off when all they wanted was his toenail clippings?

Or that she'd end up bargaining away her opal ring in exchange for a few mermaid scales? Jane had found out that one of the benefits to being a Druid-mage meant you could breathe underwater without scuba equipment. As long as she touched Ricardo, she could breathe as well. And understand Mermanese. What a kick!

Once they got to the beach, Ricardo put the ingredients in an old iron pot they'd found in an army surplus store. It currently bubbled away over a fire they'd built in a secluded cove. The concoction smelled horrible. The wind caught the steam and brought it toward her. The scent was something between rotten eggs and really bad body odor. Ugh! Quickly she moved to the ocean side of the pot so the light breeze would blow the smell away from her.

Each second that passed she could feel her heart speed up. She wanted this to work. Wanted Marissa to step out of the ashes and do a little pagan dance right in front of her. Jane wasn't sure if she should pray for help or not. Would God have a problem with her asking for help in a non-Christian ritual? In the end she didn't figure it could hurt.

· "It's time." Ricardo walked over and kissed her softly. "I've done a dampening spell so the wind won't interfere with the ritual. If you would just open the urn and make sure all of Rissa's ashes are in the middle of the circle, I'll get the potion. Don't forget to stay out of the circle once I've closed it," he warned for the umpteenth time.

Jane nodded her agreement. She'd already loosened the wax on the urn's seal. Stepping into the large circle drawn in the sand, she carefully pried up the lid and poured the contents into the silver bowl sitting in the middle. The remains were disconcerting. They weren't all ash. Included in the mix were chunks of bone and lumpy pieces and she carefully averted her eyes.

Stepping out of the circle, she watched Ricardo tip the iron pot and let a stream of liquid fall into the sand. Earlier he'd used an ancient carved staff to trace a deep groove in the sand, and he filled that trench with the potion. Once he'd spread the fluid completely around Rissa's resting place, he closed the circle with an incantation. His voice was deep. The husky timbre seemed to echo in her mind.

Jane shivered with suppressed need as he threw his head back and slowly raised his arms toward the moon. Every hair on her body stood on end with the building energy from the enchantment. Thanks to the dampening spell, there was no wind. Yet the hair moved back from his face as if caught in a fierce gale. Silver light seemed to engulf him as he said the words of the reanimation ritual. They weren't in any language Jane recognized, and yet she felt the syllables reverberate in her soul.

Tearing her gaze away from the magnetic sight of Ricardo pulling down the magic, she concentrated on keeping her eyes glued to the silver bowl. Jane didn't miss seeing the mist start to rise from the center. She could feel the air thicken and dance with electricity, the nasty smell slowly changing to one of warm peach cobbler. The flicker of what looked like glowing green eyes stared out from the spiral of smoke and Jane covered her mouth with her hands before she screamed.

Rissa's eyes winked back from the vapor.

A sharp keening sound filled the air as the mist started to take on the shape of a woman. Tears slid down Jane's cheeks as she wondered if the regeneration was hurting her friend. Almost cell upon cell she saw Marissa's specific features materialize from the vague figure as the reformation took place in front of her.

In a matter of minutes Marissa's body filled out, solidifying before Jane's fascinated gaze.

Then Marissa looked straight at her, and Jane screamed when her friend lunged at her and grabbed her hand, dragging her back to the center with her. Almost passing out from terror, Jane remembered Ricardo's urgings against crossing the line.

The instant Marissa pulled her across the magic boundary, her body felt like it had been jolted by a direct hit of lightning. It felt as if a thousand ants crawled along her skin. Biting. Burning. Her eyes closed in agony and the fireworks didn't stop. Her ears rang from the blast of sound in her head.

Jane could have sworn she heard Rissa bitch that it was "About damn time!" She recognized Ricardo's muted shout of anger and dismay without understanding the words. But she could tell he was swearing at his sister.

Several minutes later, Jane was recuperated enough from the experience to realize she and Rissa were huddled together on the sand. Naked and sobbing, Marissa didn't look like she'd been injured. With every joint in her body hurting, Jane raised her hand to push her friend's blonde hair out of her eyes. "You okay, Riss?" she asked softly.

At the sound of her voice, Rissa lifted her head and grinned broadly through her tears. "Hell, yeah. I see you've met my brother Ricardo. Or, just to piss him off, I call him 'Dick'. Isn't that cute? Dick and Jane!"

"For the love of God and Goddess, Jillian Marissa De'Angel, why did you pull Jane into the circle with you?" Ricardo all but snarled at his sister. He paced around the circle with furious steps, his eyes flashing fire and darkness. "Since you broke the circle and subverted my magic, one of you has to erase part of it so I can get in and help you up!" he shouted.

Well, Jane couldn't move. Good thing Rissa seemed to be feeling better. Her friend stretched her leg out to cross the circle and rub at the sand with her toes. The simple act of smoothing away part of the line broke the spell enough to let Ricardo in.

Immediately he pulled Jane into his lap, checking out her eyes, running his hands up and down her arms. Looking for damage, she supposed. "I'm all right. Just a little sore," she reassured him. "And did you just call Marissa…*Jillian*?"

Ricardo ignored her question and glared at his sister. "Why, Rissa? Why pull Jane in with you?"

Marissa lowered her eyes and tried not to laugh. Like she would admit to anything? "I…I don't know. I saw Jane and just reached for her. I thought maybe Marcus… Is the bastard dead?" She changed the subject nicely.

"Yeah, I got him a couple weeks after you, ah, well…turned to dust." Jane's voice was almost back to normal.

Marissa hugged her. "Thanks, Janie. I knew you would handle him."

"Jillian Marissa." Ricardo's low-voiced warning started his sister talking again.

"Dick, don't pick on me. I've just barely come back from the dead. My head hurts, my throat is parched and I need blood." She used her tongue to feel her fangs. "Guess I'm still a vamp, huh? Thanks, Bro. I really did *not* want Marcus to win this fight."

"Why?" he asked.

Jane started to ask "Why *what?*" when she saw Rissa shrug her shoulders. "Hell if I know. Feel any different, Jane?"

Did she feel any different? Now that the pain and skin sensitivity had gone away, she realized she did feel a little different. "My butt doesn't hurt anymore from the bruises I got when Marcus knocked me on my ass. In fact, I feel pretty good right now. Strong. Very awake. Like I could run for miles down the beach." As she said this last, she waved her hand at the shoreline. And screamed when sparks flew from her fingertips. "What the hell!?"

"Ah. That explains it." Rissa grinned at her and Ricardo nodded in some sort of agreement.

"What? What explains it? Why are my fingers shooting fireworks? Is that something that will disappear soon?" She looked in horror at her hands.

"It won't be going away anytime soon. In fact, it will never go away, you'll just learn how to control it. Stepping into the ritual circle, you pulled down the magic. You're like us now, Jane. This is your first incarnation," Ricardo said wonderingly. "The initial manifestation of a Druid-mage's power is the ability to fling fire. And your body has repaired itself. Another sign."

"I'm a Druid-mage? How? Will I be able to do all sorts of magic now? Can I go play with the mermen without having to hold your hand? Does this mean we get to go have more of that Magic monkey sex? Like right now!?" she demanded. Her body began to throb in a very insistent manner and she decided a few of her questions could wait until later.

Ricardo and Marissa both laughed.

Ricardo stood up and threw his room key at his sister. Then he scooped Jane up in his arms and headed toward her bungalow.

Marissa smiled when she heard his murmured "Only every day and night for the next twenty or so hundred years, my love."

She'd been right. Jane was perfect for Ricardo. But she knew her brother. Knew he'd never allow himself to get close to a human again. The dreams of foresight had shown her what to do. It really bugged Marissa to let Marcus get the upper hand, even if Jane eventually took care of him. The weeks pretending to be infatuated with the slimy vampire had been the hardest ones of her very long life. She frequently had to remind herself she couldn't just slap him across the room every time he opened his mouth.

Ah, well. It had all worked out in the end. She'd grabbed Jane just like in the dream and pretended innocence. There was no way she'd ever tell her brother this had all been a plot to get him mated. The coming centuries ought to be a lot of fun while Dick and Jane worked on controlling Jane's magic. Her brother was in for a wild ride.

Speaking of wild rides, she felt the unmistakable and heated gaze of a were-dragon watching her from the dark. "Come out and play, little dragon," she coaxed.

She so loved were-creature blood.

Florida Tropical Storm

ℬ

12 oz. V8 Splash Strawberry Kiwi Juice Drink
1 oz. Captain Morgan Spiced Rum
1 oz. Bacardi Limon
1 oz. De Kuyper Peachtree Schnapps

Place all ingredients in a blender with a cup of ice.
Blend until smooth but still thick. Serve in two frozen
mugs and top with a dash of grenadine for color.
Garnish with a large strawberry and a slice of kiwi fruit
(peeled).
Makes two, since one will never be enough!

Also by Ravyn Wilde

෪

By the Book
Let Them Eat Cake
Men To Die For (*anthology*)
Zylar's Moons 1: Zylan Captive
Zylar's Moons 2: Selven Refuge
Zylar's Moons 3: Zylan Rebellion

About the Author

෪

Ravyn Wilde was born in Oregon and has spent several years in New Guinea and Singapore. She is married, has three children and is currently living in Utah. Ravyn is happiest when she has a book in one hand and a drink in the other—preferably sprawled on a beach!

Ravyn welcomes comments from readers. You can find her website and email address on her author bio page at www.ellorascave.com.

Why an electronic book?

We live in the Information Age — an exciting time in the history of human civilization, in which technology rules supreme and continues to progress in leaps and bounds every minute of every day. For a multitude of reasons, more and more avid literary fans are opting to purchase e-books instead of paper books. The question from those not yet initiated into the world of electronic reading is simply: *Why?*

1. ***Price.*** An electronic title at Ellora's Cave Publishing and Cerridwen Press runs anywhere from 40% to 75% less than the cover price of the exact same title in paperback format. Why? Basic mathematics and cost. It is less expensive to publish an e-book (no paper and printing, no warehousing and shipping) than it is to publish a paperback, so the savings are passed along to the consumer.

2. ***Space.*** Running out of room in your house for your books? That is one worry you will never have with electronic books. For a low one-time cost, you can purchase a handheld device specifically designed for e-reading. Many e-readers have large, convenient screens for viewing. Better yet, hundreds of titles can be stored within your new library — on a single microchip. There are a variety of e-readers from different manufacturers. You can also read e-books on your PC or laptop computer. (Please note that Ellora's Cave does not endorse any specific brands. You can check our websites at www.ellorascave.com

or www.cerridwenpress.com for information we make available to new consumers.)

3. *Mobility.* Because your new e-library consists of only a microchip within a small, easily transportable e-reader, your entire cache of books can be taken with you wherever you go.

4. *Personal Viewing Preferences.* Are the words you are currently reading too small? Too large? Too... ANNOYING? Paperback books cannot be modified according to personal preferences, but e-books can.

5. *Instant Gratification.* Is it the middle of the night and all the bookstores near you are closed? Are you tired of waiting days, sometimes weeks, for bookstores to ship the novels you bought? Ellora's Cave Publishing sells instantaneous downloads twenty-four hours a day, seven days a week, every day of the year. Our webstore is never closed. Our e-book delivery system is 100% automated, meaning your order is filled as soon as you pay for it.

Those are a few of the top reasons why electronic books are replacing paperbacks for many avid readers.

As always, Ellora's Cave and Cerridwen Press welcome your questions and comments. We invite you to email us at Comments@ellorascave.com or write to us directly at Ellora's Cave Publishing Inc., 1056 Home Avenue, Akron, OH 44310-3502.

THE
☥ ELLORA'S CAVE ☥
LIBRARY

Stay up to date with Ellora's Cave Titles in
Print with our Quarterly Catalog.

TO RECIEVE A CATALOG,
SEND AN EMAIL WITH YOUR NAME
AND MAILING ADDRESS TO:

CATALOG@ELLORASCAVE.COM
OR SEND A LETTER OR POSTCARD
WITH YOUR MAILING ADDRESS TO:

CATALOG REQUEST
c/o ELLORA'S CAVE PUBLISHING, INC.
1056 HOME AVENUE
AKRON, OHIO 44310-3502